THE LONG ROAD
SHORT STORIES

THE LONG ROAD

MATTHEW LEDREW

Published in Canada by Engen Books, St. John's, NL.

A CIP catalogue record for this book is available from Library and Archives Canada.

ISBN: 978-1-989473-50-4

Distributed by:
Engen Books
www.engenbooks.com
submissions@engenbooks.com

First mass market paperback printing: May 2014
Second Printing: April 2020

Cover Image: Tegan Mierle-Joy via Unsplash
Cover Design: Ellen Curtis

For
Ellen

CONTENTS

REMEMBERING

I've been walking for a week and a half straight.

I push my body past the point of hunger, past the point of exhaustion... past the point where I have any right to keep breathing, let alone keep up the brisk pace I've set for myself. I run until my legs get rubbery and the bones in my knees threaten to snap under the strain... and then the womb's ability to heal kicks in and I get to start it all over again.

I've just passed Waterville on Route 65 when this dance starts again, black blood pumping up and surging through my joints and muscles, moistening them where need be, strengthening them in others. It gives me energy as if from nowhere, and suddenly the dull throb in the back of my head isn't pounding quite so hard, and the feeling of the highway against the soles of my feet doesn't make me want to die quite so much. A moment later those bad things are gone completely.

Deep down inside, I feel a rumbling that has nothing to do with my stomach. A kick and a squirm against my rib cage as the womb hammers at the walls of its prison, trying to get out. I swallow back hard to fight it, and that's when I realize my mouth is full of blood. But it's not the coppery, metallic taste one associates with red blood... it's a taste only I know. It's the putrid taste of the black blood that I have to thank for the sudden boost of vitality a moment ago. It tastes like rotten milk mixed with burning hair and silver.

My eyes shoot back open, and I realize for the first time that they'd been closed for almost half a mile. I pour on the speed as the night sky begins to cloud and threatens to rain on me. As my human heart and lungs begin to ache and strain, the womb finally stops slamming quite so hard.

Not altogether, just not quite so hard.

Its taken me over twice since I left home. Each time when I woke up, I found myself eight or ten miles back from where it overcame me. Trying to get back to Coral Beach. To the friends I left there. To finish the job it started.

The pack on my back feels like it weighs a ton easily, and the stench of sweat on my clothes makes me wish to God I didn't have enhanced senses, but I block it all out. I try to focus on something else... *anything* else but what's behind me. What I'm running from.

The forests to either side of me are dark and ominous. The evergreens make shadowy faces at me, waving about in the slight breeze that keeps me cool. I try not to stare at them too much, or the faces start to look familiar. The road in front of me seems to go on forever, and it's been hours since I've seen a car. Days since one has stopped to see if I needed help. The last one that did was a portly trucker, about forty-five. Overweight and clad in a flannel shirt and faded jeans, he looked like he'd stepped right out of Smokey and the Bandit. He'd pulled over about a quarter mile from where he'd passed me and waited for me to catch up, getting out of the cab when I got close. He had a grin on that was a little endearing, with a toothpick sticking out of the corner of his mouth and wearing a baseball cap with a faded picture of a bulldozer on it. He'd asked me if I needed help, and I'd looked him right in the eyes. I didn't need a mirror to know that when I did, he saw that they were as black as ebony... maybe even blacker. He'd stumbled backward and slipped on the slick, pebble-ridden pavement, slamming his back and skittering back toward the oversized wheels of his truck.

I'd flashed my teeth at him. Not the ones I was born with, the ones that stayed hidden until I needed them. The ones that were sharp and jagged like butcher's knives, and were yellow for no right reason other than they were. The ones that usually came out of my gums dripping with my blood, and went back in dripping with someone else's.

He'd slammed the cab door shut so fast that I thought the rusted hinges would crack, and then drove off with the roar of a powerful engine and the rankness of burning rubber. It made my nose itch and I coughed once as I watched him speed away, wondering briefly why I had frightened him off.

Then I remembered the reason I'd left home, and decided that the fat hick was better off having never known me. That a hell of a lot of people would have been better off if they had never known me.

My foot hits off a big rock on the side of the road, and suddenly I'm back to reality. I feel one or two droplets against the nape of my neck, and realize that all the stars are gone. I wonder what will come first, the rain or the dawn. Not that one would stop the other, even if it could.

The road ahead takes a sharp turn to the right and I stop to catch my bearings, kicking up a fair amount of dust as I do. It dissipates into the atmosphere around me slowly as I pop the calcium in my neck, releasing the tension in the cartilage and also giving me a kick jolt of pain that helps keep me awake. I lean down, resting the palms of my hands against my knees the way my father always used to after he'd spent a few hours chopping wood, and take several deep breaths before straightening. Squinting my eyes, I hear the faint squirting sound as blackness covers them anew. It's like the sound toothpaste makes when you squeeze it from the tube, that's the best I can describe it. Suddenly my vision is alive as if it were daylight. Better than daylight, there are no shadows to me.

The lights of Waterville are a dim memory on the horizon. Even if the womb escaped right here and now, it wouldn't get back in time to do any damage to the town or its people. Not that I'm about to let it out, it's just nice to know. The pavement has begun to sparkle and shine as raindrops slowly patter against it, like the stars I watched come out a few hours before.

There's a town not far west, I'll have reached it by morning. Might be able to reach it even sooner, but running in the rain is messy business, and I'd just as soon take it slow. I wrack my brain trying to think back to the maps of the state that Mr. Miles used to have hung up in homeroom, but for the life of me I can't remember any side road that will take me *away* from this small town, whatever it is. Every other place I've been able to avoid or bypass in some way, to stay out of sight of the people inside. I'd passed through Waterville, but it had been at night, and the only people who were around to notice me were a couple of teenagers, and they'd been too drunk to notice by the smell of them. High too, but that was besides the point.

I briefly consider cutting through the forests, but one look at them makes me reconsider. The contents of my pack might not survive the trees and branches, and that was the last thing I wanted right now. Those few items were all I had of home, and I carried them on my back as carefully as I could. I let out a heavy sigh and decide that I can easily get through town unnoticed, even in broad daylight.

I hoist the pack's shoulder straps with both hands, adjusting the weight a little. It wasn't until that point, when I felt the blood rush back into the pinched areas of my chest, that I realized exactly how long I'd been carrying it. I grunt and grit my teeth, grabbing the straps even tighter, until my knuckles turn white, and start toward town.

The rain made it before the dawn, and it poured.

A big, blue sign with white letters and a dent or two on it that looked to be made by bullets had welcomed me to the town of Kannibus, Maine about two miles back. Population one thousand and eight and dropping, although the sign had not advertised the 'and dropping' part. It had, however, advertised the best apple crumble in this county, which had started my mouth watering right then and there.

As I swallow back spit, I remind myself that I don't need food. Then again, I don't *need* cigarettes either, but since I'm going through town anyway, the temptation to pick up a pack is becoming too much to ignore. I also don't need the touch of a woman, but I never once turned it down from Julie Peterson... except for that one time. So, I decide that need is something very different from want, and that a smoke and some apple crumble might provide me with some natural fuel and the will to keep going on the road ahead, even when this town is far behind.

There's no snow on the ground here, and it takes a harsh wind to remind me that it's still winter. I can't see the buildings yet, I'm still about a quarter mile from that, but I can already smell them. The sun's about ten degrees into the sky, so I measure that it's a little after nine am, and my enhanced hearing picks up the groan of engines as people find their way to work. About five minutes later, three cars pass me in rapid succession heading back the way I came, probably going to work in Waterville. Something tells me that it's as close to rush hour as this town ever sees.

My head tilts from left to right like it's on a swivel, and I feel myself starting to lose my concentration on the road ahead, but decide that's a good thing. Someone looking too focused in a place like this might draw attention that I really don't need. Or want, for that matter. The trees that surround me are starting to get thinner, and the grass and marsh that surround them are scattered more and more with the sawed off stumps of where more had been. The type of tree is getting more diverse as well. Only a few hours ago there had only been those shadowy evergreen faces to keep me company, but now they're joined by maple, oak, and the occasional spruce.

The first sign of civilization I see (besides the sign two and a half miles back) is what remains of a park. Not the type of park with swings and see-saws, and those annoying metal horses on springs that I could never quite get to work right... it was a camping park, a nature park. It had rusted red gates across it now though, and looked as though it had for quite some time. An old wooden sign had a name on it that I'm sure is Native American and I am equally sure I am not going to attempt to pronounce, followed by a declaration of the park's hours of operation that had since been scratched out. The only thing within sight that looks less than ten years old was the chain and padlock that keeps the gates together, they sparkle like they're new. Somewhere not far beyond the gates, I hear the sound of a babbling brook, its steady stream caressing small, round rocks and probably making morning foam. I stop and eye the locked gate for a moment or two, and realize one thing the welcome sign hadn't read: Kannibus, Maine: Ghost Town.

Not abandoned, just dying, but a ghost town all the same. Probably built during the boom of the steel or coal industry and left to slowly bleed to death ever since. Seems like just as good a place as anywhere for someone like me, at least for a few hours.

I'm not even five minutes' walk past the gates to the park and I see the first buildings, a small convenience store and three houses.

The store's whitewash paint has been half chipped off

its siding, revealing an odd dark blue color underneath in some spots, and nothing but rotted wood in others. It has gas pumps out front, two of those self-serve ones, but there's no sign saying the price and they look faded and unused... and I ain't smelled a lick of gas since those cars passed me.

The sign across the front reads : 'Hannah's Convenience and Garden Shop,' but there's no sign of vegetation anywhere, none of the tell-tale sights and smells that come with that sort of growth. No fertilizer, no bone-meal, and most of all: no plants. Not so much as a tulip or a turnip.

There are posters in the front window advertising movies for rent, and from what I can see through the open front door, that much appears to be true. But the posters are also advertising 'The Crow' and 'Seven Years in Tibet' as new releases, so it's obvious how much effort they're putting into it.

As I start to pass the battered old business, I catch a glimpse of snack food and bread on the shelves, and an old man wearing a green sweatshirt and Sunday pants sitting between the checkout and the cigarette display. The itch I've been feeling in my chest ever since I thought of smokes awhile back begins to get the better of me, and I feel my body turning toward the store without my knowledge. I stop myself, remembering how little money was actually in my bank account before I cleaned it out, and that there was nothing saying that this guy wouldn't be as forgiving about legal age as my home town was. But somehow, looking at the disinterested man struggling to stay awake behind the counter, I severely doubted that last part. Still, one had to admire him. He'd obviously tried every trick he could think of to keep his business alive, only to be met with defeat every time.

I know a thing or two about that.

As for the three houses, they're nothing much to write home about either. Bungalows, all three of them, each with a pretty equal stake of land. No fences, and some of the windows don't even have curtains on them, even though they're close enough together that John Smith A could probably see right into Jane Smith B's bedroom. Two of them have the same, plain off-white siding; while the other had chosen a ghastly shade of pink. That's right, *pink*. Either the person who was living there was color blind, or they had the worst taste I have ever seen in all my life. Or they'd lost a bet. But more than likely, the reason was because it was cheap. Aside from that obvious difference, the homes were pretty much the same. Roofs that peak just a little off center, chimney that hadn't been used in years, two windows on the front and three in the back and a rickety old porch that led up to the front door. One of the white houses has a barbeque accompanying its porch, and the pink house's lawn is scattered with children's toys. And they are all as quiet as a grave right now.

I think I see something move in white house number two, but choose to ignore it and keep on moving. Maybe it will do the same.

The trees are further back from the road now, but they're still there. The roads are kept up pretty good for a dying town, and I realize that's the reason it was built right on top of Route 65 instead of off of it: easy way to get the county to pick up the tab on the upkeep of your roads. These people might have been cheap, but they sure weren't dumb.

I step over a blind hill and there's another row of houses on the opposite side of the road, and trees on my side. I resist the urge to just back-flip into the cover of the brush and keep on walking, keeping a watchful eye on the windows and doors that seem to be staring at me like eyes now. Maybe I've just watched that episode of the Twilight Zone about the small town that doesn't like strangers one too many times, but I can feel the hairs on the back of my neck reach for the sky like they've been held at gunpoint, and can't for the life of me figure out why.

Maybe this place just reminds me a little too much of home.

The houses are getting more and more plentiful now. I'll be in the heart of town soon, and I try to distract myself by thinking of that sweet apple crumble in my mouth. Most of the homes seem about the same as the first two, just small dwellings for small families, some identical to the last and some with slight differences. There was one that was just a trailer, and there was a middle-aged woman gathering up children's toys out of the dirt and mud in front of its entrance. She turned and looked at me, first with surprise, and then with hallowed, sunken eyes. She glared for just a moment, then dropped the toys and went back into her house, shooing a young child back in as she went.

Then there was that house.

I'm so busy watching the woman picking up the toys that I almost don't notice. It's like it snuck right up on me, which, given its size, is no easy task. It is easily twice as long as the largest of the other homes, and the only two-story one I've seen since entering Kannibus. The bottom story is made of brick and opens to an extravagant porch which is the size of the trailer itself. Attached to its side is a three car garage with a convertible parked in the driveway. A quick glance around back and I can see a basketball court and a small workshop that's the size of the pink house down the street. It has four times the property of the other homes... and this one does have a fence around it. And not some dinky little picket fence either, one with wire and metal that was probably the most extreme thing the town council would allow. Several signs tacked to the fence warn to beware of the dogs, but I don't see any from where I stand. That doesn't mean I don't think they are there. It just means that I don't feel quite so uneasy about the other houses now.

And the very next house over is a one room with no siding that might as well be called a shack. It's easy to see which family has the money in this town.

I keep walking, and the road starts to wind and turn a little, up this hill and over that, swerving left and then veering right. I'd hate to see someone trying to drive over this drunk, which I'm sure happens more often than not.

I look up ahead and see a blind turn right next to an old bakery that looks to be still in business, next to an old gas station that clearly isn't. I smell the yeast cooking along with the distinct aroma of cinnamon rolls, and for a moment I've forgotten about the apple crumble and the cigarettes, no easy task. I lick my lips and realize how dry they really were as I pass the gas station, once again fumbling the change in my pocket, wondering exactly how much I have.

This station looks like it's been out of luck for the last five years or more, with all of the plate glass windows beaten in and scorch marks all along one side. I take the time to shake my head at the idiocy of someone setting fire to an abandoned gas station for fun, and then continue on my way, pushing the rolls out of my head and reminding myself that I'm not here to browse like some Yankee tourist, I'm here to get past this place, and get some apple crumble if it's on the way.

There's another house just past the bakery that I can only see the roof of. It's built on a plateau just a little way down from street level, with a set of hastily manufactured stairs leading down to it. There's no front yard, and the back yard is another steep drop off that seems to go on for some time, though it's hard to tell with all the trees. The house itself is little more than a shanty, with the dark green roof taking up its majority. The siding is again a plain white, the door a magenta red. The stairs (hastily built or not, on second glance appear sturdy) lead to a narrow porch which wraps around to the other side of the domicile, and I bet that the view from it is spectacular. There are toys scattered along this balcony. Nothing extravagant, just a cheap red and yellow plastic bike that looks like it could have belonged to a boy or a girl really, and a doll house which looked to be better maintained than the house itself. It was clearly a one bedroom house, and as I walk past I get a better view of it. The windows are cracked, one of them broken with panel board nailed over the front. The siding, while in good condition, did not extend over the entire house. Since winter (even the mild one this town seemed to be having) wasn't a siding season, I assume that whoever owns it had run out of money and couldn't scrounge up any more before the summer ended.

I soon have an image in my head of the occupants of the home, even though they were nowhere in sight. I picture the child, maybe three or four, wearing clothes that are ripped and much too small for her anyway, Mommy having long ago stopped trying to keep up with her growth spurts. She's still pudgy with baby fat and her first word will probably be a curse, but Mom will tell the neighbors it's something else, like 'duck' or 'shirt'. As for Mom herself, she wore tank tops and cut-off jeans, but she wasn't some 40 - something mom clinging to her youth, she was definitely young enough to pull it off. Daddy had worked on the mines and had to move to find work. First he sent checks every two weeks, then every month, then when he got around to it... then never at all and his phone was disconnected. For some reason in my mind she was a redhead, and she had a nice tan. Don't ask me why, I don't really know. Either way, I fully expect Tammy (that sounds about right, somehow, again I don't know why) to be a grandmother by the time she was thirty and a great grandmother by the time she was forty-five, and that both grandchildren and great grandchildren would end up referring to her as 'mom'.

I shake my head and just kept walking, noticing a corner store that looks far better off than the first one I'd seen just as I started to round that big blind turn, which turns out to also be a blind hill. I think for a second that this might be where my promised apple crumble lay in wait for me, but decide not, figuring that there would be some sign outside to advertise it further. Instead, there are signs promoting $3.48 Milk! And Hershey's Chocolate Bars: 2 / 99 cents. For some inexplicable reason there is a large blue cartoon cat next to the sign above the door, which proudly proclaimed: 'Neighbor's Convenience and Pharmacy' in bright red letters. I wonder how good business could possibly be. I've only seen ten houses since I've come into town, and so far two stores. This one, however, looks to be doing a little better. It's still quaint, but it's kept up well and if it had served the apple crumble I long for, I would have eaten it right off the table without a worry in the world.

I'm almost past the place, and the next house has caught my eye (again with the pink siding, it must have been a good sale) when I notice her.

She's small and fragile, having to use both hands and just about all of her body weight to push open the front door of Neighbor's Convenience, and one of those hands clutched a brown paper bag brimming with red licorice as if it were gold. She's about three, and is wearing a puffy little blue dress with white lace around the edges and up the middle, a matching white ribbon tied into the auburn hair that looks as though it might have been blonde just a while back in the summer months. I picture the girl's mother smiling as she put it in that morning, and the girl squirming impatiently as she did. Her eyes are big and hazel, and would no doubt give her some trouble with boys in about a decade's time, as they probably did her mother. Eyes like that never come from the father, I've come to discover. She's a healthy child by the looks of her, too. Plump, but by no means overweight the way most children are these days, and her cheeks jiggle just a little as she turns her head back toward the store clerk and says "Tank Hue."

I can't help but smile when she says that, my enhanced hearing carrying it over from across the road as if it were Dolby Digital. I stop walking altogether for the first time since I came into town, and watch as she trots along the parking lot toward the road and turns left once she was on it, her nose squarely planted into her bag of licorice, hair falling to either side of her face.

I get that sick feeling in the back of my throat again as the womb perks up, and I feel like punching myself in the side as hard as I can to shut it up, deciding to get out of town before I do something to this child that I pray I won't remember. My mouth has that burning hair taste I've come to dread over the last five months as I start to walk away... but then that black blood reaches my ears, and I hear something that doesn't make me smile. It's the sound of fast spinning wheels kicking up pebbles, followed by the scent of cheap motor oil and gasoline, and even a little marijuana (which shouldn't have shocked me in a town named Kannibus).

As I turn, everything's slow motion. I'm never quite sure if that's all in my head. Maybe that's just the way it happens, or maybe I'm moving that fast that everything seems to be in slow motion... but I try not to give myself that much credit. In any case, I can see the little girl in the blue dress walking along in red dress shoes about four feet too far from the edge of the road, and my eye just catches what appears to be a late eighties sport car coming up over the blind hill leading into the blind turn.

He'll hit her and not even realize it, the way these roads were made.

I take two steps and realize that I'm not going to make it, so I stretch out my arms and jump for all it's worth, my tired legs popping at the knees with the sudden elaborate use after days of monotonous walking. For a second, I'm convinced that the car is the only thing moving, getting steadily closer one inch at a time while I just hang there in the air and the child remains in mid step, still looking into her bag of candy (which wasn't that long, really. It had been about ten seconds since she had opened the store doors). The second my arms touch the girl time speeds up again, and I feel her tiny body topple under my weight, and allow myself a sigh of relief.

That's when the car's fender connects with my right hip.

As the lower half of body jolts to one side without the benefit of being followed by my upper half, the rational part of my brain tries to tell me that I'm fine. That I've felt worse than this. A lot worse, actually, and a lot more often. However, in moments such as these, the rational part of my brain is often minuscule in comparison to the portion screaming out in sheer agony as I feel what I've come to recognize as muscle pulling itself away from bones.

I hit the pavement about five feet away from where I made contact and just keep rolling, furthering the injuries even as they try and heal themselves.

In a lot of ways, the healing is worse than the original offense. Imagine the worst pain you ever felt, then imagine it happening again in reverse slow motion. Times that by ten and try to fight an unnatural organ or two from doing what comes naturally to them while keeping a lid on your emotions, and you're half way to figuring out what my day is usually like.

I finally come to a stop against a guardrail, at just the right angle to see the car speeding around the blind turn. I had been right, he wouldn't even know he'd hit something until he got home and saw the shape of my hip in his front bumper. Across the street, some old man is peering out his living room window at me, waiting to see what will happen. He probably got that house for this express reason, the same reason people go to stock car races or watch reality tv: as a people, we just love to see the wrecks.

I start to move just as the old guy reaches for the phone, no doubt to call 911... or maybe his friend in the next house over, who knows really. His eyes widen just a little. He's never seen road kill that moves before. If I could lift my arm, I'd give him the finger.

There's a whimper a few feet to my left just as my bones finish setting themselves with a wet snap that reminds me of the sound of ripping chicken off the bone after it's been in the fridge for a few hours, and I remember the reason I got myself into this mess in the first place. I look up and see her face down on the pavement, sobbing to break her tiny heart. One of those little red shoes has come off and rolled close to me, and my heart races as I pick it up.

The movement is sheer agony, always is. My body cries out in utter defiance as I force myself to my feet and take the two steps between the two of us, and that sour milk taste is threatening to burn away my tonsils. I can feel the blood pumping in my ears as I reach out to touch her shoulder. I stop, rethinking it. This isn't home, and this kid hasn't grown up two blocks down from me her whole life.

"Are you okay?" I croak out. My voice sounds odd even to me, either from disuse or misuse, take your pick as to which. I touch my throat just to make sure that didn't get damaged in the accident as well, and am pleased to find no blood on my hand when I withdraw it. That's good. Neck wounds tend to be hellish.

She turns toward me with a face filled with tears and eyes brimming with more, her lower lip looking to be set to constant vibrate, billowing up and down like a ruler snapped over a desk. Her hair is messed up now, strands of it going everywhere, and there's a small scrape across her forehead that's not even bleeding, but still was cause enough to raise warning bells within my psyche. There are now licorice scattered all over the parking lot and street, most of the sticky candy now covered with pebbles and smut, and I pray that is the only reason for her tears.

She doesn't answer me, not in any way I can understand anyway. She just shoves forward, wrapping her arms around me and shoving her salt water and mucus-strewn face into the only clean shirt I have, her pudgy little fingers grabbing the back of my shirt and holding it tightly. She starts to mumble what happened (as if I wasn't there), but I'm not really catching a word of it. Between her cute little girl way of mixing up words, the speed of her panicked speech, and the tears still caught in her throat, it comes out as one big wail with varying pitches where words begin and end.

Nobody can cry like kids can cry. They cry like whatever's going on is the worst thing that's happened in their entire lives... because really, it is. Kids have no reference for pain. They don't have that little voice in their head to says 'you've felt worse,' because they haven't. That scratch on her forehead is probably the worst thing she's ever experienced, judging by the relative lack of scars on the child.

There's no rationalizing a child's pain either, no explaining what's happened so they can just get over it. For all she knows, she's dying. No wonder she's scared. So, I do the only thing I can do: I stroke my hand against the back of her head as calmly and rhythmically as I can, and say the occasional "Shhh..." when her breathing tells me she might be getting upset all over again.

We stay there for about ten minutes before she starts to calm down, and I realize I have too. The womb isn't pounding at the gates anymore, and my adrenaline rush from a few minutes before is way down. My heart rate has slowed, and the blood in the back of my throat tastes like regular blood again.

I must be the only person in the world that gets happy when he tastes coppery blood in his mouth.

When her sobbing subsides enough that I think I can let her go without starting another fit, I take my hand off her head and back up a pace, kneeling down so that we're closer to eye level. "Are you okay now?" I ask, trying my best to make my gruff voice sound compassionate. I hope that it at least passes for human.

She nods, though her head is still turned downward, and the sobs (while few) still come, each one shaking her entire body.

"Okay," I say, forcing a smile onto my face. Those muscles haven't been used in so long it almost hurts. "My name's Alexander. What's yours?"

She sniffs once, wipes her nose in her arm, and then looks at me. "I'm Klarissa."

"Okay Klarissa. Do you want to tell me what you were doing out in the street like that?"

She huffs, rolling those big eyes of hers dramatically, her arms flapping down by her sides in exasperation. "Mummy was urking at the rest rant sos I had to go to Nannysmith's hose for little wile sos Mummy can rake enough money to boy mya pony someday and race it at nascar. She wasgonna tack me to par, but she had work and Nannysmith smells weir sos I went to par all by meself (cause eya bigurl) hen se watch stories. Not s'good as Dora tories but Nannysmith like sem. Sos I was goin two the par but I want sum candy and den I gots ome candy en den hue ushed me. And I'm spittin mad!" She stomps her foot once against the pavement, then spat milky saliva onto the ground, to show that she did indeed know what spitting mad meant.

"Okay..." I drawl, raising an eyebrow. "I'm not even gonna pretend I understood a word of that, but somewhere in there I think I heard 'Mommy'?"

She makes a very large nod of her head, and I begin to get the impression that she's patronizing me a little, which was more than a little amusing. The smile isn't fake now.

Another car passes us, and all the occupants turn their heads to look at the child and I as they drive by, even going so far as to slow down a little. The people are no doubt wondering what the stranger was doing crouched down next to one of their youth, with licorice scattered all around them. God only knows what their minds have already come up with. I turn toward the vehicle with the intention of flipping them off, but they've already disappeared behind that damned blind turn.

Almost growling, my hip still remarkably sore, I rise to my feet and extend my hand to the child. She takes it. I'm not sure if that's good thing or not, after all, I am a perfect stranger. But that's not any of my concern, really. Screw the apple crumble. I've been in this crappy little town for fifteen minutes and I've already broken three bones, been run over by a car, and looked at like a pedophile. No pastry is worth this. I'm getting my cigarettes and getting back on the damn road. "Can you take me to your Mommy?" I ask, and she immediately turns, squeezes my hand a little, and starts walking down over the blind hill the way I was headed anyway.

⋔

I walk with her for about ten minutes when I notice her start to slow down considerably, and I realize that her little feet are getting tired, so I scoop her up onto my shoulder without a word. She laughs when I do, leaning forward to rest against my head and bouncing herself every few minutes, as if to say: 'giddy-up'.

We pass a few more houses and the park that my young friend must have been referring to (which I notice has not one but *several* of those horses on the metal springs that I can never figure out), and then another store. I'm beginning to wonder if the ratio of stores to houses in this community are 1:1, but Klarissa starts to fidget and I push the thought out of my mind. The houses themselves seem to be getting worse and worse with each step I take. Most of them don't have any siding now, or half-finishing siding. One was missing a north wall, which would have been fine for a house under construction, but the remainder of the home looks well lived in, as does the rusted out Ford parked haphazardly on the front lawn. The streets themselves are nearly deserted, with a car passing by every now and again. Only now they seem to slow more as they passed Klarissa and me... not much, but enough that I could see at least one head in each vehicle turn and look me up and down. The drivers were all young. Not as young as me, mind you, but young all the same.

One overweight man in his mid-forties peddles his bike up the road in the opposite direction as me on the other side of the road. His shirt is faded and full of mustard stains, and flip-flop sandals barely contain feet stained by tar and nails that were barely clinging to their anchors. He winked at me as he rode by, twitching his head to one side as he did, and I did my best not to make eye contact until he was gone.

The next house looks gawdy even by the standards that this town has set (pink is in season this year, after all). This one's color was normal enough, though (white with a dark blue trim), but everything else about it simply cried out for attention. On the lawn, three flamingos are perched in a semicircle facing one another, and they look somehow as if they're having a conversation about me. To the right of that is wooden cut out of the baby from 'Who framed Roger Rabbit?'. Three mannequins are sitting around a large fountain which spouts blue water, and there's an entire Smurf village which I can't help but think Mike would either love or be terrified of. There also appears to be a painting the size of a movie screen of a train on their back yard, actually sprayed onto the grass.

"That's Missusus Flarity's house," Klarissa states matter-of-factly, pointing a finger at the house. "She gives out candy apples for Hall oh wean."

We come upon a big hill on a very steep angle when we make the next turn. My young friend starts to squirm to get off as if she's used to having to hop down at this point, but I keep her up there, mainly because this is yet another of those blind hills, and I'm not keen on the idea of jumping in front of another moving vehicle. The march up isn't easy. It may not look like winter here at the moment, but it certainly is. You can tell by how slippery the roads are, and maintaining my footing on them hurts the backs of my heels like nobody's business... until the healing kicks in, that is. There's that odd slurping sound as a sore I hadn't realized was on the back of my left foot heals itself over, making a new layer of hardened, tough skin right there on the spot.

There's a little stream running by both sides of the road on the hill. The one on the other side of the road looks to be fed by the rudimentary sewer systems in the town, the water clear but still mossy and not something I would even stick my hand in, let alone drink out of. The water on my side, however, looks to be natural, and falls down over little rocks that stand in its way, making little splashing sounds as it did, this little babbling brook. I watch it intently, completely absorbed by its tranquility as

I make my way up the dirt path on the side of the road.

Klarissa seems to notice me watching the water and starts to watch it herself, laying her head down on mine and sending a few strands of her auburn hair into my face, which I blow away without a care. As she watches the brook and listens to the rhythmic sound of the water pouring, I feel her little body relax, and it's only then that I realize just how shaken up she had been by the events of a few minutes before.

We reach the top of the hill and I continue straight, passing a post office with a battered and bruised American flag out front and graffiti all but covering one side. Klarissa taps me twice on the head with her full palm and I crane my head to look at her, stopping in mid stride. She points down a side road that I've passed, and I see a little take–out restaurant there, just a minute's walk into the road. I nod, then follow her instructions and turn around.

The establishment looks simple enough from the outside, a twenty-foot cube with wobbly wooden steps leading up to the front. The whole thing is painted a brick red and has two large windows on either side of its plate glass door. A large painted sign across the side facing the road proclaims: 'Marie's Restaurant and Take-Out, the best food in the county.' I'd begun to fear that that might not be as big a stretch as I would've initially thought, but my nose was picking up the scent of fried chicken and gravy (and fresh bread too, no doubt made at the bakery up the street), and suddenly my mouth is filled with more saliva than I can choke back in a simple gulp.

There are two signs hanging in the window to the right of the door, placed outside the white curtains patterned with roses. One gives the hours of operation (which, curiously, proclaims that it always closes for lunch), the other is hand-drawn and taped to the window itself: 'Home of Marie's Apple Crumble Special.' My eyes nearly bug out of my skull as I put Klarissa down next to me and open the door, its rusted hinges squeaking in defiance. I missed Christmas this year... but this little turn of fate will do just fine.

The inside of the diner looks a little better than the out, but not much. To be fair, they did wonders with what they had to work with. There are only four tables and eight chairs, all painted the same brick red as the outside. Someone tried to dress up the walls and make them look pretty, putting flower trim all around the center, but the tiled walls and the odd underlying odor that it wouldn't take my nose to smell tells me that this place was a butcher shop no more than five years ago. Just like the video store out on the edge of town, it had to change just to survive. Through an open door that reads 'employees only' I see the large sheering saw that used to be used for cow, and was now used chiefly for chicken. In all fairness, it was remarkably clean. A place this small with a cutting room, a kitchen and a bathroom should make a guy like me want to hurl from what I can smell, but all I get is the familiar scent of pine cleaner that makes my nose twitch just a little.

Behind the counter are racks of potato chips and soda, and another door into what can only be the kitchen, a phone attached to the wall next to it for taking orders. The door opens, and a tired looking woman comes out.

"Mommy!" Klarissa yells, holding out her arms wide

as she runs under the counter and jumps up into the woman's arms. She hugs her mother tight, clutching at the apron patterned with the same roses as the curtains, but stained with grease and blood.

The woman smiles and laughs, running a hand through her daughter's hair and not realizing that she just left a gloop of some unknown black substance there, probably oil from one of the stoves in the back.

I feel ashamed for an instant as I look at them. Not thirty minutes before I had had her pegged as another neglectful teenage mother with more condoms in her pocket than common sense in her head, letting her child run free in the yard like an animal. Christ, I'd had her pegged as a great grandmother by the time she turned fifty, for crying out load. This girl was nothing like that. First off, she seemed older than I'd originally thought. There were lines around her eyes from either laughter or pain (or both). Her hair wasn't red at all, but a golden blonde that made her look positively angelic. I had been right about her daughter's eyes at least, those same hazel spheres glistened in her eyes too. Her smile was the best part, though. She had nice, freckled cheeks that moved at even the hint of happiness. Even a small smile for her reached from ear to ear, and made me realize what those lines around her eyes were really from. Her teeth weren't what you'd call straight but they were definitely properly cared for, never touched by nicotine and rarely by coffee. The only make-up on her face was on her lips, a pink gloss that made them shine and sparkle. Suddenly, the apple crumble didn't seem that appetizing anymore.

I'm about to estimate her age as actually being mid-thirties, when the rotary fan behind her finally turns and sends her scent in my direction. Behind the grease and sweat, she has a scent like marmalade. A natural sweetness that starts my mouth watering again, and I change my mind on her age. She's no more than twenty-five, probably a little younger, just aged a little too early by stress and a few too many disappointments.

"Klarissa," she tisks, getting down on her knees to face her daughter at eye-level. "What are you doing here? You're supposed to be at your Nanny Smith's house until after supper." Her voice has a hard edge to it, but it's natural and unintentional. Each word is doused in so much love, you'd have to ring them out by hand to make them mean. "Didn't she take you to the park?"

"See was gonna," Klarissa sighs, again slapping her arms against her legs dramatically, rolling those eyes of hers, "but see had to visit her friend Jack Daniels, but she never done that either... see just fell asleep watching stories, so I went to the park all by myself cause I'm a big gurl, but then on the way I wanted to go to the store sos I did an got some candy, but then the man pushed me."

Klarissa's mother turns toward me, as if noticing me for the first time. I'm leaned against the counter, trying my darndest to look casual, my hands clasped out before me. "You pushed her?" she says, her voice accusing as she gets up, dusting off her apron.

I back up a pace, stuttering a little as I do. "I - I mean - - there was a car! I pushed her out of the way of a car that was coming over the hill. It was a car, right Klarissa?"

Her mother looks down at her, and the child shakes her head slowly back and forth. "I din see no car."

My face goes white, and I realize that after everything, my chances of getting that apple crumble are fast fading away.

She looks up at me with dead seriousness, her eyes squinting in a way that doesn't look natural for them. I wait for a swift kick to a place where even my healing won't help me, but instead I see a smile begin to grow on her thin lips again, her cheeks rising until they nearly overtook her eyes. "Had her nose buried in a bag of candy, did she?" she asked, ruffling her daughter's hair.

I breathe a sigh of relief, feeling all my muscles relax, then nod. "Yeah. Some idiot in a car almost ran her over. Wasn't really her fault, but you might want to rethink your choice in sitters all the same."

She nodded knowingly. "Mm. She was a bit of a last resort. Usually Marie, the owner, looks after her when I'm working for her, but she had to go to a funeral upstate so Nanny Smith was really our only option." She looked me up and down, then extended a hand forward the way people do when they're not sure what else to do. "My name's Sandra. You can call me Sandi."

"Alex," I say simply, taking her hand and shaking it twice. Her hands aren't smooth like most girls her age. Lots of hard work and labor have turned their velvet touch into leather way before their time, but there's a softness to them that nothing on this earth can take away, I'd wager.

"What brings you to Kannibus, Alex?" she asked, trying not to sound as though she was prying even though she was. She might have been grateful, she might have been kind... but she wasn't stupid either. I was a stranger that had been alone with her daughter and I must have smelled like a pit bull by now. She had every right to have questions, so I decided to answer as best I could.

"Just passing through. Been keeping to the highways mostly, but this little place cuts right through it. If I keep going on the main road, will it take me back out again?"

She nods, even as she hands Klarissa a box of orange juice from the cooler and starts to wipe down the counter tops. "Yeah. Should only take you about an hour's walk to be completely out of town."

"Any place I can pick up smokes between here and there?" I ask, taking a quick glance around the place a realizing that not only are there none here, but I can't even smell that herb musk of nicotine anywhere close by.

"There's the gas station. It's the very last thing you'll pass when you're leaving the town limits. They're really expensive here, though. They know you can't get them anywhere else, none of the other stores sell them."

I nod in understanding, jingling the change in my pocket.

"So, what can I get you?" she asks as soon as she's done cleaning the counter, placing both hands on it and leaning forward, smiling. The top button of her checkered blouse is undone from the heat of the kitchen, and when she leans forward I can smell the sweat from her body.

"Nothing for me, thanks. I gotta get on the road and I haven't got much money." I say, turning back toward the door. It's time for me to get out of here, before something bad happens. Because with me, something bad *always* happens.

"Wouldn't dream of charging you. I think saving my little girl's life earns you a piece of chicken. Or at least some of Marie's apple crumble, there's a fresh one in the fridge, not even sliced yet."

I stop in mid-step. I remind myself, not for the first time, that I don't need to eat, strictly speaking. But my stomach starts to roar at me as it eats away at itself, and my dry tongue longs for the taste of something other than my own spit on it. I take my hand off the door and turn around, and before I know what I'm saying, I ask: "Ice cream?"

Sandi smiles again, as she gestures toward the cooler. "Your choice of three of the thirty-one flavors."

I walk back toward the chairs and sit down as she starts cutting up the promised apple crumble I've waited so long for. Every so often, Klarissa pokes her head up over the counter and grins at me as I wait, and I realize her eyes weren't the only thing she got from her mother.

She got her smile, too.

The apple crumble tastes like heaven.

I wolf it down like a savage, and it still takes me the better part of fifteen minutes to eat it. I think she gave me nearly half the whole pan, and she hadn't skimped on the ice cream either. It was vanilla and it was homemade by someone local or close to local, I guessed, and it's cool goodness in contrast to the steaming hot crumble makes the whole world disappear each and every time I shove another spoonful in my mouth.

She watches me eat the entire thing, head rested on her hand behind the counter. I apologize once or twice for my table manners, but she insists that she's enjoying watching me enjoy it. I smile at her (a feeling that if I'm not careful my mouth may get used to) and put another bite into my mouth, this one drenched in melted cream.

Klarissa's eating her own smaller version of my meal from a dish at the next table over, and I turn to her and wave my spoon in the air in a mini 'cheers.' She reciprocates the action, waving it a little bit too hard and sending droplets of melted ice cream spraying to the floor. The both of us laugh, followed in suit by her mother, who quickly wipes one of those droplets off the counter.

"So," she asks, smirking at me again. "What're you doing out on the highway in the middle of winter anyway?"

"Wandering," I say in a non-committal voice, motioning toward my pack in the corner. "Trying to keep warm and keep fed. Been on the road about a week and a half."

"Coming from the north or the south?"

"Neither," I answer, and don't elaborate.

She's polite enough to take the hint and get off the topic quickly. "Any idea when you're heading out?"

I put the last piece of apple crumble in my mouth and start to chew. I almost feel bad that as soon as I swallow I'm going to say: 'now,' then grab my stuff and leave, but it's not like I owe this girl anything. I don't know her from Adam, for god's sake. I can see both suspicion and curiosity in her eyes, and know that if I stay, one or both of us will end up hurt. Probably just her, and not in the way she would be worried about.

I swallow down and I'm about to make my exit, when I hear the roar of a suped-up engine pull into the driveway outside. Sandi hears it too, and the smile disappearing from her face just confirms what I already know : trouble.

I see dirt settling through the window, most of it being taken up and away by the breeze coming in from the north, probably bringing some snow with it, too. I can see just enough of the roof of the car to tell that it's red, shiny, and that the owner of the vehicle was definitely overcompensating for something. I hear shoes against the gravel outside as the scents start to make their way in through the doors before the men themselves. And they are men, I can smell the testosterone from here. I can also smell cheap motor oil and gasoline... and marijuana. More of it this time than the last time, I smelled it. My eyes narrow and my blood starts to pump, my fists clenching until the knuckles are white.

Sandi waves Klarissa over, ignoring me now as if I wasn't even there, the way any good mother would. Klarissa runs under the counter again and her mother shoves her into the kitchen, closing the door shut behind her, just as the door to the diner opens. Through it, I can see the red car, eighties model, suped up, with a dent in the front bumper where my right hip had hit.

I was expecting to see some stupid thug wearing army pants and a black tee-shirt with tattoos going down both arms like sleeves. I've really gotta stop assuming things like that, because for the second time since I marched into town, I'm dead wrong.

He's about a head and a half taller than me (which doesn't really take much), and he isn't the built up muscle man I was expecting, but he isn't weak either. It was hard to tell under that suit and tie he was wearing, the top button undone in a vain attempt to look casual. He looks like someone who works out, but not someone who thought working out was their life. He has short hair that's combed neatly to one side and gelled there so that it stays that way the entire day, and a perfectly groomed smile that looks like one a used car salesman gives you before he tells you the price. His hands were hairy and the veins were popping out of them at the knuckles, which were scarred in some places and scabbed in others. His eyes were that cobalt blue that made girls melt, made it so they couldn't see anything but those eyes until it was too late. People used to call eyes like that 'bedroom eyes.' I had another word for them, but not one I care to say.

Yeah, it's safe to say I don't like this guy right away.

Behind him is the big trouble, though. A walking mountain that looks to have the intelligence of half a mule and none of the charm. This one was wearing army pants, but he was wearing a white wife-beater instead of a black tee-shirt, and if the clothes ever made the man, they look to have with this guy. He looks like an ex-marine that beat his wife. He also looks like he would have no trouble taking me a round or two, and I'm glad when he hangs back outside.

"Get out of here, Kurt," Sandi says, pretending to be relaxed as she wipes down the Pepsi cooler frantically. "You know you're not allowed to come in here anymore."

"Sandra, baby," he smiles, his voice smooth and calm as he lifts up the door to the other side of the counter and walks in behind as if he owns the place. "I can do whatever I want, you know that."

They're both ignoring me, which is fine for now. I keep

watching to see what I can learn, but with every second that passes I become more and more certain of what this is and where it's going, and I become painfully aware that my knife is in the pocket of my bag in the corner.

"You can't come in here, Kurt. I don't want you around Klarissa. She doesn't need to see you, not now." Sandi is backing up two paces for every one step he takes forward, and before she knows it her back is against the cooler. She jumps a little as the condensation hits her back, and suddenly she's sweating and looking downward as he closes the distance between them. The fan behind her moves again, and I can smell the fear coming off of her in waves.

"I'm just here to make sure she's okay. Old man Hickey says that he saw her almost get run over by a car today while she was alone. Is that any way to take care of our daughter?"

I remember the old man in the window and curse.

"She was supposed to be with Mrs. Smith!" Sandi yells, pleading now, tears ready to come at any moment. The only way she would have broken this fast is if this wasn't the first time, but more the latest of many.

This is where some people would make a discreet exit, and I hate to say that I'm tempted. This mess isn't any of my business after all, and in an hour I could be on the outskirts of town smoking a Marlboro with a full stomach for the first time in recent memory. Then again, it wasn't my business to jump in front of a speeding car to save that little girl either, but I'd done it. Far be it for anyone to say I don't see things through.

I get up out of my chair and it squeaks noisily, and

suddenly both Kurt and Sandi realize that I'm here. I pick up my plate and fork in one hand and walk over to the counter, looking around it for a tray or something where I can put them. "Where do I lay these?" I ask stupidly, making eye contact with Kurt for the first time since he came in.

He glares me down, and suddenly I'm in a contest to see who'll blink first, and it's him. "Just put it anywhere and get out of here," he snarls, that salesman smile long gone as he pokes a thumb toward the door, then turns his back to me and pushes both of Sandi's shoulders against the cooler.

"Fine," I state, then toss the plate at his head. It hits just to the right and shatters against the cooler, sending sharp shards everywhere but where they intended to go. I realize I've gotten rusty, but try my best to make it seem like it happened just like I wanted it too.

"Fuck!" Kurt yells, brushing the bits of plate out of his perfectly groomed hair and messing it up in the process, making him look like a wild man. "What the fuck is the matter with you?"

"Throw a dart at a word that describes crazy, you'll probably hit one that fits me," I quip, smirking a little out of the corner of my mouth. "Now get the hell out of here."

"You've just made a really big mistake," he snarls, pointing a finger at me accusingly. There is no boasting in his voice, none of that wavering that usually comes with the empty promise of an evil man. "I own this town."

"Yeah, well I'm new," I say, feeling a little like Clint Eastwood. "So you'll have to pardon me."

He squints, making his blue eyes shoot fire if they could. "There are no pardons in my town," he says, then turns and walks toward the door, slamming his fist against the wall before he leaves and shaking one of the tiles down. The big guy outside looks as though he wants to come in after me, but he gets a slap upside the head and follows like any good lackey. It's almost comforting to know that no matter where I go, lackeys are still lackeys. Almost.

The engine roars back to life and he pulls away, the stench of dope staying in the air for a long while. When I'm sure he's gone I turn to Sandi, walking around the counter to where she's still got her back against the Pepsi cooler, as if he never left, shaking like a leaf.

"Hey, sorry if I was out of line..." I start, raising my hands in surrender, again ready for the possibility of a swift kick.

It doesn't come. "It's okay. I'm just sorry you had to see that," she says, voice quivering even as she reaches for the broom and starts sweeping up the plate I shattered. This time I help, bending down and picking up some of the bigger pieces. "Don't," she says, her voice full of concern, "You'll cut yourself."

I chuckle and meet her gaze. I don't know what my smile looks like, but whatever it is, it brings hers back. I don't bother explaining that it would take a whole lot more than a bit of plate to make me bleed. There's still no reason to get into that, much as part of me would like to.

"Thank you," she says finally, when all the little bits are in the pan. She opens up the door to the kitchen and dumps it in a hidden garbage, letting Klarissa out at the same time. "I don't know how I can repay you."

"That's fine," I say, and I feel my smile fading. I'm starting to get itchy to leave. I know where this conversation is headed, and I'm anxious to get out before it goes there.

"Do you have anywhere to spend the night?"

Too late.

Her shift ends a few hours later, and we go back to the little white house with the magenta red door next to the bakery. The walk doesn't seem so long this time, as she points out all the little houses that I noticed on my way up and tells me things about the owners. Nothing too scandalous, just cute little tidbits that one hears in a small town. The only house she doesn't even glance at is the one across from the store where Klarissa almost got run down, but I do. That same old man is in the window again, phone pressed to his large, swollen ears. You don't get ears like that by leading a peaceful life, you get them by taking as many hits as you dish out over the course of years.

She doesn't cook, and that's fine by me. She'd done enough of that over the last few hours I guess, and a microwave dinner was still the nicest full meal I've had in ages (but still didn't top the apple crumble).

Her home is small. The front door opens right up into the kitchen / dining room, which barely has enough room to walk around the table. Off of that is a living room with two doors in it, one for a bedroom and one for a bathroom. Only one bedroom, and that one had Klarissa's name on it in stick-on star letters. It was well cleaned, though, and warm despite the cool wind from the north that was only getting worse. All said, I was glad I wasn't on the road tonight.

After dinner, Sandi starts clearing away the table and Klarissa and I go play in the living room. We watch an episode of Dora the Explorer and then Sponge Bob Square Pants while playing a few rounds of shoots and ladders. She wins twice, I win once. I'd love to say I let her win, but when I suck at something, I really suck.

After a quick game of ker-plunk, I ask her if she'd like me to tell her a story. Her face lights up and she all but jumps into my arms, and out of the corner of my eye I see Sandi turning away from the sink and smirking at the two of us over her shoulder. I try not to smile back, but I can't help it.

I tell her the story of Klarissa and the Beanstalk, a classic. I change certain key things in the story and she eats it up. Klarissa doesn't sell a cow for magic beans, she sells licorice, and she buys it from a used car salesman that remains nameless. I get to the part where the giant (who I name Derek) says he smells the blood of a little girl, and I notice the fright in her eyes. I ask her if it's too scary, and she shakes her head no so quickly and furiously that her hair whips at my face. I turn to make sure that Sandi isn't watching, and then continue, pounding my fists against the floor to simulate the giant's footsteps.

I turn on the T.V. when Sandi goes into the room with Klarissa to put her to bed, much to the child's objection. There's nothing really good on, so I channel surf for about thirty minutes until a news station from the west coast catches my eye. There's a story on about the robbery of some high-tech industrial complex, followed by one about three homeless men found burned alive after they were caught scavenging for food. I turn the channel a few more times, landing on some sitcom and lean back on the coach, pretending to watch it. Over by the front door, my bag is calling to me again, telling me to take the opportunity and just leave. Now. But I don't, and a few minutes later, Sandi comes out of the bedroom wearing pajamas.

"Is she down?" I ask, smiling and poking my thumb out in the direction of the star-covered door.

"Yeah," Sandi smiles, taking her seat close to me even though there was plenty of room on the couch. "I had to listen to her retelling of Klarissa and the Beanstalk, but she fell asleep about half way through. I do hope she got out of it alive."

I blush a little, then smile. "I think that's a safe bet."

She reaches out and touches the short hairs behind my ear, and my entire body feels tingly.

"So, what was that guy's deal today?" I blurt out, trying desperately to change the topic and hoping it isn't obvious.

Her fingers stop, and she rests her arm across the back of the couch and sighs. "He's Klarissa's father, but I guess you figured out that much."

"I did, yes," I admit, that and more, but me telling her what I already know won't help her. She has to tell me before it eats her alive. Maybe someday I'll learn to take my own advice on that front. But I doubt it.

"I met him about four years back, right after he and his father had come into town. His Dad was some big shot Texas businessman with what seemed like all the money in the world to us. This community's been dying ever since the mine closed, and he promised he was going to make everything better."

"Did he?" I ask, raising an eyebrow skeptically.

"At first. He got everyone jobs at this factory in Waterville, everyone that didn't already have jobs, that is. And he started pouring money into the community. Like that playground down the street, or the baseball field up by the gas station. Everything seemed so great, he was like a father to the whole town... but he wasn't a kind man, by any means. He'd yell at kids if they made too much noise when he was trying to think. And the businesses, he started buying them up one by one, and those that didn't sell seemed to shut down pretty fast. There'd be some accident or they'd just run out of money. Or both."

I remember the abandoned gas station just up the road from here, the one with scorch marks all over one side, and understand what she's talking about.

"While all this was going on, I was dating Kurt. He seemed really nice at first. He'd take me on dates into the city and all over. He told me that when his father left for Texas in a few months, he was going to run this town, and he wanted me with him." A frown came over her face, and I knew what was coming. "But I wouldn't... you know. He said that didn't matter to him, that he loved me. One night I got mad with him when he wouldn't leave the video store on the other side of town alone, and he just... took it. Me, I mean. He just..."

Against my better judgment, I reach out and touch her shoulder. I don't say anything to coax her on, though. She'll tell all she wants to tell, and not one word more because of me.

"I went to the police. They took down every word I said and made it all really official. They said they'd get him. Then a week went by. Then two. Around the time I realized that I was pregnant, I noticed that all the county policemen for this area were driving new cars... and then I knew. It's been everything I can do to keep Klarissa away from him. He wanted nothing to do with her at first, but then a few months back he saw her at the county fair when she was eating cotton candy, and ever since then, he's been trying to take her away from me. And almost everyone in town helps, because if they don't..."

I nod, thinking back to the glares I got from the few people still in town when I walked through.

"I just know he's going to use this accident today to take her, I just know he will." That was it. As strong as she was (and she was, stronger than I'd be, or any of you, for that matter), the idea of losing her child was too much. It was too raw. The salt water finally came from her eyes in great rivets, and it was like a dam had burst inside the ducts. I wonder how long she'd been holding it in with nobody to talk to. I don't think a year would be a over-estimation.

I do the only thing I can think to do. I pull her close and lay her head against my heart, stroking her hair that still smells like grease over shampoo and let her cry a river onto my shirt. She's only there a moment before her arm is around me, clutching me as close as she probably did her pillow every other night. That marmalade smell fills my nostrils, and despite everything I've had to eat today, I find myself hungry again.

As if she's reading my mind, she takes her head off of

my chest and looks at me with those hazel eyes. I hadn't even noticed that the sun had gone down until I noticed the way the moonlight sparkled against her lip gloss, making them so beautiful and succulent. I don't lean into her. I don't encourage her in any way. But I don't stop her, either. She leans in and kisses me, and suddenly that sweet nectar smell is everywhere, as is the taste as I feel her tongue, slow, then fast inside my mouth. Still embraced, I lean her onto her back and she wraps one leg around me, pulling me toward her. Her skin feels so smooth, her clothes so warm.

I break off the kiss and move my head back as she tries to continue it, her lips still moving as if it is. "I can't do this," I say, but she can feel my body rising, making a liar of me.

"Alex, I feel safe when you're here," she says, her voice equal parts seductive and innocent. It's almost more than I can bear.

"That's why I can't do this," I explain, getting up and helping her do the same. "It wouldn't be right. You have enough people taking advantage of you lately."

She smiles, then laughs as she starts to cry again. "You really are a nice guy," she beams, leaning in and giving me a peck on the lips and then a hug.

"No, I'm not," I say, but I'm smiling when I do, and I squeeze her tight.

"I feel so stupid," she laughs again, wiping away the moisture that the last hour brought to her face, and I'm happy to see that no more is coming.

"Don't," I say, rubbing both her shoulder as we part our embrace. "Believe me, it was my mistake."

She laughs again, and it's as if it didn't happen. We talk for a few more minutes and then she goes into Klarissa's room to sleep on the floor, giving me the couch. I try to say I won't sleep anyway, but that's another one of those things that would require too much explanation.

I turn the television volume down to zero, which is more than enough for my ears to pick up, and start flicking through the channels again. I watch an action movie until late, then get up to get myself a cup of coffee. A cigarette would make everything superb right about now, but what can I do? I sit back down and flick through the channels a little more, as the couch gets more and more comfortable and I feel myself starting to drift. I take another shot of coffee and continue to channel surf until I find a horror movie in black and white from the thirties and settle in, hoping that I can keep my attention occupied until morning. It crosses my mind that I can just leave whenever I want, but I don't want Sandi to think that there are hard feelings, so I stick it out.

It's about two a.m. and my eyelids are starting to get heavy. I hear a car go by, it's the fifth one this hour, and I wonder what these people are *doing* at this hour in the morning on a Tuesday.

My nostrils perk up as a familiar smell comes across them, and suddenly I'm more awake then I've been in weeks. Down at my right side, the womb perks up and starts to throb. This time my knuckles only turn white for a second before I let my fingers relax and the claws come out, one by one. My blood drips onto the floor from the wounds the talons make, and the pain makes me feel awake and alive. It's the same tingly sensation I got when

Sandi kissed me, as grotesque as that sounds.

The smell of motor oil and marijuana is everywhere now, or at least it seems that way to me. I can feel the pressure in my veins building more and more with each and every breath I take it in with, both my hearts beating so fast I should be in pain, but I'm not. It's a strangely relaxing feeling, that little bit of calm before all hell breaks loose. In that moment, everything is clear. There's no right, there's no wrong. There's just me and the person in front of me, and the knowledge that in a few minutes only one of us is going to be left standing. There's a strange purity in that.

The knob to the front door clicks twice, and then the door comes open, almost off of its hinges. I hear the sudden gasps of air coming from the bedroom as Sandi and Klarissa awake with a start, and Sandi's knees scuttling against the floor. The door hits the kitchen counter, sending splinters of wood twirling to my feet as I take my first steps forward toward the barbarians at the gate. I feel the rumble of base in my throat that begins every growl, feel its vibrations against my chest and jaw. All of this happens in less than two and a half seconds after that second click of the door knob. At the three second mark, I'm facing off against a mountain with legs.

He's still wearing those damn army camouflage pants from earlier today, but he went shirtless rather than wear the wife-beater. Hard to dispose of blood-spattered shirts, way easier to just jump in the shower. His skin is the tan brown of someone that's been out in the sun just a little too long, but the lack of tan lines told me it was his natural color. I don't think this guy's a local, maybe a friend of

Kurt's from around the south Texas border. His hands are clasped together tightly, combining to make one big fist that's the size of my head. His low, cave-man like brow (with a curious lack of eyebrows) rises as he lets out a long bellow and brings his hands across the side of my head, sending me flying across the room.

I hit the wall doing a forty, I think, and I somehow manage to leave a dent in it the size of my entire body.

As the room spins and the womb fights to give me back some semblance of control over my sight, I barely notice as Kurt walks in behind his thug, that used car salesman smile of his grinning smugly at me. I make a promise to myself that by the end of the day, he won't be smiling anymore.

We're six seconds in, and the world stops spinning just in time for me to see those two clasped hands connect with the bridge of my nose. It's one of those moments when I hate my enhanced senses. They make everything more real. I can hear the bone snap as well as feel it, and the sickening crunch as the healing factor rights it again. All said, a single, thin line of blood escapes my left nostril before it's completely healed.

The man-mountain looks at me, a perplexed expression on his dim-witted face.

"Get used to it," I bark, slamming my heels into both of his knees. He bellows loudly, but I don't hear anything break, and before I know it, he's struck a blow to my side. He hits even harder when he's angry, and that was my *right* side. My brain howls in agony as the impact makes the womb organ skip one beat, then another. It's not really hurt, but it's rhythm is just off enough that it's pumping air into my veins rather than that black tar that tastes like burnt hair.

The lucky fuck has gone and fucked me.

Sandi's eyes go wide as she stares at the silhouette of the man opening her bedroom door. Backlit the way he is, he looks as though he's all black... except that wide smile. That toothy grin of his is still pearly white. The combination of those two images is quite unsettling.

"Give me my daughter," he barks, and the smoothness is gone from his voice now. It's just demanding, like a child stomping his foot and demanding a new toy. It was the same tone he'd used the night he'd gotten her pregnant.

"No, Kurt!" she screams, holding her hands close to her heart. "You can't have her! She's the only thing you can't have. You can have anything else you want!"

He takes a step forward, reaching out and grabbing her around the neck and lifting her to her feet. "There is *nothing* that I can't have!" he yells, glancing into Klarissa's bed and seeing that she wasn't there. "Now where is she?"

Finally, Sandi understands, and smirks a little. "The only reason you want her is because you know you can't have her. Just like me," she smiles, looking him directly in the eye for the first time since she had dated him.

His upper lip curls as he grabs her by both shoulders and shakes her violently once, then twice, then lets her go, slamming her against the closet door.

I'm down but I'm not out. I've been without the power of the womb before, and I will be again. That does not mean I'm about to get my behind handed to me by some lummox with the intelligence of a gnat. I wait for him to rise for another strike (I think this is the third one since he made the womb-organ do the labamba, but I'm a little woozy on that point). He does with another of his massive grunts, and I slash out with my claws, raking them across his chest and stomach. He staggers back, confused and in shock. I didn't get very deep, but he definitely felt it. He looks down at the red coming from the four lines I've made across his torso as if this were the first time he'd ever seen his own blood, pressing his hand against them and hissing gingerly under the pressure, then looking at his blood on his hand in the moonlight.

He looks back at me and roars in anger, sending one fist forward. I swerve my head out of the way just in time, as he puts his hand through the wall as far in as his elbow. Turning toward me and bellowing again, he tries to remove his hand and gets about an inch. He's stuck, and I feel myself grinning. I slide under him and bring my knees up to my chin, then let loose with about thirty double-kicks to his chest and gut, around the same area where my talons tasted his flesh. He screams with every impact, and I pray to god it's not scaring Klarissa too much. But that thought's minor, I'm sad to say. Mostly, I'm just enjoying lacing into someone that actually deserves it for once. That's the one thing I love about thugs. No matter what I do to them, I never feel bad.

His eyes begin to water as my legs begin to ache, and I'm starting to have a massive headache because of all the air the womb pumped into my system, but it's well worth it. Out of the corner of my eye I see something coming out of Klarissa's room and stop, turning toward it just in time to see an expensive shoe coming toward my eye.

I regain consciousness no more than a minute and a half later, but they're already gone. The stench of their aftershave and that cheap dope still hangs in the air though, and it's better than smelling salts for waking me up. I get to my feet quickly, aching as the womb finally starts back at a normal beat, healing the bruises all over my body. I can't see out of one eye and my depth perception sucks, but I stumble my way over toward Klarissa's room.

My heart sinks.

Klarissa is still there, god bless her soul, curled up against her mother's breast and crying. There's a stream of blood going from the metal handle of the closet down to where Sandi's head is resting against the wall. Try as I might, I can't hear a heartbeat. It doesn't take a genius to figure out what happened, and that's good, because I might never have if it had. He'd pushed her way too hard. He probably hadn't even tried it the way it happened. Not that that mattered to me one little bit. Her hand is still wrapped around her little girl, just under the nape of her neck. Her last action had been trying to make the child feel better, to comfort her in some way. Her face is lifeless now, the muscles relaxed and fixated in that position. Still, I want to believe that I can still see that smile on her face.

I know it's not really there, but I swear I can see it, just under the surface.

The cops arrive way too fast. Faster than anyone but me and Kurt could even know there's a crime. I kiss Klarissa on the forehead and bring my finger to her mouth. She nods in understanding as I slip back into the shadows of the room.

I'm there for an hour and forty five minutes. In that length of time, three cops and a coroner come through the place. None of them notice me. I could stay in this position for days if I had to, luckily that long isn't necessary. They talk about pressing charges and against who. There have been reports of a stranger in town they say. He attacked Klarissa, they say. I listen to it all, but more than that, I listen to the words behind the words. I listen to each of their heartbeats as they talk amongst themselves, to see which of them is lying. I'm surprised and gratified to find that none of them are, each of them deluded enough to believe what they were saying.

It's four thirty in the morning before the last of them leaves, and I finally step out of the shadows, stretching my stiff back muscles. I go immediately for the dresser and open it, rummaging around for something I smelled almost an hour before, but had no way of getting to. Something that smells like marmalade and skin moisturizer.

Something that smells like Sandra.

My hand hits something solid amidst the socks and shirts, and I haul it out immediately. It's a diary, brown with a coiled metal spine and a picture of a elk on the front cover, leaping over some tall grass. There's a pen sticking out of it to mark her page, and I open it with quivering hands.

'... the only nice person I ever met. He's so kind and gentle, and he gets along with K. really well. He told her this hilarious story about Jack and the Beanstalk, but he changed all the names and things for her. I know he's going tomorrow, and that nothing I do can make him stay, but tonight he kissed me and made me feel special, because he cared enough to stop. He's the nicest, gentlest man I've ever met. And I just hope he remembers me after he's gone...'

I feel the true womb start up again. Taste that burnt hair in the back of my throat as the black blood rises. Hear the soft squirting noise as that blood fills my eyes, rupturing the vessels there and turned them coal black.

"Black Womb lives."

ʌ‹›ʌ

"I'm telling you, it was that guy that attacked Klarissa yesterday," Kurt yells into the phone as he takes a puff of his cigarette, leaning forward in his chair and resting his elbow onto his knee. He reaches forward and doubts the smoke, joining a pile of ten within the last hour. "Who else could it be? Nobody else in our town could do such a thing. This is a good town, sir, with good people. Yes." He pauses, listening to the person on the other end of the line, then smiles. "Definitely. We'll start a full search in the morning. He won't get very far." He hangs up the phone and sighs, looking forward into the fireplace. It has started to snow outside, and he watches it fall for a moment before he sees something behind him in his reflection.

"Wasn't too hard to find the place," the Womb spits, grabbing Kurt by the collar and hoisting him up out of his chair. The room is filled with hunting trophies and expensive looking artwork that all looks positively ridiculous together, a mish-mash of culture from a thug trying to look better than he is. There's a picture of Sandi on the mantle, and it almost makes me throw up. "Just looked for the biggest, gaudiest house in town. Yours was the only one that fit the bill. It was also the only house whose owners could afford real siding."

I bar my teeth at him. I'm not quite sure what that looks like, really. I've never been able to sum up the courage to look myself in the mirror when I'm in Womb-mode... but judging from the expression on Kurt's face, it's the worst thing you've ever seen.

"Please, please don't kill - -" he doesn't even get the sentence out before I throw him against the mantle, his head bashing against its metal. It would be terribly ironic if I accidentally killed him like this, the same way he killed Sandi, but somehow I don't think I'm that lucky. It shuts him up though. He's not dead, but he's pretty out of it. I know that because his hand fell into the fire and he's not even twitching it to get it out.

I pour myself a drink of whiskey from a mini-fridge and sit in his chair while I drink it, watching his arm burn. When the skin starts to bubble I fish him out and sling him over one shoulder, and start toward the door.

ᶺᐸᐟᐥ

I push his head under the water, and the son of a bitch finally wakes up. His eyes jut open like they're spring loaded, and bubbles start to come up from his every orifice. I know he can't really see me through the water. It's almost dawn, but with all the cloud cover, you wouldn't know it. There's a heavy weight of snow on the ground now, but that's not what's making me act so cold. It's the thought of two young lives ruined by one moron's temper. I've changed back into my human face. For some reason, that was important to me. It's not very stealthy, but at this moment, I don't care. I hear him curse beneath the current and pull him up by the collar, watching him as he gasps for air.

"What the fuck!?" he yells at me when he's got enough air in his lungs, although he's still coughing up water. He gets his bearings and looks around, seeing nothing but evergreen and elk. The only sounds are that of the river, the rustling of the trees, and the steady creak of the park gate as it swings back and forth on its rusty hinges. For some reason, I thought this would be as good a place as any to do this, though I don't know why. Maybe because it's the first thing I saw when I came into Kannibus, maybe because I didn't want people interfering... mostly I think it's because it's the one place I'm certain that Klarissa won't wander off to by herself. That girl's seen enough death for one lifetime. "Help!" he screams, and I smile a little.

"Yeah, like that's gonna happen," I snap back sarcastically. I'm sure there's something real meaningful I could say to him here. Make some kind of Biblical reference about the washing away of sins and re-baptism and all that jazz... but somehow, I'm just not in the mood. Grinning, I push him back down under. His eyes shoot open again, like one of those porcelain dolls whose eyes open and close depending on which angle you tilt them.

His arms rise above the surface of the water and start grabbing at me, punching at my chest and pulling at my arms to try and get free. Once again I realize I was wrong in my earlier assessment: he's actually as weak as a kitten, and I almost feel bad about what I'm doing.

Almost.

He starts to kick as the bubbles get fewer and fewer, but his blows are getting less potent with each passing second. Finally, his eyes roll back into his head and the bubbles stop. I wait an extra moment and then haul him out of the freezing winter water quickly, laying him on his back. His lips are already blue and his digits are losing color fast, but that enhanced hearing of mine tells me I have plenty of time. His heart's slowed down and beginning to stop, but its beats are still strong.

I lace my fingers together tightly and press them against the center of his chest, timing it at five pumps every four seconds. I pause for a moment and look at him, realizing that there's no response. Again, I pump at his chest. One, two, three, four, five. Then I lean forward, pinch his nose and take in a long mouthful of air, then cover his mouth with mine and blow in until his lungs are full. He coughs, squirting water upwards as I move out of the way. He sits up, holding his chest tenderly. When he does I notice the pack of Marlboro's sticking out of his breast pocket, and reach out quickly to grab them. They're still dry, miraculously enough.

"What is the matter with you?" he coughs, turning toward me.

I grab him by the throat and push him back under the water again, using my free hand to push against his chest just like before, except instead of forcing the water out, this time it forces the air out. There's not as much of it left in him this time anyway. As soon as the bubbles stop, I pull him out again. That perfect hair of his is an absolute mess now, the moss from the stream freezing to it.

Again, I pump the water from his lungs and give him mouth to mouth, until all the water is gone.

Then back under he goes again. I marvel at how shocked he looks each and every time. I couldn't have hoped for as much.

Bubble... bubble... ... .

One, two, three, four.

Breathe in, breathe out.

Cough.

Bubble... bubble... ... .

I repeat the process eight more times before letting him go completely. That last time I held him under, he hadn't lasted more than a few seconds, and it was getting to be more work than it was worth to bring him back. I let him cough all of the water out of his lungs, and then he just sits there for a minute in the snow.

"If you're going to kill me," he says, and his voice is shaking from fear and the cold, "just do it."

I smile. I reach into the pack of smokes I just stole from him and light one up, taking a long steady drag. The smoke travels down and makes me feel relaxed, and for a brief instant, this moment is perfect. I know the way that sounds. "Kill you?" I chuckle, ruffling his hair as I crouch down next to him, blowing smoke in his face. "Who said anything about killing you?"

He looks at me with confusion, his eyes squinting with

the effort of trying to understand what I've just said.

I decide to save him the effort. "See, if I kill you, then your pain's over. That doesn't sit too well with me, not after what you've done." I snarl, grabbing him by the collar and forcing him back into the water. I don't submerse him this time though, I just leave the back of his head in, in case he forgets his place. "I've got something much better in store for you. I'm going to *almost* kill you, again and again. And then I'm going to bring you back every time... just so you can feel what she must have felt all over again." I bring my face in so close to his that our noses touch, and that vibration of a growl happens in my throat again. "That's something you and me got in common, Kurt. See good people get to die just once... bad ones like you and me, we get to do it over and over again." I pull him out of the water, then turn my back to him and start walking back toward the street. "She said she wanted me to remember her... and I will, though I don't think this is what she meant. I want you to remember her too, Kurt. Remember what you did to her. Remember what it feels like. Remember that that's what you have to look forward to every day for the rest of your life."

As I walk out the trail toward the highway, I hear the seethe of a knife I hadn't even realized he had on him. I'm worried for a moment, until I hear that faint heartbeat of his.

A moment later, I hear his body hit the snow, and the soft squirt that only a jugular can make. The wind changes direction, and I catch the scent of blood, motor oil, cheap marijuana... and raw, primal fear.

It snowed pretty heavy that night. They didn't find his

body until spring.

On my way out of town I stop by the take-out again. I don't go in, but I see Klarissa with a big plate of ice cream and apple crumble laid out in front of her. A middle-aged woman with a name tag that says Marie is talking to a woman dressed the way only a social worker can, and they're both calm, but sad. Klarissa looks up at me, and she smiles a little and waves. When I wave back, her smile gets bigger, almost hiding those perfect hazel eyes of hers. Sandi's eyes.

It occurs to me that maybe it's not just bad people that get to live over and over again, like I told Kurt. Maybe good people do too, just in a different way. A better way.

I carry the memory of their smile with me as I go, and somehow it lightens the load and keeps me warm through the snow and the cold. I remember them both fondly, and when I do, it doesn't seem like I'm walking alone anymore.

MIKHAIL

Black Womb slammed against the tree trunk, shaking tufts of snow from its branches and down across his lap. The creature growled angrily, rising back to its feet to meet the person who'd dealt it the blow.

The assailant stepped off of highway ninety. He placed one hand on the guard-rail post as he crossed over it, one leg at a time. A car sped by and made his shoulder-length blonde hair flapped about in the updraft, but he didn't pay it any mind. His cobalt blue eyes remained locked on the Womb, burning with anger and fury. His lips, barely visible between the static scruff he'd let get too long, curled in disgust. He dressed in rags, a ripped-up suede jacket covering half a dark blue shirt underneath. His jeans were ripped apart too, one leg ending at the knee to reveal hairy, frostbitten skin. "Murderer," he spat as he started to cross the ditch that separated them.

Inside the Womb, Xander groaned. When the sound came out of the Womb's throat it was a deep and feral growl. *Now what the fuck did I do to piss this guy off?* he thought, rubbing a hand across his scalp as he stood. His skin still ached from the transformation. The black ooze completely covered his body now, and his red eyes allowed him to see everything in the forest around him. There were no shadows for him. He raised his head and tested the air before whipping out his hands at his sides to reveal eight claws, one at the end of each finger.

The man stopped in the tracks, half way between the road and the tree line where his blow had landed the Womb. His eyes danced over the talons, each one an inch and half long. They looked clear from here, and he could see the cuticles attaching them to the creature's fingers. Several drops of blood came from each of them, even though they had yet to slice anything. The blood was a thick black and looked even more so when it landed against the mid-morning snow. The blonde man squinted, as if trying to see through the Womb into the man inside, but made no progress. "You don't scare me," he said through barred teeth.

He reeks of rum and sweat, Xander thought as the wind changed direction, blowing the mystery man's scent toward him. *He's drunk and he's tired. But the one thing I don't smell on him is fear. Whoever this guy is, he's not afraid of me one bit.*

The man ran forward with his mouth wide in an unintelligible battle cry as he raised both his fists high above his head, then slammed them downward toward the thin black demon in front of him.

The Womb leapt quickly, its powerful legs coiling and then releasing in a heartbeat, sending it skyward into the branches. More snow fell to the ground.

The man's fists hit the trunk, rending the flesh on his white knuckles and turning them a ghastly red. He howled with no humanity in him anymore, craning his head up to look into the tree branches.

The Womb looked down at him from between its legs, bracing itself on two thin arms of pine. Its chest heaved up and down as it met the eyes of the man below, its own opaque red lenses squinting, studying the man for flaws and weaknesses. *He's not carrying himself very well on his left side,* Xander noted as his eyes continued to flutter about in their pupilless sockets. *There's something going on with the back of his neck, too. A stiffness. This isn't the first fight he's been in lately. He's probably a drunk.* "Look pal," it said in a rough, grainy voice. It sounded odd to hear such a visceral looking beast say things like that, even to him. "I don't know who you think I am, but..."

"You're the Womb," the man snarled, jabbing a finger in its direction.

Black Womb's head leaned back a bit, as if the finger had actually poked him. The sentence left him breathless as he struggled to regain his composure and respond. He didn't get the chance to.

"The Black Womb. Xander Drew I believe you're going by these days, aren't you?" the man continued, smiling sinisterly when he perceived the distress that his words were causing.

"You're... really good at this game," it replied, steadying itself with its claws and lowering its head, trying to get a better look at whoever this was. "Mind sharing the wealth?"

The man glared at the Womb, and then suddenly his gaze softened. He chuckled heartily and honestly, shaking his head and smiling as he braced himself against the tree.

"I'm sorry. I don't know what came over me there. My name is Mikhail."

Xander raised an eyebrow, lowering himself another quarter inch. What that translated to one the Womb's face made it look like its right eye was going to explode, growing larger suddenly as the muscles expanded and contracted, black goo swirling about unseen to the naked eye. "Did you just say... Michael?" it asked, taking another look at the man's long blonde hair.

Mikhail grinned again. "Have you killed him yet?"

"What?"

"Don't worry," he scorned, grabbing the creature around with one massive, hairy hand now that it was within arm's reach. "You will."

He pulled the Womb to the ground and pinned it there by the neck. He punched it repeatedly in the back of the head until his fists were covered in black blood. He let go, unleashing a brutal kick to the Womb's side. A rib broke free and punctured a lung, and Xander could already feel it filling with bile as he rolled several feet in the freezing snow, coming to a stop in the ditch between the road and the forest.

"What the hell?" the Womb muttered, spitting out muddy water and pebbles as it tried to rise to its feet. "What did I do to you exactly?"

Mikhail stared down at it from atop the snow drift, his fists clenched by his sides and dripping with both of their blood. His hair billowed magnificently in the wind. He didn't look like a bum now, he looked like some ancient warrior disguised as one. His brow furrowed as he stared silently, as if pondering whether or not to answer the question. "You kill my wife," he said finally, a bitter hatred to his speech.

The Womb rose to stand ankle deep in the near-freezing swamp water. One of its hands lay limp, while the other caressed its aching side. Inside him, the Womb was crying out for sleep and release... but more than that, it called out for blood. *It's not really what this guy just said that bothers me,* Xander thought, getting ready for the attack he knew had to be coming. *It's the phrasing of it. He said it like it hasn't happened yet, like it's something I'm going to do. That really raises more questions than anything.*

Mikhail lunged at him, but this time there was no elaborate battle cry. He was silent and driven. Somehow he'd become more focused. Xander could still smell the rum on him, but he couldn't see it in his movements anymore. The Womb ducked under his attack and then vaulted, spinning once in mid-air and landing upright, trying to get at least a few feet between him and the enigma that was assaulting him. Mikhail's upper body was turning even before he'd finished landing, his fist spinning back around and slamming the Womb in the left temple.

It growled as it turned, and suddenly they were both facing each other from a few feet apart. The scales over the Womb's body slithered and danced as though they were alive. Tiny bits of aqua started to find their way into his red retinas, but he blinked hard and forced them out.

"Red eyes bad, green eyes worse," Mikhail recited, the way people remember rhymes from their youth. "Beware the demon pain has cursed. He tries to trick he tries to sway, don't be the fool don't be his prey."

The Womb stared, the only indication that he had

even heard it was the slight tilt of his head as Xander tried in equal parts to figure this guy out and fight off the migraine that always accompanied warding off the aqua-eyed true-womb.

"I never realized that was about you before," Mikhail chuckled, rubbing one hand against his shirt.

"Yeah, me neither," It said sardonically.

Mikhail regarded it with some fascination. The look reminded Xander of the way his father used to look at rabbits when they escaped his traps in ways he'd never considered possible before. "You're very flippant here," he said, his eyes traveling from the Womb's head to its feet and then back again. "And not as strong. When you kill her, you'll be brutal. And as silent as a rock. All because that blonde bitch told you too."

Livid blood pumped its way into Xander's cheeks, and he had to fight twice as hard to stop the real Womb from taking over. He knew that would be a mistake. Whoever this guy was, he had taken things one step too far, and now he wanted to see this through without any help from his other. "You want to run that last bit by me again?"

Mikhail smiled, licking his parched lips. The saliva flattened down his mustache and made him look like one of those evil characters from silent films, tying innocent girls to train tracks. "You can't fool me. We both know what you're going to become, and what you're running from."

The Womb's shoulders slumped as Xander thought back on the events of the past few weeks. His blood pressure dropped back down and his mouth went dry as he remembered the things he'd done, and who he'd done them too. "That wasn't me."

Mikhail took a step forward and thrust his finger out again. "It isn't yet, but it will be someday. The Womb may well be unkillable boy... but you aren't."

Again, the words struck Xander worse than any punch ever could, but this time they got in deeper. He had no defense for this anymore, the walls had been broken down the second Mikhail had mentioned the blonde woman.

Sara.

"One day," Mikhail continued, seeing the effect his words were having, "years down the road, your human self is going to die. The red will switch. When that happens, there will only be the Womb left... and when that day comes, I pray I'm not around anymore."

Each word went deeper then the last, like a knife that just kept plunging further and further into his gut. He didn't have a comeback. He'd been worried for months about what this man was saying, but his friends had always told him different. Now he had no friends, and this Mikhail was spelling out his worst fear as if it were written in stone. He closed his eyes and held onto his gut, wanting to just curl into the fetal position and die. He heard Mikhail take a step forward, and then another, and made no effort to stop him.

How does he know all this? he caught himself thinking again. After a moment his eyes shot open, glimmering brightly with the answer his mind had returned to him with. "Tell Hale it isn't going to work," it said, standing back up straight and realizing that Mikhail had closed the distance between them, and they were now nose to nose.

Mikhail raised an eyebrow, regarding the Womb with

confusion. "What?"

The Womb brought up its claw swiftly, but not to strike Mikhail.

Mikhail flinched anyway, his hair bobbing when he did.

The creature dug its claws into its own face and pulled, blood spurting out from the holes it made until its face took on an pliant appearance then fell off completely, falling into the mud and mixing with the water there with one sickening plop. It was like watching something out of a horror film right before your eyes. What was left when it was over was the face of Xander Drew, the rest to the womb-flesh slithering into the appearance of a black tee shirt and jeans all around him. There was blood matted onto his face and hair as he glowered at Mikhail, the last of the blackness spiraling back into his pupils, like dye washing down a toilet bowl. "Tell Hale it's not going to work," he repeated, his voice closer to normal but still raw and bleeding from speaking so much as the Womb. He could already feel the lining of his esophagus healing, making a taste like bad cough syrup in his mouth.

"Changing the look doesn't change the soul inside," Mikhail said, spitting toward Xander's feet. "Doesn't matter what color you wear, your heart is still blackened."

Xander shook his head, then turned to walk away.

His eyes bulging, Mikhail drew back and punched Xander in the back of the skull, forcing him to the ground.

Xander spat out mud again, along with the damaged and abandoned portions of his throat, looking down at his reflection in the water. In the distorted image, it still looked like Black Womb. *He's with Hale and the Circe,* Xander thought, watching Mikhail's shadow fall over him in the water. *He has to be. There's no other way he could know this much about me. I don't know what kind of game they're playing... so I'm just not going to play. Not going to make the same mistakes as last time. They give me a choice of two doors... I'm going to pick the window. I'm through playing things by their rules.* He pushed off with his hands in the mud, sliding backwards in the grime. He ducked and slid right between Mikhail's legs, jumping to his feet and kicking him quickly in the small of his back.

Mikhail went down into the mud almost exactly where Xander had been, his hair getting tangled and matted instantly. He coughed, glaring back over his shoulder at Xander. His eyes widened when he did not find the boy behind him, but nearly five feet above him, almost at the top of the gravel embankment leading back to highway ninety. "No!" Mikhail cried, scrambling to him feet quickly. "You can't leave. This is my one, best chance to stop it, don't you see that?"

Xander paused at the guardrail and watched another car go by. It was a blue minivan with a small family inside. One boy that looked about eleven stared at Xander as the car sped by, his clothes looking fine while his head was covered in blood and dirt. The boy tugged on his father's shirt and pointed, but he was out of sight before the Dad looked, assuming he even did. Xander turned back down toward Mikhail, and from this angle he didn't look quite so menacing. Maybe it was just the positioning, staring down at him from above, his suede jacket soaked and his hair a tangled mess, standing in ankle-deep filth, but it seemed like the man had gotten smaller somehow. "That's not who I'm going to be." He mumbled, but he knew that Mikhail could hear.

Mikhail sighed, his chest heaving with panicked breaths and his eyes showing an emotion they hadn't yet in their brief encounter: despair.

"And if you are working for Hale... tell him I am becoming something. It's not going to be what he wants, it probably won't be what I want... but it definitely won't be what you think." He turned his back on the rum drinking derelict one last time, hopped over the guard rail and picked up his backpack, then started down the road again.

Still wading in the ditch, Mikhail watched him go. He started to rub his head as he felt another one of his migraines coming on, barring his teeth in preparation for the pain he knew from experience was about to overcome him. He hissed and fell to his knees with a splash as the pure white snow suddenly became too bright for him, forcing him to shut his eyes tight.

"You're right..." he said to nobody, forcing out each syllable. His tongue felt like it had swelled to twice its normal size, as if it were a balloon someone had filled with too much air. "You're going to end up much, much worse. The Mistress calls. Evil calls..."

He chuckled, fighting back tears from the pain. "Red eyes bad, green eyes worse, beware the demon pain has cursed. He tries to trick he tries to sway, don't be the fool don't be his prey."

He almost broke out into a fit of laughter, then buried his head into his hands and sat there in the mud until

Xander was far off into the distance.

SHORT STORY

He was trying to enjoy his beer.

He had been in Illinois two hours before he had come across a town. Twenty minutes after that, he had found a bar. Another thirty and he'd found a bartender that would serve him something other than club soda. Then a final twenty-two seconds explaining to that bartender that he'd ordered a beer, not a lager, and that there was a difference between the two.

He sat with his back hunched and his elbows on the bar, trying hard to peel the label off of the long neck of his drink without leaving any scraps of paper behind. He paused this activity long enough to take another sip, and then started again. The wrapper made a soft crinkly sound as it reluctantly released itself from the condensation laden bottle every few millimeters, then jumping in his grasp where it had been glued on inconsistently.

The bar counter itself had this wonderful smell to it that you could appreciate from halfway across the room. It was old and pine with stains on it that had been varnished over but never quite disappeared, showing that someone who knew a little bit about carpentry had shown it some love once or twice every few years. It smelled like the very back section of a library, where all the books were old and musty but sparked memories every time your nostrils took them in. It had a million other scents too, but they took a little more work. There was a dry, sweet taste that he associated with his father from where someone had spilled their whiskey and coke the night before. A lemony scent he first mistook for cleaner was pegged as the smirch from an actual lemon, one with quite a bit of large-grain salt on it and was probably from a margarita. There was another salty taste, but that was just sweat. That was typically everywhere, and he'd learned to block it out for the most part. A smell that reminded him of his mother baking bread was actually the yeast from the head of a beer. There was also an aroma remarkably like peanuts which turned out, unremarkably, to be the bar's complimentary peanuts.

The rest of the establishment was quaint and cozy enough in nature. It was all one room with one large window in the front, tinted to keep the light out. People didn't like seeing the sunlight as they drank, it seemed. There was a cartoon of a leprechaun holding a pitcher of beer painted on the window, with backwards letters which when read the right way read Over the Rainbow Pub and Services. There was a faded navy carpet that contained all of the smells of the counter and more besides. There were several tables scattered throughout, a juke box that looked like it hadn't been used in years, two dart boards and a pool table. There was a door in the back that barely blocked the itchy smell of dryer sheets and urinal cakes, and a steady rolling sound indicated that the services mentioned in the name of the bar included a laundromat.

There was another smell back there too, one he knew that he knew yet could not figure out.

Xander took another sip of his beer, finally getting the label off and shaking it from where it stuck on his forefinger. It released itself after a moment and traveled quietly to the floor, half leaned against the empty barstool next to him. He laid his bottle down, then immediately tipped it back up to his lips. There wasn't a lot of alcohol in it, not as much as some of the drinks he could have gotten, but with the yeast there was just enough. Each sip dulled his senses just that little bit so that he could block out the world for that one moment before his metabolism kicked in and reversed the effect. It was like playing tug-a-war with intoxication. Still, after a while his head would start to get a little woozy, but he always attributed that to being psychological. Like the time he had swiped his father's vodka and orange when he was twelve, only to find out later that it was orange juice and sprite. Is brain would get fuzzy and it would become harder to maintain several thoughts at once, but those he did retain he grasped onto with some clarity.

In more ways than one, it literally helped him escape his world.

Which was something he was in desperate need of these days.

As bad as the smell was, it wasn't the only thing.

There was a guy standing pretty close to the door playing darts with a limited amount of success. Each time he threw one of them there was a slight whistle of air followed by a soft, dull thunk as it embedded itself in the sisal of the board. Sometimes there was also an excruciating squeak if the head of the dart came too close to the metal of the board. As the guy playing got more and more alcohol into himself, every so often the thunk was replaced by a sharper and louder thwack when the dart hit the plywood that had been nailed around it to protect the wall. It was like listening to a clock tick out of rhythm. While it was going steady you could drown it out, but every so often when it slipped it made your arm twitch and you'd have to get adjusted to it all over again.

The man himself made sounds as well, most of them even less pleasant than the darts. There was a slurp every time he sucked back some beer from his mug, and as he got steadily more intoxicated each slurp was accompanied by the patter of beer against the floor as he missed his mouth or kept it open too long after he'd taken the glass away. Before every few shots, he'd wipe his nose quickly with his sleeve and snort, and Xander wasn't sure if he had a cold or if it was some kind of superstitious tradition to help his aim. There was even a sound when he scratched his head, but that was minor.

The look and smell of him didn't help matters either, but at least they complimented each other. He was wearing a button-down forest green shirt with a pack of cigarettes poking out of the back pocket. It was covered in grease and oil stains, as were the faded jeans with the knees worn out that he wore unbuttoned. He was clean shaven at least, about twenty-nine, and there was a cut above one of his bushy eyebrows that had been recently stitched up by a doctor. There was also a confusing mix of garlic and roses coming off of him, the two smells combined together as if from the same source. He checked his watch and sighed, going back to his game of darts.

A couple in one of the corner booths watched each other intently, the man fumbling his thumbs together nervously, the girl smiling wide and playing with the straw in her absolut vodka, bobbing it in and out of the glass and bringing the tip to her mouth every once and a while. This action on her part seemed to make him more and more nervous, and he scuffed his feet more and more by the minute as his heart rate went up. She made noise just by sitting there and doing nothing. Her earrings jingled and her heels clacked every time she did anything with her feet. She had applied her lip balm too generously, and every time she spoke or even breathed they smacked together, although lightly. The real pain in the neck was the conversation. They were speaking just loud enough that the tone of their voice could be heard, but none of the words understood. That constant repetitive drone of cadence and syllables was enough to send any man over the edge. They sounded like the teachers on a Charlie Brown cartoon.

The guy had a goatee and was wearing a suit, he looked like a lawyer but he didn't act like one, lacking all of the swagger and arrogance of posture that all the lawyers Xander had met in his life had possessed. His aftershave was both nauseating and copious, like it had been caked on with a sponge. He was pre-law, Xander guessed. The girl was cute at about twenty-two, with auburn hair highlighted with blonde streaks parted on the left side and swaying down to the other, where it became one meticulously created curl on an otherwise straight-haired head. There was too much eye-liner on her upper eyelid and not enough on the bottom, and some of the goop from it had somehow attached itself to the white of her left eye. Her eyes themselves were big a pretty, and kind of mix between hazel and blue that he assumed were colored contacts. She reminded him of what his friend Mandy Peterson might have looked like, if she had lived to drinking age. The makeup itself had a fragrance to it, a kind of dry, pancake smell that you tasted the second it hit your nostrils, and had the effect of making your tongue feel dry and sticky.

The lawyer-type guy turned casually, laughing at something the girl had said. He noticed Xander eyeing the two of them and his gaze immediately turned a little cold. Xander turned back to his beer and took another long swig. Two men in a bar were like two wolves in the wild: when eye contact is made, someone has to look away first and admit defeat or disinterest.

There was that smell again, the one he couldn't identify. It was weaker now, but still there and still repugnant. Part of it was coming to him now, though. It was a mossy smell, like mold or the mushrooms that used to grow wild on Cathy's back stoop. Before he could identify it further, it was gone again.

There was one other patron in the bar, and she was by far making the most noise and the most annoying noises. She was also the only person in bar that Xander knew the name of, as she repeated it in some way, shape or form every other time she pulled down the arm of the video lottery terminal by the pool table.

"Come on, come on. Work for Patience," and then:

"Give me the money, give Patience the money," and finally, "Big money, no whammies. Patience wants big money, but no whammies..." And so on, and so forth. Mix and repeat those phrases and you've summed up the last hour and forty five minutes of Patience's life. That would have been bad enough on its own, but every time she pulled that lever a barrage of bells and whistles assaulted Xander's senses, clanging and shrieking happy little tones and chimes. The few times she won, there was a short period of closely repeated clangs as her winnings spewed out in quarters into the steel tray by her knees, and then the scraping as she scooped them up into her bucket. She was about forty and smelled like urine that was not her own, and he wondered briefly how she had come across the odor but decided some things were better off not being known. Her hair was a salt-and-pepper of silver and black, and she wore big, black-rimmed glasses that one usually saw young boys from the forties wearing. They made hers eyes look like they were under magnifying lenses. She won again, this time apparently a bigger pot, as a small swirling light Xander hadn't noticed before sprung to life for a few moments, sending flickers of orange light snapping over the bar in tune with the even louder noises it made, most of them in the key of C.

Xander tilted his head to one side until he heard his neck crack, the sound from inside his own body and the sudden rush of pain drowning everything else out for one moment. He turned his back on the other customer's completely, hoping that the old 'out of sight, out of mind' adage would hold true, but of course it didn't. If anything, it made them seem louder. He could feel a vein near his temple throb, and that seemed to only add to the noise and clatter all around him. Sighing heavily, he took another swig of his beer. It was room temperature by now, but that was fine with him. He'd been walking now for weeks on end, barely ever stepping foot into towns, let alone stopping in them. At this point, he was quite content with having any liquid in his gullet, whether it was cool and fresh or not was besides the point.

The door in the back opened, and that dry dryer-sheet smell came in with the draft and filled the room for a brief instant. A man stepped in from the door and shut it quickly behind him. His eyes darted across the room at the patrons, glancing over the couple and the gambling addict but lingering slightly on the dart player and Xander before breaking off eye contact. His mouth smiled warmly at the bartender, but his eyes held onto his frown long after he had forced it away. He made a quick double-fingered motion to the man behind the bar, who nodded once in return and put down the box of beer he was stocking in the cooler, heading toward the tap and starting to pour up some fresh draft for the man.

Xander looked at the cold, foaming liquid hungrily, realizing now just how warm and flat he'd allowed his own drink to get while playing with the label. "Beer should be like coffee," he muttered under his breath. "You should get free refills."

The bartender shot a look at him from the corner of his eye as he poured the new man's drink, not giving the statement the justification of a response.

The man walked over to the bar on heavy feet, each footstep sounded like a sack of hammers falling against the carpet floor. He took the seat next to Xander, smiling politely as he took his mug in hand and gulped down a quarter of the drink in one long slug.

Xander watched him without realizing it, holding his own beer in the air mid-way to his mouth as the newcomer wiped a foam mustache from his.

The man sighed and looked down at the floor from between his legs. "Jeez," he tisked, reaching down and picking up a white piece of paper he saw stuck to the leg of his barstool. He held it between his thumb and forefinger, then flipped it over and revealed it to be a beer bottle label. He motioned to Xander, again forcing that same smile. "Litter-Bugs, all of them. They got no respect for any..." he stopped, noticing the glue smudges where the label had been peeled off Xander's drink. "Er..."

Xander smiled, waving the comment away with a gesture. "It's okay. You're right, I was just bored. Wasn't thinking."

"Huh," the man smiled, more naturally this time but still not quite there all the way. "That's definitely allowed, then."

Xander laughed at that, smiling wider than he had in weeks. He took his hand off his beer and extended it toward the man. "The name's Xander Drew."

The man looked from the offered hand to Xander's face, and then back again. Wiping more foam from his mouth and setting down his mug, he took the younger man's hand and gave it one hearty pump before letting go. "Kenneth Tribb," he said simply, as if he somehow didn't like the taste of his own name in his mouth.

Kenneth was a blocky man, not skinny but by no

means fat either. His torso was almost shaped like a rectangle and his arms were thin and wiry with very few defined muscles, but Xander guessed that he could handle himself in a fight if he had too. He didn't seem the type, though. He was wearing a pasty-colored shirt that was somewhere between off-white and sky blue with well pressed, paint-stained jeans. It looked like clothes that he barely ever wore, except when he was going out to a bar for a quiet drink and just didn't care what people thought of his appearance. He was wearing a red baseball cap with a picture of a tractor and a gear on it over jet black hair that needed to be washed, but not too desperately. He had about two-days worth of stubble all over his face and dark blue eyes, and the type of big nose that comes from a little too much drinking.

He had smells with him too, of course. The day Xander met someone who didn't he'd be very, very worried. He smelled like sweat and fresh dirt, and Xander guessed that he worked in outdoor construction of some kind, but he could have been wrong. For all he knew, Kenneth had been helping a friend dig a ditch all day. There were other smells there too. His hair smelled like oil. His hands reeked of that sterile alcohol flavor of hand sanitizer and soap. That dry, sticky scent of dryer lint was all over him too, but mostly Xander noticed that other odor, the one he hadn't been able to pin from the back room. Kenneth must have gotten something on himself back there. It definitely had a fungal nature to it, but there was also a sort of citrus-like lime affiliation with it. A tang that left a bitter sweet feeling against his teeth after it overloaded his olfactory senses.

Xander brought the bottle to his lips once more and tipped the bottom toward the ceiling, watching through the brown glass as the last of the liquid poured down his gullet. He let out a sigh as he placed down the beer, staring at the empty bottle for only a moment before the bartender took it away.

"Another?" the bartender asked, raising an eyebrow in his direction.

"I'll have what he's having," he answered curtly, feeling a little like a character from a movie for a moment as he poked his thumb into Ken's general direction.

The bartender nodded once and headed back toward the tap, scooping up another mug by the handle as he went.

"That's a hard beer," Kenneth warned, his voice both paternal and a little bragging at the same time. "A lot of men find it too bitter. Not too late if you wanna get another of what you're having."

Xander threw him a glance without really looking at him, a smirk on one edge of his lips. "I think I'll be fine."

Ken raised his hands momentarily in surrender, chuckling at the obviously younger man sitting across from him. "Just saying... if you're doin' it to be a big shot, you picked the wrong fellow. I couldn't really care less about what a man drinks, as much as I care about how he acts after he drank it."

Xander pondered that for a moment as the bartender slid his new mug up next to him, foam curdling down the side, the bubbles in it popping upon contact with air. After staring at it for a while he gripped it by the handle, feeling the icy glass cool his fingers, then took a long swig. He'd been right, it was a strong beer. It dulled his senses for nearly twice as long after that first mouthful. When they finally kicked back in after a minute or so, that weird, unknown smell was back again, and it was like the equivalent of getting kicked between the legs for your nose. He laid the glass back down and began to pat his pockets, finally finding his pack of Marlboro's he'd been milking for weeks now, ever since he left Maine. He opened it up and saw that there were only three left, and frowned. Taking one out, he grabbed a book of matches off the countertop and lit it. He took a long drag, letting the smoke exit his mouth of its own momentum rather than exhaling.

Beside him, Kenneth took another sip of his own beer, watching Xander smoke out of the corner of his eye. "You'd better watch it with those things," he said between gulps. "They'll kill ya."

Xander smirked, taking another quick puff. "I'll take my chances."

"Suit yourself," the older man grumbled, shrugging his shoulders.

Xander eyed him for a moment, then extended the nearly empty pack toward him. "Care for one?"

Kenneth let out a breath of relief, smiling from ear to ear to reveal teeth that were slightly yellowed. "Thought you'd never ask."

Xander smiled back as Patience won another spin on the video lottery terminal, clapping her hands and hooting as quarters filled the tin tray at her waist and colors flashed exuberantly upon the screen. Both he and Kenneth turned to look at her, and they both started to chuckle.

"Every damn night." Kenneth said, motioning discreetly toward Patience. "Every night she's in here, and every night she leaves with fifty dollars less than when she started, but that doesn't stop her from coming back the next night. I think there's a bug in that VLT, too. You can almost set your watch by when she wins, amazing she's never picked up on it."

"Some things you can't really see until you step back," Xander reasoned. "Maybe she's a little too close to it to see is all."

Kenneth looked to consider this, then motioned his drink toward the couple. "That young law-type. He's in here at least once a week with a new girl."

Xander cocked an eyebrow. "Now you're pulling my leg. He doesn't seem the player type. I should know, I've met a couple."

"He's not," Ken laughed, slapping his knee. "Dumb kid never gets any further than second base. Never. Every week they always seem so into him that you'd have to be a world-class fuck up not to seal the deal... but every week he still manages to do exactly that."

Xander laughed, making smoke come out of his nose. It was a horrid smell, but it helped block out all the other horrid smells, which was what he was trying to accomplish. "What about dart-boy, there?" he asked, gesturing toward the man trying for a bulls-eye even as he spoke.

"Never seen him before," Ken admitted, clicking his tongue against the roof of his mouth. He shifted uncomfortably in his chair, then scratched the back on his head.

"That's what that look was about when you came in."

Xander smiled, giving himself a little smack against the head.

"Sure," the older man said under his breath, taking another mouthful of beer. He turned and gave Xander the once-over with his eyes again, finally really looking at the man sitting next to him. "You look like you been on the road awhile."

He didn't respond, just took another sip of beer.

"Been thinking about hittin' the road myself, lately. This town's startin' to get old, if you can understand that."

Again, Xander did not respond. His nose twitched though, and he took a fourth puff of his smoke to try and keep his senses in check.

"If I'm bothering you..."

"No," Xander said, shooting him an obviously manufactured smile. "Just something's bothering me. Can't quite pin it down. You ever get that?"

"All the time," Ken said solemnly. He got up and started walking toward the pool table, grabbing a stick from off the wall as he went. Upon reaching the table he turned to Xander and motioned for him to grab a stick as well.

Xander waved his hand, trying to dismay the idea. "Sorry, friend. I don't think I'm even going to be in town long enough for that."

Ken grinned at him, then motioned toward the sticks again.

Xander sighed, then allowed himself a smile as he grabbed up his beer and started to walk over to the table. The blonde girl in the corner booth watched him as he first lurched off his chair, then glided on his feet across the room to the pool table. After a moment the lawyer-boy she was with started a new topic of interest, and her eyes immediately snapped back toward him, wary of being caught wandering.

Xander applied some chalk to the tip of his cue, then some between his index and middle fingers, as he'd watched his friends back home do many times when they were playing for big money at The Factory. He understood that there was some logic behind the tradition, but mostly he thought it was just superstition. Either way he'd picked up the habit and didn't even realize it until it was done, looking down at the blue streaks on his hand as if he had no idea how they even got there. His face sunk with somberness as he handed Ken the chalk without even looking at him.

Ken glanced at his own hand too, but there was nothing there. He scratched his forearm underneath his shirt for a moment, then chalked his own stick. "Your break, or should I?"

"Don't really care," Xander shrugged, noticing that whoever used the table last had left the balls racked. This eliminated the standard 'I rack, you break' escape.

"Your break then," Ken said, laying the chalk against the table's edge near the side pocket.

Xander frowned, moving to the edge of the table. He grabbed the cue ball, taking note of a chip in it next to his thumb, and moved it almost completely to the right edge, taking aim at the eight in the center. He knelt in close to the table for his shot and slid the stick between his fingers a few times in preparation. He couldn't help but take a breath, and it was like taking the table back in time. He could smell the tequila that was spilt as recently as the night before, the cigarette smoke that had been caked in for years and the tiny amount of blood that he wouldn't have thought had a place there, but made sense when he thought about it. Alcohol plus idiots plus competition sometimes ended in blood, after all. Not only that though, he could smell the nylon and wool from the green cloth that covered the table as though it were brand new. From his perspective, it was like being the first person to shoot at a new table when the moving person had been smoking, drinking, and managed to cut himself while bringing it in. That coppery smell of blood was unconscionably strong and it itched at his nose, making it twitch.

He also had a better smell of Ken from here, and there was a part of it that was a little like wet dog. That could actually have been from a wet dog, but it seemed too intermingled with the other scents. After a moment, he decided it was definitely part of the equation, but still didn't know what the sum was. There was a dry feeling as he breathed it in at close range as well, and it made his mouth pasty like when he'd just eaten a peanut butter sandwich.

He smacked the cue hard and straight, but that chip on the ball proved more of a factor than he'd initially thought. It hit just a little right of its target, still scattering the balls rather nicely around the table, but not sinking any. The eight, however, stayed in the center of the table where he meant for it to.

"Nice break," Ken said, pacing around the table a little to look at his possibilities from all angles.

Xander stayed stagnant in his position, leaning against his stick a little and deciding to go for the thirteen if Ken didn't sink a high ball. "Eh," he replied, teetering his hand from side to side.

Ken tapped his foot for a moment, then leaned in over the table near the lower right corner pocket, taking aim. "One ball, corner pocket," he stated simply just before hitting the cue. It smacked the slightly small yellow ball gently and sent it rolling toward the opposite corner. It looked like it was about to stop right at the edge, then fell in and hit the leather strap nets with almost no sound at all. He smiled, pumping his fists just a little, not really meaning for Xander to notice the action. He immediately took another shot toward the three, again barely touching the red ball, sending it rolling across the grass toward the side pocket. This time it looked as though it were going to stop on the edge, and did. "So, you running to someplace, or away from someplace?" he asked, applying just one more scratch of chalk to his tip.

Xander didn't look at him, just lined up his shot with the thirteen. The eight was kind of in the way now, but that was the way he liked to play. He'd pick a ball and go for it, regardless of the changes in the shot. It was something his friends had always criticized him for, especially when he won. "Don't know what you're talking about. Thirteen, side pocket." He almost stood completely straight when he made the shot, grinning at the last second as something caught his eye and he put a slight backspin on it. The cue hit the thirteen and it went in simply enough, but it came back and hit the eight afterward, sending it slowly toward the other side pocket.

"You fucked yourself now," Ken laughed, slapping his knee.

"Wait for it," Xander hummed, holding up a finger for patience. The eight rolled slowly, like Ken's ball had before, stopping just at the edge of the pocket and blocking what would have been an easy shot at the three for Ken.

"Son of a bitch," Ken said, but there was no anger in his voice. It was said as though it were a compliment, and Xander took it as one. He stepped aside, letting Xander walk around the table to figure out his next shot. "I'll ask again, cause this is a small town and the 'tender knows all the underage guys here and not to let 'em in. Since I got more sense than him to know how old you're not, mean's you're not from around here. Nobody stops in this town unless they're on the road. Nobody. Most kids don't get out of this town, but those that do don't come back. So, are you running to someplace, or away from someplace?"

Xander found a shot at the ten and started to work out how he was going to make it, pretending to ignore his opponent. "Little of both, I guess," he said, finally. "Ten ball, top left corner." He took his shot quickly, and the ball flew in the right direction, ricocheting off the corner and going in the wrong direction, ending up in the right corner pocket. He sighed, then picked up the cue and handed it to Ken as he walked toward the offending pocket. He reached in and pulled out the ten, then planted it squarely in the middle of the table and back into play.

Ken frowned, looking for a new shot as he walked to the head of the table and rested the cue against the faded white line. "You know where you're going?"

"No."

"Then you're mostly running from someplace, by my definition," he said in an informative way, trying the cue in different positions before planting it almost exactly in the middle of the line. "Don't fret on it. Lot of men made their mark runnin' from somethin'. Don't mean you're a coward... don't mean nothing, really. Just means you don't know what you want in life, but you know you ain't gonna get it where you were."

Xander smiled at that, nodding slightly. "Not quite," he corrected, his voice a little smug. "But I like it all the same."

Ken nodded, then lined up a shot at the six. It's green was almost the same color as the table, and for a second he had to blink in the low overhead lights to see it properly. It was pressed neatly up against the side of the table, its shadows obscured by the overhanging felt. "Six, bottom corner," he called, motioning toward the corner at Xander's right. This time he shot hard, sending the cue flying toward the front of the table and spinning like a top as the six bounced off the side it had been against, then off the opposite side, finally rolling along toward the pocket that he had indicated. For a moment it grazed alongside Xander's red-striped fifteen and looked as though it might sway off course, but then it plopped into the pocket as soundlessly as the others had.

Xander crumpled his chin and nodded, impressed. "Nice shot."

"I've made worse," Ken agreed heartily, as he quickly surveyed his shot at the three again, still almost completely blocked by the eight. He sighed, then took aim at the two. It lay almost dead in the upper center of the table, and he took aim just to its right. "Left corner," he said almost as he shot, softer again this time. The cue hit the two and it went into the pocket just as he had planned, the cue coming to rest about an inch away from the top right pocket.

"What about you?" Xander asked, as he leaned back against the table next to them.

"What about me?" Ken responded, his voice a little less welcoming than it had been before. He cleared his throat, and was back to his soft-spoken self. He tossed a glance at the three again, finding this angle no better than the last.

"You said I had to be running... what are you doing here tonight? You're here alone, and you don't seem like any of the alcoholics I've met." Xander grinned, trying his best to make his question inoffensive.

"Met many, have you?" Ken replied, almost patronizingly, the words again coming out harsher than even he had anticipated. He saw the seven lingering near the bottom left pocket and took aim at the brownish ball. "I came to do laundry. Drink was just a bonus. Seven. Left."

For the first time this game, Ken made a few practice strokes before actually firing. The cue hit the seven near the left edge of the ball, sending it in the opposite of the intended direction and over toward Xander's fifteen. The cue stayed near the bottom left pocket, making either ball an easy shot.

Xander pushed himself off from the table, his eyes growing distant again as he looked over his options. "Didn't mean to pry," he mumbled, not making eye contact with the older man and he moved toward the cue.

Ken frowned, stepping back from the table to give Xander some room. "You didn't," he said apologetically. "Just been a bad day, is all. Rather just forget about it."

Xander leaned in to take advantage of the easy shot at the fifteen, reminding himself that easy shots can become hard ones if left unchecked. As he stepped into the space that Ken had occupied a moment before his nostrils flared and something he didn't want to think about deep inside him twitched. It was that fungal lime smell again, but there was more to it. The smell reminded him of the bad taste in his mouth if he forgot to brush his teeth before going to bed, along with a stale, sugary sensation not completely unlike tasting flat coke he'd left next to his heater for too long. He shook it off after a moment, focusing the ball in front of him. "Fifteen, corner," he stated, and Ken nodded.

He shot softly, the cue ball rolling forward as if it had been sent of its way by a stiff breeze rather than Xander's stick. It nudged the dark red stripped fifteen ball, sending it the few inches it needed. It fell into the bottom right corner, clacking noisily against the six when it did. The sound rang through Xander's head, and it was only then that he truly realized how high his senses had dialed themselves up. He brought his finger to his temple and started to rub it, drawing an intrigued and concerned look from Ken.

"Are you all right?" he asked, reaching out to put a hand on the child's shoulder and then stopping himself, staring down at the back of his hand again for a moment before letting it fall limply to his side.

"Fine," Xander said, trying to feign chipperness. "Why

wouldn't I be?"

Ken shrugged, keeping an eye on Xander as the boy walked around to the opposite side.

Xander gritted his teeth, taking aim quickly at the ten in the center of the table. He did not verbally call his shot, merely gestured to the upper right corner with his cue before firing as hard or harder than he had on the break, slamming into the ten and sending it racing toward the pocket. It hit the corner and bounced between the two for a moment, looking like a pinball rather than a pool ball before it finally rolled casually away from the pocket. He sighed, then chuckled to himself. "Guess that's what I get for playing angry."

"You should never do anything angry," Ken nodded, his voice taking on a gravely wise tone. "No matter what it is, it'll almost certainly turn to hell once you do."

Xander nodded as he stepped away from the table. Something in the man's voice let him know that he was not speaking out of speculation, but from experience. It made him think hard about the choices that had led him to this bar, before and after leaving home. After a moment, he forced them out of his head.

Once again, Ken stepped toward the table. He took a scan of it quickly, finally grinning slyly at the seven as it sat by itself near the center of the table. When he shifted his body a little to the left, it lined up almost perfectly with the top right pocket. Both Xander's nine and fourteen were dangerously close to being in the way, but he thought he could make it. He stuck his tongue out of the corner of his mouth without even realizing he was doing it, then closed one eye and took the shot. The cue hit the brownish ball hard and sent it careening in the direction of the desired pocket, narrowly missing the fourteen before slipping in with that soft patting sound the balls made when they hit the leather.

"Nice shot," Xander said, clapping his hand against his stick once in a gracious form of applause. He looked over the table just as Ken did, looking at his five balls compared to Ken's two. A smile spread over his lips. "We can call it a draw now, if you want."

Ken cocked an eyebrow at Xander, trying not to laugh as he took aim at the four. It was a kind of navy color very close to the stripe of Xander's twelve ball. They should have actually been exactly the same, leaving Ken to think that they'd actually come from two different sets. "What have you been smoking and where can I get some?" he joked rhetorically, tapping the cue with his stick slightly. It rolled forward and hit to four, sending it softly into the lower right pocket. It landed with a hard clang that seemed too loud for the minimal effort put into the shot, banging off the fifteen and the six when it hit.

Xander laughed and flicked the tip of his nose. "Just saying," he said simply, as he backed up from the table an extra pace.

Ken eyed the three again. It was still sitting near the side pocket but obstructed by the eight. He scoffed, turned his attention toward the five, and saw that he had no clear shot at the bright orange ball. "Your balls keep getting in the way," he grunted.

Xander snorted. In his head, he could hear Tommy saying That's what she said. It was odd. He never thought he would miss a Machiavellian jerk like Tommy Irons, but at least once a day he could almost hear one of his sarcastic quips in his head.

Ken turned and tried to bank the cue off the rail to hit the five, but it barely grazed it and spiraled toward the opposite cushion and came to a rest. He grumbled and tapped the fat end of his stick against the floor in a quick show of anger, then yielded the table to Xander.

As he stepped forward he took a deep breath to try and calm himself, determined to go for the ten again and hoping that all that would be necessary was calming himself, as Ken had mentioned. When he did he caught a new smell, a decidedly better one. It smelled like roses after a cool spring rain, the way they used to grow in his grandmother's garden when he was very young. It sparked a memory of her smattering his cheeks with kisses despite his protests and made him smile. This smell was more processed though. It was probably some form of rose-oil perfume, most likely worn by the girl with blonde-streaked hair. It was still mixed in with the bad, fungal-soda smell that had been bothering him since he came in though. The two smells seemed unique and separate, and yet they now seemed to occupy the same space. There was bleach with it too, he realized (almost as a side note). He remembered it from the time Cathy had tried to dye her hair, with disastrous results.

Crouching down, he lined up his shot with the ten. It was almost lined up perfectly with the top right, but he still took well over a minute sliding the stick back and forth between his fingers, making sure the pressure was just right. When he finally hit the cue it rolled effortlessly toward the ten as though it were meant to, like a planet in orbit around the sun. It barely made a sound as it tapped the other bakelite ball. The ten rolled the six inches to the edge of the pocket, appearing to hover there for a moment before toppling in and tapping the seven when it did.

He smirked to himself and gave Ken a little nod before setting his sights on the nine and moving to the far side of the table to get a better angle on it. He bent down to take the shot again, closing one eye an lining it up with the right side pocket. "Last chance on that draw," he said musically, sliding back the smooth wooden pole.

Ken chuckled and waved his hand to dismiss the idea.

Xander shrugged, then shot the cue. The stick skipped and grazed the side of the ball, sending its blue-smudged surface rolling harmlessly to one side of the nine. It spun a little as it went, coming to rest almost in the center of the table. That thing deep inside him surged as he stepped away from the table again. He bit the inside of his cheek to help himself ignore it. He stopped for a moment, the strangest sense of deja vu coming over him, then forgot it and continued. "So, you married?" Xander asked, again applying some chalk to the end of his cue after the last debacle of a shot.

Kenneth laughed and shook his head, stepping forward with his stick with the brashness of a man who knew he had won. He carried it as if it were a sword and he were stepping onto a battlefield. "Naw... naw I was never the settling down type."

"Still," Xander said slyly, raising an eyebrow. "There must be somebody."

Ken became very quiet for a moment, his eyes dancing

along the floor around Xander's feet. "No. Not for a while now."

"Sorry to hear that," Xander said honestly, leaning against the next table over.

Ken peered at the five. The cue had it lined up almost perfectly with the right side pocket Xander had been aiming for a moment ago. He smiled to himself, making sure to check the angles that the ball would travel in after the shot was made and for the backspin. Satisfied, he walked around to the left side of the table. He leaned over, lining up the end of his staff with a sapphire smear on the cue ball, then fired.

The two balls clacked together softly, the white one stopping in its tracks the second they touched and the bright orange one lurching toward the pocket and dropping in. Ken smiled and snapped his fingers triumphantly as he marched around to the other side of the table to take his shot at the final ball.

When he passed by Xander, the boy was smirking devilishly to himself but made a motion of admiration for the shot Ken had made all the same.

Ken got to the other side of the table, his gut touching the edge of the pocket his ball had just sunk into. From there he stood straight across from the only one of his 'solid' balls left on the table: the three. The coral red ball stared back at him, the glowing bulb from above reflecting off of it and into his eyes. Behind it, so close that the two actually touched, was the deep black of the eight ball. They both looked ready to fall into the pocket at even the slightest breeze, let alone pressure from the cue. They glimmered and shone in the light and seemed like two eyes staring Ken down in a contest of wills he couldn't win. He took a step to the right, getting the balls from a different angle. Frowning, he went back and then took a step to the left. He glowered, twisting his hands around his stick as if to strangle it. He turned to Xander, managing a smile. "You had this planned from the first shot you made, didn't you?"

Xander smiled, shrugging playfully. "I don't need to beat you, I just need you to lose," he joked, thumbing a little of the chalk off the top of his stick.

Ken sighed, then lined up his shot with the three as best he could and then touched the cue slightly. It rolled over and barely touched the three, but even under that minimal exertion the eight slammed into the pocket like a sack of bricks, gravity finally taking hold of it after so long teetering on the edge. Ken cursed softly, then walked over an extended a hand to Xander. "Good game," he said simply, unable to keep the grin off of his lips.

Xander took his hand and pumped it heartily. The second he did, the odor came over him again. All of the previous elements were there again, that taste of bleached fungal lime morning-breath mixed with flat coke and rose oil. This time he again identified something new, and kicked himself for not getting it before. It was garlic. Not a smell like garlic, but definitely garlic itself. It was the same smell that had been coming out of the Italian restaurant he'd passed coming into town. Xander was sure now that the stench hadn't just gotten on Ken while he was in the back room doing his laundry. The smell was coming from him. It was on his skin and in his pores. The more his new friend perspired, the more the scent wafted into the atmosphere. There was something else, too. It was a rich smell, like cornmeal. It might not have actually been cornmeal, but that was the memory it created in his head. "You too," he responded finally, releasing the man's hand.

Ken smiled, laying his pool stick back on the table. "You're not much of a pool player, but you're a heck of a strategist. I'd like to play you in chess sometime."

"Never was much for chess," Xander admitted, putting his stick away as well. "Don't have the patience for it."

"You should try it sometime. If you learn a little patience in the process, well, there are worse things that could happen."

"Mmm," Xander hummed, squinting at the man. "I guess that's true."

Ken shifted uncomfortably, jingling the change in his pocket for a moment before checking his watch. "Well, I guess I should be going."

Xander smiled, checking the time himself. "Now who's running away?" he half-joked, pointing a finger at him.

He chuckled, nodding. "Nothing like that. Just time to be hittin' the road is all." He stopped and looked Xander up and down. "You don't want a ride out of town, do ya? Got no problem helpin' you on your way."

Xander eyed him for a moment, then nodded. "Sure. Yeah, sure. You mind going west?"

"Headed that way myself," Ken smiled, motioning toward the door with one hand.

The both of them walked out together, Ken patting Xander on the back almost paternally. Xander passed by the window advertising the bar and other services and turned to look over his shoulder at the other patrons just as they opened the door to leave.

The lawyer and his date were gone now, but their scents were still there, indicating they hadn't left long ago. Xander smirked as he pictured the man striking out again as Kenneth had described, it brought him some sense of odd satisfaction.

Patience cheered and clapped happily as the one-armed bandit she was sitting at let out a string of c-note chimes and spat quarters into the stainless steel tray by her waist. She thrust her hands into the air triumphantly, hooting and hollering as she did.

The man that had been playing darts had stopped some time ago without Xander's knowledge. He was surprised that he hadn't noticed the halt of steady thunks and thwacks as the darts slammed into the board and the wall around it. The man now sat on the chair next to his table, a few more empty mugs of beer there then there had been before. His shoulder was covered with long red and white hairs, even though his were neither. He let out a string of curses as he looked at his watch, then pressed the redial button on his cell phone and brought it to his ear, tapping his foot impatiently. When he burped the sound filled the room, followed a few seconds later by the stench. It was a smell like yeast and bile, but carried with it the smell of bleach and roses again.

Giving one last silent goodbye to the people that occupied the Over the Rainbow Pub of Stoke, Illinois, Xander Drew left with Kenneth Tribb, closing the door behind him and letting the bell at the top of it jingle softly when he did.

Once outside, one would think that the smells wouldn't have bothered him as much anymore. Anyone who thought that were obviously talking out of an orifice other than their mouths. Not only did the sounds of several streets now assault his ears anew before he could tune them out, but the gust from the west made him downwind from Ken. He got that smell so bad and strong that it was almost like it was something tangible. Like it had been given form and shoved in his mouth, and now he was tasting it. All of it. His brain felt like it was overloading with information as each bit of the aroma triggered a different memory, his mind yelling the different components to him all at once.

There was that cornmeal taste first this time. It had definitely been cornmeal, there was no question now. He could see the box with the word printed on it in his mind's eye, his Mom baking something just out of his field of vision. There was a dryness that he associated with his high-school sweetheart Julie for some reason. Like the taste of her makeup on his lips whenever he kissed her cheeks. There was the smell of limes and bleach, followed by the morning breath. Hot, horrible morning breath. The type he'd always described as toxic. The rose oil and the fungus seemed intertwined now, which produced an odd mental image. He'd never seen mold on a rose or any flower for that matter, yet his mind had no problem calling up the picture as if he had. There was a new smell, one he hadn't identified previously. It was starch. Pure, simple starch. He was amazed he hadn't gotten it sooner. The garlic wasn't as bad as Ken had stopped sweating in the cool winter air, but it was still there nonetheless. Finally there was the tinge of flat coke in his throat, so clear he could almost hear his Dad complaining about it as he threw it in the garbage. One final element came to him, a sick taste he remembered. It sparked a slew of memories ranging from smell to taste to touch, and he had no idea how it had literally been under his nose for so long without his recognizing it, blaming it on the cigarette he'd had before the pool game.

"You okay?" Ken asked, placing his hand of Xander's shoulder.

Xander opened his eyes, only now realizing that they'd been closed tight. He heard a buzzing noise in his ears that he couldn't pin. His hands were pressed against his temples and he took them down as his brain stopped the onslaught of images matching to the smells coming at him. They were all identified now. Each one mentally tagged with its origin. He could practically see them waving about in the air. It was only now the he realized that these were not separate odors, but all the same thing. The smells had all come from the same source, made up of many smaller sources. Just the way everything was worth more than the sum of its parts, he supposed. He blinked twice, focusing on Ken. "Sure, I'm fine," he said finally, forcing a smile. "Night air got to me, I guess."

Ken nodded, motioning toward an old persimmon pickup truck parked a few feet away, the bottom covered with rust and salt stains from the road.

They both walked toward the vehicle in silence. Xander waited by the passenger side door for Ken to go around to the other side and let him in, tapping his foot slightly as he did. He could see his breath in the cool night air, the sight of which made gooseflesh trickle over his body. He knew he wasn't actually that cold, but it was psychological. Like drooling at the sight of food when you're not even really hungry.

Ken fiddled with the keys in his pocket and finally produced a ring, then located the proper one. He slid it into the lock and turned it. When it did not move, he slammed his free hand against the door near the latch, then tried again. This time it turned freely, the door opening when he pulled up on the lever. He scrambled in quickly, then leaned across and pulled up on a plastic knob to unlock the passenger side door.

Xander entered and got settled in his seat and slamming the door behind him as Ken started the engine.

The smell was even worse inside the vehicle, now joined by the smell of gasoline fumes and pine air freshener. He balked as soon as the smell hit him, but tried his best to hide it.

The car itself was in bad shape, with a dozen empty potato chip bags and bar wrappers crunching at Xander's feet. There was a large chunk of the seat actually burning away in the space between the two of them. The road below could be seen from several places through the floor, and there were mounds of paper and bills strapped to the driver's side visor with elastic bands.

There was no radio in the dash, only a few exposed wires where one should have been, but there was a stereo held down to the top on the dash with velcro. Wires sprung from the back of it and trailed all along the cabin, meeting with a few speakers behind them to create some semblance of surround sound. There was a buzzing sound from behind his head, but it wasn't coming from the speakers.

Xander laid his arm against the rest, feeling the stickiness of half-dried soda when he did but ignoring it.

Ken pulled out of the parking lot, causing a splash as his tire sunk down into a pothole and sprayed muddy water up onto the windshield. He clacked his gums together as he turned from side to side to make sure nothing was coming, then pulled out onto the main road. Smiling, he turned to Xander. "Down by the tracks okay?"

Xander still had a far-off look in his eyes, not really focused on anything but staring at the speedometer absently without realizing it. "The tracks," he answered after a moment, then nodded slowly. "Yeah, that'll do fine."

The pair drove in silence for a few minutes, Ken staring alertly out the front window as Xander stared lazily out the side. Xander's eyes darted back and forth, watching the buildings get fewer and fewer with each mile they traveled toward the outskirts of town.

"So, where you headed to next?" Ken asked finally, chuckling to break the tension that had somehow found its way into the vehicle.

Xander's head snapped around, his eyes startled for a moment as if he'd forgotten where he was. "Nowhere in particular. Always wanted to see Salt Lake City when I was a kid... might head that way."

"Was there, once," Ken nodded. "Visit the Rice-Eccles Stadium if you get the chance."

Xander nodded, watching the headlights beam their way out in front of the car. There were very few houses now, and no more businesses.

Ken tapped his hands against the steering wheel to the beat of some unknown song, glancing into his rear view mirror every now and again at the pan of his truck. "So, you're headed west means you're coming from east. Judging by your accent, I'd say you're a Maine boy, huh?"

Xander said nothing, rubbing his finger along the bit of fuzz along his upper lip.

"You came this far runnin' from somethin. Must be a girl, huh? Yeah, bet it's a girl."

Again, Xander remained stagnate and did not speak.

"Is it because it went too fast... or because she turned you down cold?" he laughed, but there was a bitterness in his voice.

"That why you killed her?" Xander asked abruptly, not even turning toward him.

Kenneth's face went white all at once, stretching out in despair as his eyes grew extra rings to show how shocked he was. After a seconds worth of silently gaping, he finally found his tongue. "What... What are you talking about?"

At that, Xander actually chuckled a bit, turning and smiling at Ken for the first time since their drive began. "You ate tonight at Michelin's, that Italian place on the way into town. You had spaghetti and a coke and way too much garlic bread. You were eating alone. Somewhere close to you a man and a woman were sitting and eating. They're early in their relationship, only the first few dates. The guy had on a button-down forest green shirt with a pack of cigarettes poking out of the breast pocket. He was covered in oil stains, probably went out straight from work.

He was clean-shaven and about twenty-nine. The girl was younger than that, about twenty-four. She had natural red hair but it had been dyed bleach blonde not too long ago. She wore rose-oil perfume and she was beautiful. Way too good for the guy she was with, I'm willing to bet. How'm I doing so far?"

Ken stared at him, but said nothing. They were in the middle of nowhere now, only trees surrounding them as they whizzed past.

"Whatever. Anyway, she caught your eye. You were done up all right and he was here with this wonderful girl that smelled like roses with oil stains on his clothes. Guy didn't know what he had. You started thinking that you should have a girl like that, not him. Or something along those lines. I been there, believe me. I got a nice few bloody noses in high school taking on guys twice my size because they looked at a girl that wasn't even mine. So, believe me, I get it. What I don't get is that instead of going after the guy and just being a royal dick, you went a different route.

"You overheard them saying you were going to meet in the bar back there tonight. I think you showed up early and caught her having a smoke out back and made your move. I don't know what happened then, but I don't think you meant to hurt her... much less kill her. I do know that's what happened, though." He tapped his finger against his right nostril twice. "The nose knows."

Ken stopped the car in front of the tracks, the red warning lights flashing on and off as he did. Tears had already begun to flow down his cheeks freely, dribbling onto his pant leg. "I swear, I didn't mean to. I caught her out back having a smoke and walked up to her. She thought I was going to hurt her and tried to run so I grabbed her. I wasn't going to hurt her, I just wanted to explain that but she wouldn't listen and she kept screaming and..." he closed his eyes, sobbing uncontrollably.

"Brick?" Xander asked, reaching over and laying a sympathetic hand on Ken's shoulder.

Ken nodded, his lower lip quaking. "I don't even know how it got in my hand. Didn't know what was happening until she was dead."

Xander pursed his lips, sighing. "There were a lot of smells that got me here. The dry smell of her make-up... but the kicker was copper. That coppery smell blood has. When it's mixed with a fungal citrus smell and a weird taste like morning breath... well, that's how I describe the smell of death, anyway." He paused, squeezing Ken's shoulder to lend support. "Hate to tell you man, but she didn't die behind the bar. There's a lot of that coppery blood smell in the pan of your truck. Dead bodies don't bleed like that, believe me. She wasn't dead until just before we came out, I'm guessing."

"Oh, gawd," Ken urged, vomiting a little onto the seat between his legs.

"That's the real reason you were in the laundry room out back, to try and get the blood out of your clothes. It's also why you glared at the guy playing darts when you came in... he was the guy she was supposed to meet. He started calling her while we were playing pool. I can still hear her phone vibrating against the pan of your truck."

Ken stopped and listened, the low buzz reaching his ears as well. He balked again, more tears then he'd ever cried in his life now tumbling down his face. "Get out," he said sternly, not looking at Xander.

"Not a chance," Xander sighed, removing his hand and leaning against the door.

Ken nodded, then slammed the truck out of park and pulled forward slowly. The car bumped up and down once as it moved up onto the tracks. When it straddled them with its chasse he put it back into park and turned to Xander with eyes that were red and puffy and bloodshot. "Get out," he repeated, but his voice wasn't able to hold onto the sternness. Now it was wavy and pleading, full of guilt.

Behind Ken's head, Xander could see the glow of the train's spotlight. From this angle it made it look like the driver had a halo. "You're a good man, Ken," Xander assured him, smiling and nodding with respect. "You just made a mistake. A horrible one. Now... you're paying for it."

The train's horn blared with urgency as the tracks and truck began to shake with the vibrations of its motion. "What about you?" he asked, his voice crackling from sorrow and pain.

"I'm still paying for mine," he said, smiling.

"I just hate that I'm taking you down with me." Ken said, his voice almost a whisper now.

Xander reached into his pocket and pulled out a Marlboro cigarette. He brought it to his lips and lit it, then took a long drag.

Eyes wide with fear, Ken turned toward the driver's side window of his truck and watched as the blinding white light barreled down upon him, the horn blaring in his ears.

He closed his eyes.

INTERLUDE

Sometimes it stank in Los Angeles. Stank like ashes.

She wasn't sure if it was the factories spewing out smoke or the millions of cars or the smog, but some parts of the town smelled like they were burning even when it was pouring rain outside.

More than that, it made her skin feel dirty. As though she'd been covered with dust or grime. She kept moving to brush at it but found nothing there each time. She did this even now, stroking her fingers over her left shoulder where she thought she felt the tickle of sand or some other debris. When she looked and saw that it was clean she rolled her eyes at her own lack of impulse control, then stared forward at the building in front of her.

It was a rather large teal townhouse, three stories high. Bay windows on the front showed that the first floor alone had ceilings of well over ten feet, with several fans placed around to combat the heat that dominated this city even in the depths of winter. There was a balcony circling all the way around the front, going wide on the west end to make a large gated porch used for barbecues and tanning. Stairs went up from it to a second entrance on the third floor, which looked dark and dusty from what she could see from across the street. She'd done some research on the place before coming. Hot-water heating with a propane back-up system, the three-acre property had a reported five underground tanks of water and contained enough stored food to last several months if need be. Apparently the owner had designed it personally to be completely self-sufficient after being taken in by the Y2K hysteria. She supposed that even though the world hadn't fallen into economic collapse, it still made for a hell of a conversation piece.

The woman's name was Leigh Blackheart, something that not many people got to know personally. She was slim and beautiful, but there was also something about her that was off-putting. The angle that her back bent at didn't seem quite right. Her limbs seemed to be able to move regardless of the limitations of her joints and her eyes quivered as though their hold to her face was tenuous at best. Like yolks shaking in the centers of fried eggs. She hadn't been on many dates in the last few years, but those she had been on had ended rather abruptly when the man (or woman) in question had gotten a real good look into those eyes. They were as black as tar yet somehow glowed in darkness, a glint in their corner even when there was no light around.

The skin on her face was a chalky white that looked more like a balloon shaped like a face, filled with too much water. Even though she wasn't chubby, her face still shook every time she moved as though she were. Her lips and eyelids were painted black and her raven hair was cut short, held down close to her scalp.

Other than her face, her shoulders were the only part of her body uncovered and were just as pale. The rest of her slender form was covered in a form-fitting sable jumpsuit that covered even her hands and feet. She looked as though she had been poured into it, like something out of a spy novel.

She spat out the gum she'd been chewing as she glanced in both directions (pausing to let one last car pass by), then stepped off of the sidewalk and onto the road, heading toward the house she'd been watching.

Her footsteps barely made a sound as she walked. When she was certain nobody could see her she broke into an run toward the far east side of the property, ducking behind a fur tree that had been planted there. The foliage looked out of place in the otherwise barren and rocky yard. There was still an orange ribbon with a price tag wrapped around the center of its trunk.

She peered through the house at the darkened windows, searching for any sign of movement or life. Another car sped by, illuminating her for a moment. She turned in its direction and the driver caught a glimpse of her pasty white face and starkly black eyes, but he was in such a rush to get home that what he had seen would not register until later that evening when he was home in bed next to his wife. The sight would give him nightmares for three weeks.

Once it passed she ran toward the house. She pressed her body against the concrete foundation and lowered herself until her eyes were flush with the basement window. Again, she saw nothing but darkness within. She frowned and squinted with concentration as beads of sweat formed on her forehead, her pupils widening to take in more light. After a moment, the basement den of T.J. Evans faded into existence.

It was quaint. In a different situation, it might have made her smile a little.

There was an old dusty-rose couch just a few feet off from the window she was looking in through, with a host of science fiction novels and popular mechanics magazines on a wire rack next to it. Just beyond that was a table that looked as though it might have been hand crafted, a few spots on it a little less varnished than others. It was either the least impressive professional job she'd ever seen, or the most impressive amateur work. She wasn't sure. On it was a stainless steel chess set with a few of the pieces moved about as if it had been left in mid-game, as well as a picture of what she could only assume were Evans' parents in a dark purple frame.

On the opposite side of the table was a chair that almost matched the couch, but not quite. This one was more of a pink, and had faded roses stenciled all over its cushions. They had definitely come from two separate sets, and had probably been picked up at a yard sale. Against the wall behind it was a powerful lamp with one of those energy-saving bulbs in it, aimed directly over the shoulder of the chair. The wall behind it was covered in pictures of family and friends, as well as some shots of random objects with black-and-white film. It was obvious that somebody in his family fancied themselves an artist of some sort.

Leigh turned her gaze away from the room once she was satisfied that it was empty, looking down at the hard white plastic that surrounded the glass pane. There was a crack running along the outer edge that terminated itself after a foot or two, as well as several growths of mold in each of the corners, but other than that it looked sturdy enough. She slapped her hand against both sides, then pushed on the hatch of the window just enough to make sure it wouldn't have come undone all on its own. Satisfying herself that there was no other way to enter the building, she closed her eyes and got ready.

Sitting down in the dirt and crossing her legs Indian-style, she rested her hands against her knees and tried to stay calm. She took a deep breath and then slowly let it exhale the way she had done many times before, feeling a tingly numb sensation work its way down through her body and then out through her fingertips. The way it felt always reminded her of electric energy, the way it surged right through her.

She pushed the thought away, inhaling again through her small black lips. To a casual observer she would have looked very odd sitting that way on the side of a stranger's house. With her eyes closed, she would have looked much more normal now as well. It was much easier to see just how long her eyelashes really were now as they lay pressed gently against her cheeks. She exhaled again. When she did she felt something move next to her ear. She had experienced this before but never the exact same way twice. She had found the hardest part to be not breaking her concentration to turn and look at what the movement had been. When she filled her lungs again a lock of her hair fell from its place against her scalp, bouncing gently next to her earlobe. It itched at the tender skin and sent more shivers through her, making her mouth twitch a little as she struggled to keep her concentration.

The hair began to move.

On its own, with no help from her or the wind, it started to curl upwards like a piece of plastic curling away from a fiery log. The tip narrowed to a point as it moved, swirling over and over with increasing speed as if being spun around some invisible finger.

She had to remind herself to continue breathing, suddenly letting go of a mouthful of air she'd almost hung onto for too long. When she did her mouth began to vibrate, as if it might fall right off her face if she wasn't careful.

Her hair had curled itself up almost to her head again as one last surge of electric energy shot its way underneath her skin. Suddenly the hair melted together and dripped, like two dewdrops meeting on a leaf and then tumbling off of it together. The greasy liquid fell to the ground where it landed with an audible -plop!-, seeming to hang in the air for a moment before finally splashing.

Leigh took one last breath and held it as her entire body erupted in one large splash, like a water balloon that was filled too tight finally bursting. Liquid shadows spread out in all directions, laying in one massive puddle in the mud next to the house. Another car passed by, its headlights shimmering off the trees in the distance. Other than that there was no movement and no sound.

A ripple made its way through the surface, its rings growing until they reached the edge and splashed up onto a nearby rock. The puddle started to flow toward the house slowly but surely, as though it were on a slope even though it wasn't. It pooled right under the windowsill, defying most of the laws of physics as it did, and started to flow up the concrete wall. Ripples began from some unknown place in its center and waved out, growing with every inch until it crashed forward like a tidal wave. Every time it did this it gained a hold on whatever it had landed on, pulling itself along the wall like that until it covered the entire window.

There was an odd sucking sound as it conformed to the shape of the glass, like when you open a jar of jam for the first time. At first there were air bubbles, but even they slowly deflated until it looked like someone had painted the glass black.

It stayed like that for several moments, with no movements or sounds except for the patter of rain all around the house.

The blackness covering the bottom right hand corner of the window seemed to twitch, no more than a heartbeat, and was followed closely by a loud slurping sound that seemed to drag on forever. It was like someone trying to suck the last bit of cola from a straw. A bubble popped where the twitch had been a moment ago, leaving behind a hole in the black sea.

The rest of the tar started to swirl around the hole like a whirlpool in a bathtub, that slurping sound getting louder and louder with every bit that got sucked up. The goop glistened as it slowly disappeared, pebbles and raindrops falling from it as it unstuck itself from its place on the window. One last sliver swirled around the edges of the hole for a moment before being sucked in, and then it was gone.

After several long moments, a car went by on the road,

its headlights beaming into the trees again. Between the branches, they illuminated something the driver didn't see at all. Something whose eyes held onto the glow of the lights long after they were gone.

∞

The last of the black ooze ran down the wall on the other side of the window, leaving a stream of moistness in its wake as it rejoined the rest of its mass on the floor. It had congealed together in a large lump rather than a puddle, like half-formed clay tossed onto a spindle. It didn't have any specific shape, just lumps on top of more lumps of darkness. Suddenly two eyes opened in the center and Leigh's head jutted out of the darkness. She struggled at first to get free as it clung to her cheeks and she gasped for hair. Her face almost blue at first, then slowly faded back to the pale white it had been a moment ago as she got more and more oxygen into herself.

Slowly her body began to take shape around her, the lumps and mounds folding inwards until she was back to her paper-thin figure. Her hair had once again taken on the close-cut style it had before she had melted. She gasped for air, afraid to close her mouth for fear of missing some even though she was drooling onto the homeowner's wooden floor. When she raised a hand to wipe off her chin it splashed against her face. She opened her eyes for the first time since the ordeal had begun and saw that it was still just a maw of dripping tar at the end of her wrist.

"Fuck," she cursed as she stared at the disobedient appendage, dark sweat dotting her forehead and cheeks. After a moment the liquid bubbled upon itself, boiling up until it had enough girth and then falling back, leaving a pale white hand with ebony fingernails behind in its wake. She smiled, nodding her head back and forth the way she did when she was proud of herself, but only when it was just her around. She stood and took a look around to make sure everything was the way it had looked from outside.

She picked up the top science fiction novel off the wire rack, the mostly red cover showing two starships passing by a small asteroid, each of them backlit by a star behind it. She rolled her eyes and tossed it back onto the pile, then turned her attention to the stairs that twirled up from the center of the room. At the top, almost obscured from view, was the outline of a doorway. From here it looked like a rectangle made of light painted onto the shadows.

Taking one last cautionary glance around the room, she moved up the stairs as though she were gliding off them, her legs not bending so much as arching. Each step stretched just a little too far, as if her body was ready to let go of her legs at any given moment.

She stopped dead in her tracks just as she reached the door, turning back down toward the floor. Her lips were drawn up small as she stared into the darkness at the bottom of the stairs, the faintest mist of light floating in from the window. Once again the rose-colored couch had been reduced to an outline to her, the metal pieces of the chess set claiming most of the light that had filtered in.

She squinted, waiting for her eyes to focus and holding her breath as long as she could. She couldn't see anything, but she was almost sure she had heard something upon reaching the top of the stairs. It had almost been like the pit-pat of the rain outside, but there had been more to it.

It had been followed by a hissing sound like the one a cat made, only faster. She waited for it again, then turned and opened the door.

She barred her teeth as the door creaked, stepping through it as quickly as she could. She stared at it for a moment, debating whether or not she should risk making the sound to close it again, then decided to leave it open.

The house she had opened up to was as different from the one she'd peered into downstairs as murder was from suicide. The walls were a dark navy that usually showed dirt but in this case emphasized just how clean and pristine the home really was. There was a shelf with a narrow rectangular mirror behind it on the wall opposite her, her reflection fading into the dark blue within the white frame. On the shelf were tiny pictures of children in heart-shaped frames. They each seemed to have the same coffee-brown eyes and angular nose regardless of gender. She thought maybe they were siblings, but they were definitely all related in some way. The floor beneath her was hardwood and was freezing against the soles of her feet.

Using her thin frame to slide between the open door and the wall she passed into the main hall. It was wide and spacious, with plenty of scrapes and gouges in the floor that resulted from children's play. They had been touched up with varnish, the same type of almost-professional job that had been done on the table downstairs. Pictures hung on thick wires all around her. A set of french doors led into a room that looked like a sitting area, but was so immaculate she thought it likely that it had never been used.

She turned another corner and almost bumped into an end table, coming face to face with another long, winding staircase that led to the upstairs bedrooms. She smiled to herself gleefully, then started up them two at a time.

No matter how many times she did this, it still had the same effect on her. It was like the world's best drug and never lost its potency or dulled its edge the more she did it. Her heart doubled its pace by the time the arch of her foot touched the fourth step, adrenaline coursing its way through her bloodstream. She felt her calve muscles pump harder as more oxygen and glucose was fed into them, sending her up the stairs even faster.

She reached the top and stopped suddenly, steadying herself on a round oak banister when she slipped on the smooth floors. Her smile beamed wide. These were the only times she ever had on a real, genuine smile and she usually wished she had a picture of it to prove that it did happen from time to time.

The hallway up here was thinner than it had appeared from downstairs. Where the main floor had been open and lavish, this floor was far more utilitarian. The walls were still navy blue with white trim but boasted none of the elaborate hangers or pictures that the downstairs had. Instead there were a few scratches and scrapes on the walls, probably from children as well, that hadn't been tended to yet. The fact that these weren't a priority made her believe that very few people got to see this floor that weren't spending the night.

There were four doors, each one nearly identical to the next. They were all the same eggshell white, all with the same round gold knobs. Her eyes went over them one at a time from left to right, examining each one meticulously before moving on to the next. Her brain was still juiced from the surge she had felt a moment ago, moving a mile a minute to process the information before her. She stopped at the second-to-last door and smiled, her eyes focusing in on the knob. It was exactly like the others, with the exception of a thin vertical slit in its center.

It was the only bedroom with a lock on it.

She chuckled softly and shook her head as she walked toward the door. She reached out and grabbed the knob, twisting it sharply to the right. It turned ten degrees, then stopped with a hard -click!-, refusing to go any further without its key.

Leigh rolled her eyes and pointed at the lock with her right forefinger. It seemed to wobble on the edge of her knuckle, like a sword made out of silly putty. She pressed it forward into the lock and grimaced as it slid in, the jagged metal winces slicing at the liquid flesh. She felt something inside it snap and pushed the door with her free hand. It slid open gently, her finger sliding out of the lock. She watched it as it became solid again, sucking in air as bones and nerves re-knit themselves.

She stepped into the room slowly, her eyes darting everywhere. It had been months since anything had truly taken her off guard in either her professional or personal life, but she never stopped being careful.

-tak-

She spun around so fast that she felt her hips become liquid again for just a moment to accommodate the motion, almost leaving her legs facing the wrong direction. She stared back down the stairs into the hall. It was fed by a light in the adjoining room, casting odd shadows and reflections back at her. The light seemed to dance like a wild flame for a moment until her eyes got used to it, her pupils larger than a normal persons were capable of being to make sure she saw everything.

The tiny hairs on the back of her neck stood on end as she again felt that sudden rush when her adrenal gland pumped more and more epinephrine into her system. What had felt wonderful a moment ago now felt like too much of a good thing, her mind now working overtime to come up with different things that could be waiting in the dark for her. It didn't take much imagination. In her life she'd seen many amazing things... but many horrors as well. She'd seen a child that put her own darkness to shame sprout teeth and claws as if from nowhere and dive at her. She'd seen men that looked meek and gentle overcome her in one shutter-fast instant. She'd seen things large enough to flatten houses barrel down toward her at speeds they shouldn't have been capable of. At that moment in her mind, whatever was downstairs was all of those things and more.

After a moment of silence she smiled and laughed a little at herself. Still, she closed the bedroom door behind her as she turned around.

The room was small and windowless, its walls a pale cappuccino color. There were no scrapes on the walls here, or anything else out of place for that matter. The floor was hardwood with a single, multi-colored Vietnamese rug running up its center from the doorway. On either side of the rug were three large cases, each one perfectly shone to magnificent glory until one could barely tell where the air ended and the glass began. At the end of the felt walkway was a small table with three stainless steel boxes laid carefully upon it.

She took a deep breath and stepped forward. She almost expected alarms to ring out the second she stepped onto the rug, but they did not and she chided herself again for being so worrisome. If anyone had been watching her, they would have thought it was her first job.

It was, however, an important one.

Each of the six cases held items that on any other day would have given her (and any other thief in the country, she imagined) a wet dream. There was a curved blade accompanied by a jeweled holster that had been lifted from Saddam's fortress after the American occupation. An unfired bullet from the gun that had shot Adolf Hitler and Eva Braun. A suit of armor that had been worn by Genghis Khan.

She stopped by the last two display cases and turned to look at the one on the left. It was a small blade, only about ten inches long. The small card in the display window said that it was diamond-etched titanium, but that wasn't what had caught her eye. On the grip was an upper-case 'I' incased in a golden circle. On the card it was misread as the letter 'H', but she knew better. Had in fact seen one like it before, if not this exact one. When she leaned in a little closer, she thought she could actually still see a little blood spatter in one of the grooves.

She scoffed, curling her upper lip in disgust. She debated just reaching in and taking it, then thought better of it and turned back toward the table at the end of the hall, doing her best to ignore the display cases lest she get distracted again.

The desk was a deep black oakwood and looked to have been hand carved, although it was anything but ancient. Symbols representing Vlad the Impaler, Musolini Trepes and Judas Iscariot had been carefully engraved there along with too many others for her to count now, though she wanted to.

There was no doubt anymore. This was a War Room.

She had heard that T.J. Evans had descended from German war-criminals but hadn't believed it and still wasn't quite sure if she did. As bad as all of this looked in light of those rumors, it could still have been a healthy obsession with history and its battles. Either way, she tried not to think about it. Convincing herself that Evans was one of the bad guys would only serve to make her feel justified in what she was about to do and although she felt no guilt, she had no delusions of Robin Hood syndrome, either.

-sisssss-

She turned around, wondering if she'd tripped some alarm after all. There was nothing, not even a bug or shrew on the floor. The room was immaculate. She shrugged, then turned back to the desk.

There was a dark silk cloth laid elegantly over the table, upon which sat three identical tin boxes, each about the size of a cigarette case.

Pursing her lips together, she reached for the case furthest to the left and tapped it firmly with her index finger. A clasp inside came loose at the top and opened slowly without a sound, its inside lined with the same red silk as the cloth.

Laying there, staring up at her from a sea of red, was a floppy disc. Its metal slide-guard twinkled and winked at her even though it must have been ancient. She doubted it would even read in a computer anymore, but the words scrawled across it made her want it anyway. Even if it was worthless, just the idea of having it in her possession gave her the shivers.

It read: Srebrenica.

At the time the largest genocidal mass murder in Europe since World War II, killing over eight thousand Bosniak boys and men. It had been a specific and intended plot to obliterate Bosnian Muslims in the area of Srebrenica, a United Nations safeguarded area.

Some people had long suspected that there were other factors involved in the massacres, the answers to which were probably on the disk in front of her. That information could give tens of thousands of grief stricken families the peace they deserved... as well as fetch her at least eight mill on the international market.

Leigh reached out to touch the disk, but stopped short of it and moved on to the next case, tapping it once.

A smile spread across her black lips.

A slender piece of metal sat in the center of the box. It was almost devoid of anything with which to identify it with, except for the small USB connection sticking out of its head. A small piece of paper next to the flash-drive had the word Unstable printed on it in calligraphy.

She reached out and picked up the drive carefully between her thumb and forefinger. Smiling, she brought it to her lips and kissed the cold steel softly before tucking it into her blouse and turning to leave.

She stopped before she even made it a single pace, clenching her teeth as she tried to fight the thought that had just occurred to her. Letting out a hefty sigh she turned around, rolling her eyes at herself as she did. "One of these days you're going to run out of lives, Leigh," she scolded herself, even as she stepped back to the table. "And your curiosity will get the better of you."

Pausing only for an instant, she tapped on the cover of the last case and watched it slowly open to full view.

Her eyes widened.

"Oh, no shit," she whispered, leaning in to make sure she was actually seeing what she thought she was.

It was a mini- cassette tape of the kind that was popular in the mid-nineties for recording home movies on. They would be slid into larger, master tapes and played in any household VCR but were much more compact and easy to store than normal VHS tapes.

This one looked to be a security tape rather than a simple home movie awaiting Bob Sagat's approval and had been kept in remarkably good condition. She imagined it had already been exported to DVD at some point, but one never knew with things like this. There were no words on the label, just one hastily drawn symbol. It looked like a figure-eight with the bottom half of the lower circle missing and a line cutting diagonally through the top. Not a lot of people in this world would have recognized it and even fewer would have known what it meant, but she did.

It was the Zyphrius symbol.

Her mind racing, she reached out toward the tape. She stopped herself again, almost immediately. There were places in the world where you could be killed simply for having seen something like that, and this was one of them. How Evans had gotten away with having it out in plain sight like this for so long was beyond her, although she suspected that she would spend the next few nights laying awake thinking about it.

Biting her lip, she turned away and started back toward the door.

Thick, grey smoke barreled out from the crevice between the door and the floorboards, circling upwards in loops and spirals.

Leigh froze in her tracks, the drive almost popping out of her shirt as she did. "Oh, fuck," she cursed loudly, making no effort at stealth. Either she'd been caught or this was all some massive coincidence, either way she was still trapped in a burning room with no windows.

Wincing, she reached out toward the doorknob carefully, trying to see how close the fire was to the door. She felt nothing at fist, but then it was like her nerves woke up and realized what was happening. Searing pain scorched through her arm, traveling like a bullet through her system and exploding out the back of her brain. She screamed, yanking her hand away as quickly as she could.

Her wrist stretched, like a piece of chewing gum pulled in two opposite directions.

Her hand remained clasped to the brass knob, still firing bolts of pain every few seconds.

"Argh!" she screamed again, tears now running down her pale grey face as she fell to her knees. The space between her wrist and hand had become a long black rubber band.

When she looked at her fingers, still clutching the knob, they looked like they were boiling. A bubble grew on one of her knuckles and then popped, sending spurts of liquid flesh in all directions.

Shaking with fear and adrenaline, she clenched her jaw and forced her upper lip stiff, glaring at the misshapen mass that had been her hand a moment ago. She tried to will herself not to cry and failed, even as sweat started to pour down her face in droves. Her cheeks became bloodshot as they puffed in and out, trying to take in as much air as they could. The pain made it difficult, but she reminded herself that she could take it. That she'd experienced worse.

"Fuck you," she whispered, glaring one final time at the doorknob before she exploded in a vibrant splash of black tar, hand and all.

For a moment the puddle just lay there, still bubbling in some places. Then, slowly, it started to seep through the boards of the hardwood floor. An instant later, fire burst through the door and into the room, shattering the display cases and charring everything in sight.

Leigh dripped into the living room one floor down from where she had been, tumbling over a toy truck as she did so.

The walls were painted a rich mustard color, the lower foot of which was covered in finger paint and crayon masterpieces. Hundreds of children's movies lined the shelf along the far wall, a large television in the corner standing poised and ready to play them at a moment's notice. A large chest lay open, brimming with action figures, dolls and hundreds of small green toy soldiers. Some still lay arranged in mid-battle beside their case. It looked to be displaying Blitzkrieg.

Smoke had already begun to waft its way into the room, finally reaching a detector and howling out in alarm. The sound filled the home as other alarms joined in the call, even though the flames hadn't made it to this floor yet.

Leigh's body took shape around her, lumps and mounds bubbling to the surface until her slight form began to restore itself. She gasped for air, taking in a lungful of smoke and erupting into a hacking cough. Large bulges had formed under her eyes and would not go away no matter how much she willed them to.

"No, no, no..." she chanted, panicking as she reached a hand to her chest and began to fidget with the fabric frantically. After a moment, her hand touched the cool metal and she heaved a sigh of relief before rising to her feet and moving for the door.

She paused, tapping her fingertips against the metal twice before grabbing it outright. It was warm, but nowhere near the searing levels that the one upstairs had been. She smirked smugly to herself as she opened the door and turned the corner toward the basement again.

She slammed her head on into his chest. If her nose had not been as malleable as it was it would have broken almost instantly. As it was it had become a deformed lump in the center of her face, spewing out clear liquid and blood by the bucket load onto her chin and chest. She landed on the floor so hard that it shook a picture from the shelf on the wall and sent it crashing to the floor, spreading glass everywhere. It melted into the hardwood immediately.

He glared down at her from on high, scowling with such ferocity that she didn't think the devil himself was capable of as much hatred. He was well over six feet tall, his spiked red hair dancing along the ceiling. It seemed to move of its own accord, like flames moving about over a smooth surface. His skin was ashy and white, cracking and peeling around the eyes and mouth like someone who had been out in the sun for far too long. Parts of it flaked away while she was watching, tiny bursts of steam puffing out and joining the atmosphere as his meat was exposed. The eyes were so small they almost weren't even there, saved only by an orange glimmer that got just a little brighter as he made eye contact with her. They were covered with soot like charcoal almost all the way down to his cheeks, outlining the patches of his rough-hewn face. He wore a long brown trench coat that appeared to be rubber, but was far too dirty to be sure. He was topless, his chest and shoulders exposed to reveal massive scars, holes and especially burns. Hundreds of small, circular burns covering his abdomen and sides. When he looked at her the room appeared to get hotter, sweat pouring from her more than ever now.

His hands were nearly devoid of all skin, one knuckle ripped clean to the bone.

They were smoking.

"Well, you're hot," Leigh laughed, forcing a smirk. Her voice wavered when she spoke and did not sound like her own. It was scratchy and dry, even though she couldn't remember the last time she'd gotten thirsty. Ever.

He stared at her. After a moment his sneer faded and his face became an emotionless void, yet still he stared down at her.

"Yeah, whatever," she groaned as she climbed to her feet. Her nose had finally stopped gushing blood and water, looking to have reset itself. Now that she was on her feet she could see him a little better. The jacket wasn't dirty, it was sooty. As though he'd been upstairs when the fire hit. She could see that his eyes pulled upwards at the corners a little. He was Asian, or at least of Asian descent. No more than two-generations removed. His face was devoid of any hair whatsoever, his eyelashes and eyebrows having been burned off at some point. She maintained eye contact for a moment, then turned toward the basement again. "Fuck you."

He grabbed her by the shoulder.

Leigh fell to her knees as pain soared through her body, all of her nerves screaming out in alarm all at once. Her neck and arm broke out in postulant boils almost instantly upon his touch, while the rest of her body appeared to go limp and rubbery. Her legs wobbled and she braced herself against the wall, finding it hard to stand. It was like being dipped in a deep fryer, an experience that up until this point she could only have claimed she felt in the pinky finger of her right hand.

Her skin became hard and cracked, much like the flesh around the stranger's eyes and mouth. Worse, it felt like it was spreading in as though he were cooking her slowly until there was nothing left. One of the boils on her shoulder burst, sending a hissing packet of steam into the house where it joined with the tumbling smoke and disappeared.

She wanted to cry, but tears wouldn't come. They evaporated the second they escaped from their ducts. Her cries were hoarse and dry, not sounding at all like her usually bubbling tone.

A foul stench filled the air as she lost control of her bladder. The urine was so hot that it boiled its shape into the hardwood floors, warping them.

"Why --" she managed to gasp legibly, her neck cracking as she slowly turned up to face him. Her bones and joints felt like there was sand between them.

He did not speak. He barely even moved, save for tilting his head slightly toward her.

Suddenly his hand got even hotter, something that she would have thought impossible even just a moment before. The tips of his fingers began to glow bright white.

Before she knew what was happening, she felt like she was flying. Despite all the amazing things that she could do, flight was not one of them. For an instant, she remembered what it was like to feel the whoosh of air against her face as she propelled herself skyward on her swings as a child, imagining what it would be like to let go and just keep going.

Then she hit the wall with enough force that she blasted through it, landing in T.J. Evans' back yard. She landed three feet away from the house but slid an additional ten, digging a long trench and ripping swatches out of her flesh as she went. The night air stung at the open wounds, the contrast of the cool breeze and her hot flesh sending a new kind of electric pain sizzling through her skull as she started to go into shock, clenching her teeth.

The light orange trail left in her wake arced upward after she fell to earth, flashing as brightly as a solar flare before blinking out of existence as quickly as it had come.

The Asian man stepped up to the hole he had made in the wall and casually jumped down, his coat billowing behind him as he fell. As silently as a grave, he began to walk toward her. He stopped a foot from where she lay and raised his hand, pointing his palm at her evenly as smoke began to churn from the cracks in his fingertips.

Even her eyes began to sizzle, shrinking in their sockets as she gasped for air and got nothing but humid steam that scorched its way down her esophagus into her lungs. "Why?" she croaked again, grabbing at her throat. When she tried to pull her hand away, she found that the two bodies of flesh had melted and fused themselves together. She could almost feel her fingers wriggling inside her own neck and felt like vomiting, although she did not know how the logistics of such an act would work at the moment.

"Justice," he said simply, his eyes glowing brightly when he did. "Is like fire. It consumes all that stands in its way."

Slowly, Leigh forced herself to her feet, glaring at him. If there had been enough moisture in her mouth to accommodate, she would have spit her blood-tainted saliva right into his face. As it was, she settled for sneering at him as his hand began to glow white again. "Who are you to... justice?" she forced, a long gasp in the middle of the sentence masking half the words.

Its message however, was clear. The man raised one

side of his hairless brow as he regarded her, nodding slightly as he considered the will it had taken her to merely stand at this point. Her legs looked like they were going to melt away at any time. "Shadow Flame," he answered, bringing a second hand toward her as well.

"Well, Mr. Flame, let's have a lesson in nature, shall we?" Leigh smiled, her eyes finally sparkling to life again. "What happens when you pour water over a fire?"

She leapt at him even as her body finally lost control of itself and became liquid again, descending upon him like a tidal wave.

His eyes went wide with shock as he let out a massive howl, bringing up both his hands to block the attack.

There was a brilliant flash of light that was seen all throughout the city, which meteorologists would later attribute to dry lightning.

When he opened his eyes again, there was nothing there.

The only sign of Leigh Blackheart was the odor of burnt flesh and tar, and a smoldering piece of metal on the ground at his feet.

He reached down and picked it up, crushing it between his fingers as he walked into the shadows of the forest surrounding the home.

Sirens blared in the distance, but the house was almost burnt to the ground by the time they got there.

One week later, meteorologists reported a freak occurrence of what was dubbed 'black rain' in the L.A. area, which they assured the media was not acid rain and just a naturally occurring phenomenon.

Sometimes I get uncomfortable. Sometimes for no apparent reason at all other than I am. I get fidgety and nervous and I'm pretty sure I start to sweat a really putrid stench, although nobody has ever commented on it.

Sometimes it's just me being stupid, other times it's legitimate. The problem is telling the difference. I still haven't mastered that one yet, but I'm getting there.

I've been walking the same road for so long that I'm starting to think that I'm actually walking in place. Everything looks the same. There's just marsh and bog in every direction for miles and miles. There are mountains in the distance, but they don't seem to get any closer no matter how fast I walk and I'm not totally convinced they're even really there. My mind aches every time I try to think about anything. I'm half delusional, but I keep thinking that this is the road I've been on my entire life and I'm only now realizing it.

It's the long road. The one that only ends up one place.

I grunt away the thought, reminding myself that I'm actually on Interstate 80. I crossed into Utah not too long ago. I've never been here before, but I know of it. Can't wait to get out.

Utah does not allow alcoholic beverages to be sold on Sundays, which I believe it to be. Now, that's bad enough (especially considering I've been on the road for almost a month now and could really go for a drink) but they also happen to be the only state in the country that still allows guns to be brought into their schools.

It's that precise type of backwards mentality that I think is going to put me at odds with the good people of Utah.

Not only that, but the cold is unbearable. Even for someone like me, it's absolutely rancid. It was minus five last night when I slept. When I woke up I think I left half the skin on the side I slept on frozen to the ground. There's still a chunk of skin missing that used to cover up my ribs along my left side. It hurts like I can't even describe every time my shirt rubs up against it. Every few meters it spits some kind of clear liquid I really don't want to think about out of the gash there and I have to feel it trickle down and soak into my jeans. It's healing, just a little too slowly for my tastes. That probably makes me sound spoiled.

My hair feels disgusting. Every time I run my hand through it it comes back soaked in sweat and just want to puke. I think I might literally give my left nut for a shower. It'd probably just grow back anyway. I'm not sure on that, and I'm not really in the mood to find out thanks.

It wouldn't be so bad if all the water around here wasn't bog water. At least in Maine there are lakes and rivers and things that I can use to clean myself up a little. I guess this place must have them too, I just haven't come across any yet.

All in all, it's safe to say I'm not a fan of Utah. I really don't see myself settling down in any one place, but if I do it won't be here. The only saving grace is that I haven't run into any people yet, thankfully.

No sooner do I think those words do I hear the familiar sound of rubber spinning against asphalt. That would be the Drew luck kicking in. I swear, all I would have to do to become a millionaire is to scream the words: "I don't want to be a millionaire" at the top of my lungs. Money would fall from the heavens, I'm convinced of it.

The car that drives past is a pink caddy that's spitting out enough fumes to wipe out the ozone layer all by itself. That said, it's a beautiful car. It wasn't perfect, but you could tell it was still a work in progress. What I had seen of the grill looked to have been ripped to pieces and the antenna was a coat hanger, but the body was smoothed to a mirror-shine and the hubcaps gleamed like tiny stars. I almost expected to see a blue cloud coming out the back of it, or for some guy in a Hawaiian shirt to pop his head out and ask me for directions.

That didn't happen.

The car continued to putt along for about another half mile, enough that I let out a sigh of relief. I'm tempted to throw my head at the sky and curse, but I'm not that dramatic. I just shove my hands deep into my pockets and keep walking, steeling myself against a cold breeze that comes across the marsh.

The car gets about a hundred feet in front of me when the brake lights snap to life. The treadless tires skid a foot or so on the slick pavement before the vehicle comes to a complete stop.

I actually curse this time, spitting out a word that would make any woman in earshot slap me. I hate saying that word actually, but it seems appropriate. Trying my best to remain respectfully passive I shove my hands just about through my pockets and keep walking, not even so much as glancing at the caddy as I come up on it.

The back bumper gleaned at me as I walked past, making me squint my eyes. I'm hating this, partly because I know what's going to happen and partly because I can't really avoid it. I'm almost at the passenger-side door when I start to think that maybe - just maybe - it's a coincidence… then I hear the slow buzz of a small motor coming to life as the tinted glass lowers itself and lets me look inside.

"Hey stranger!" comes a perky, happy voice from inside. The sentence is so drawled together that it takes me a moment to decipher it. People from Utah have this odd, amalgamated accent, somewhere between sweet southern slang, long-syllable central and a drunk orangutan. I couldn't see the driver yet, but I pictured him as an older gent that people called sir with a smirk on their face. His face would be unshaven and his mouth would hang open even when he wasn't speaking or doing anything at all.

It crosses my mind that I could just keep walking. Keep walking and keep ignoring this lookie-lou until eventually he gets the hint. Even if he has to follow me along the road a few hundred meters, eventually he will get the hint. But one of my first priorities right now is to avoid attention, and a strange man crossing the state line who venomously opposes the idea of a ride does attract some. Plus, I'm not really in the mood to be a dick. It takes too much effort.

I plaster on my best scowl as I stop and lean into the window, hoping that if I look annoyed enough the driver might just take the hint and drive away. "Yes?" I sigh, trying my best to sound unpleasant. The sound of my own voice almost makes me jump back in fright. I think it has been almost two weeks since I've used it and its gone all hoarse and stringy. It almost sounds like the Womb's. I think the shock is evident on my face, because the man behind the wheel raises an eyebrow at me quizzically.

"Care for a lift?" he asks, a lot clearer this time but still with the drawn-out A's of West Virginia. I wonder if he's actually from Utah or if I'm just trying too hard not to like him. Could be a little of both, for all I know. In any event he looks nothing like I pictured. He's clean shaven and young, no older than twenty-five. His eyes are blue and his hair's cut short, spiked a little in the front with aerosol spray instead of gel. Even though he's sitting I can tell he's tall and lanky, and while he may not be built like a tank like some of the folks I've come across he looks to at least be in shape. He's wearing a red button-down suit and some faded jeans under a green corduroy jacket that looks as though its seen better decades. "I'm only going as far as Indigo, but you're welcome to join."

I almost ask what in the Holy-Godfuck Indigo is, but don't. Just the context it was used in should have tipped me off to that, but I'm tired dammit. Cut me some slack. It's the same exhaustion that prevents me from coming up with anything even remotely sounding like a plausible excuse for why I wouldn't want a ride... besides the fact that a not-small section of my brain is screaming to accept.

"How far is that from Salt Lake?" I ask as I lean against the window, though I don't much care what the answer is. Still, in the city there would be motels. I've discovered that around the outskirts of towns there were no-tell motels where it was easy for a person like me to break into an empty room and grab a hot shower. On the road that could make all the difference, might even get a few extra miles a day out of myself if I felt fresh enough.

"Few miles, nothin' big. Few more years of expansion and we'll practically be a suburb." He says the last bit as a joke but his voice as the twang of bitterness to it. Despite all appearances he's just another backwards redneck afraid of change.

There's a nip in the back of my throat that won't go away. Something about just being around people makes me nervous and I'm not sane enough to hide it at the moment. He's looking at me with one of his preened eyebrows raised again, like he's trying to figure out what I'm all about. Probably thinks he's picked up an axe murderer or something, the way I keep shifting from foot to foot. "Sure," I say finally, pulling the rusty door open and climbing in. It squeaks loud as I slam it shut and so many of the springs are gone that I drop what feels like a foot the second my behind touches the imitation-leather seat. There's a fluffy white pair of dice hanging from the rear-view mirror and a dancing hula-girl on the dashboard. It looks like it has been handed down by Elvis Himself. Even though nothing's really wrong, I start to feel it. It starts off small (always does) just this dull ache in the back of my head that won't go away. Makes it so that my skin doesn't feel right on me and my stomach gets a little queasy.

"Name's Jay," he said, extending an open palm toward me.

The movement again makes me jump. Jesus, I curse at myself inwardly. You wouldn't think that just a few weeks away from people would cause you to forget so many of the intricacies of human interaction, but it does. Just having a conversation with this guy feels as natural as walking with both shoes on the wrong feet. "Xander," I say, taking his hand and giving it one stern pump and nod at him.

He nods back, then turns toward the road and puts his foot to the gas.

Almost instantly I'm exhausted. Even a seat this uncomfortable is better than the rocks and swamp I've been resting in for the last little while. There's heat blasting out of the air vents directly into my face and it feels like I'm on cloud nine. I feel a smile creep over my face that isn't at all forced, which is a miracle.

We're about two miles further down the road when he starts thumping his hands against the steering wheel in a steady, fast rhythm. After a moment his mouth joins in, curled up in an 'o' and making noises that sound like the letter 'b'.

-Ba- -Ba- -Ba Ba- - Ba Ba Ba Ba- -Ba- Ba- Followed by seven slams against the wheel with his right hand.

Now it's my turn to raise an eyebrow at him, as I turn my head toward the action slowly and deliberately. Even through it's rudimentary, the tune feels very familiar. I knew immediately that I'd been hearing it off and on for the better part of my life, though I couldn't quite put my finger on from where.

-Ba- -Ba- -Ba Ba- - Ba Ba Ba Ba- -Ba- Ba-

"I wanna be sedated," I finished finally, not quite on the beat.

Jay turned back to me, grinning up one side of his face. "Had that stuck in my head for the last three hours."

I chuckle and lean forward a little.

"Ever notice you never get songs you know stuck in your head? You only get ones that you know, like, one line to?"

"Yeah. I'm usually getting a Disney lyric jammed up in there somewhere. The bridge to Part of Your World or something stupid like that."

"Never been that bad," he laughs.

I laugh too. It's an interesting feeling. I should be relaxing, but I'm not. Something about him puts me on edge, even though I'm not sure what. Like when the Womb organ in my gut freaks out into overdrive when I catch Derek's scent or see the glean off a knife before I really see the blade itself. Except this isn't coming from the Womb, it's coming from me. Some part of me recognizes something that the rest of me doesn't, past the cleanly-pressed shirt and neatly styled hair. Though I can't quite pin down exactly what it is, I've been through too much to ignore that feeling.

"So, what brings you to Salt Lake?" he asks in that fake, high-pitched way that everyone phrases that question.

"Just passing through, really."

"Where you headed?"

I almost want to answer nowhere in particular, but I remind myself that I'm trying not to be terribly rememberable. I don't think my little trek is being followed by anybody, but better safe than sorry. "Boise," I say, almost as a knee-jerk reaction to the question. Seems like as good an answer as any.

"What for?"

"Visiting family."

He took his eyes off the road for a moment, glancing me up and down. I hate when people give me the hairy eyeball like that, especially when I'm already unsettled to begin with. Too many people have used that same once-over glance to size me up for coffins. "No way do you have family in Boise. Or anywhere in Idaho, for that matter."

I fake an amused smile at the brashness of the statement. It almost sounds like something I'd say, calling someone out on their bullshit. "What makes you say that?"

"Your hands are smooth and you're dressed in all dark colors. You look like you've been on the road at least two weeks, so you're not coming from anywhere close by... and your accent's pure North-East. Could be Boston, but I'm guessing Maine. Probably not too far off of Bangor."

In give an impressed nod, my lower lip sucked in a little from embarrassment. I didn't realize I could be read quite that easily. "Caught me," I admit, dropping my hands to my knees in defeat. If he'd been even a little off I would of flat out denied it, but that was just too close for comfort. Somewhere in the back of my head, the extra-paranoid Xander wonders if he has been following me since Maine. I instantly regret telling him my real name. Stupid. In this day and age, a name and a state are all you need to find out everything you'd ever want to and more about anybody. "I'm a Pirates fan. Didn't think you'd approve." I try to sound casual. I'm not. Mind and body are both on edge now, teeth barred, every muscle tensed.

"Don't really follow sports," he tisked, tilting his head to one side. "Though I've been known to take a swing at bat every now and again."

"Baseballs not really my sport. Used to play with my Dad when I was a kid, guess I just kinda grew out of it." I almost jolt forward with surprise after the words are out of my mouth. I'd answered so honestly and reflexively. Again. Have to watch that.

Jay chuckled at his own little joke, his tanned cheeks turning a little red.

We drove in silence for another few minutes, only the steady roar of the engine breaking the silence between us. It sounded like it might sputter to a well-deserved death at any second.

"Why you stoppin' over in Salt Lake?" he asks, clearing his throat. The mountains that are in the distance are gone now and the lights of a town can be seen. There aren't many, but it's not the hovel I was expecting either.

I don't like the question. I know exactly where it's going and try to stop it in its tracks right then and there. "Looking for a cheap motel, been making a point of stopping in one in every state." It's a lie, but it's a good lie. Keeps him from offering me a spare bed or a couch if it seems like it's my quest to stay in a Motel 6.

"No need to go all the way out there. I own a little motel around center of town. Called it The Buzzing Sign. Get it? The Indigo Buzzing Sign?"

He waits for me to respond, so I give him a polite smile but make no effort to hide how campy I think the name is.

I think that's the point.

"Anyway, there's always vacancy. I'll let you have an end room for free."

Dammit, I think, as I try my best to keep my nod-and-smile looking genuine. Sometimes there's just no way out.

About thirty minutes and three eighties' tunes played on the steering wheel later we arrive at The Buzzing Sign. As roach-motels go, it's actually pretty upscale. Just a long rectangular box with a roof covered in a reflective tarmac to try and diffuse some of the non-existent sunlight. There's a porch that goes all the way around that seems like it's kept up pretty well and some daffodils and bleeding hearts hanging from planters every few feet.

It looks almost... homey.

Except there's only one set of fresh tire-treads in the lot and as I get out of the car I don't get a strong whiff of ammonia and pine. Means the rooms haven't had a fresh cleaning in a while. Means they haven't needed a fresh cleaning in a while. It's my experience that no matter how well you dress up a place, if you know that there hasn't been anyone there for a while, it gets creepy. Every sound becomes more acute when you know that whatever's making it is not of human design.

I slam the door to his car shut and step out onto the dusty brown gravel lot he uses as a driveway. He does the same just a moment later and now we're both walking toward the motel's office on the far right side with our hands covering our eyes from the gravelly wind.

Jay motions to the door all the way to the right of the building. It's painted red when all the others are a sea green, I suppose I should have taken that as a hint. I hurry in as fast as I can, waiting by the door for a moment as Jay comes up from behind. There's something tacked to the door, a pendant or something made from cloth. It's composed of a straight line at a forty-five degree angle meeting at its tip with another that hooks at both ends. I'm convinced I've seen it before, but Jay pulls it down and tosses it to the balcony before I can figure out from where.

"Darn it," he says under his breath as he fumbles with his keys, finally selecting the right one and shoving it into the deadbolt. I get the impression he doesn't curse very often. Even the word darn seemed forced and unnatural coming out of his mouth. He pushes the door once and it doesn't budge, then slammed his shoulder against it. It swung open, crashing into a chair as Jay stumbles twice on the loose mat. He catches himself on the counter-top just to his right. He lets out a long sigh, then chuckles a little at his own clumsiness. "Sorry I'm such a klutz."

I shrug the notion away, stepping into the office and closing the door behind me.

Just like outside, it's nice enough. He obviously did the best he could with what he had, like we all do. The walls are an odd color blueish-green that I don't think I've ever seen before, like the color of a seasick Smurf. Even though the paint smells fresh its already starting to chip and peel around the edges of the baseboards. The humidity does that, staying on top of it's probably a full time job in and of itself. There are more plants hanging from the ceiling, one a fern and the other is some kind of chive that makes the whole room smell like Chinese food. The counter-top is a little too high, coming up to the middle of my chest, and the cash register on it looks like it was taken from Leave it to Beaver.

"As you can see, Utah has many different season's worth of bad weather," Jay half-jokes as he walks around to the other side of the counter a presses the NO SALE button, opening the register. He lifts out the empty cash shelf and lays it to one side, then picks up a key from the bottom of the drawer and holds it out to me. "Room C, right on the other side of the lot. Don't want to crowd you."

"Thanks," I grunt, nodding to him as I stare down at the key. It's old and worn from use, the metal bending at its base to the point of breaking. Even though it's silver, there's a scent on it like copper that I can't seem to shake. There's a tag on it with the letters BS-C scrawled on with a pink pen, a single piece on clear tape laid over it to keep it from fading.

There's silence for a moment as Jay leans over the counter, tapping out some tune on it with his knuckles as he pops his tongue back and forth in his mouth. "You want a bite to eat? I haven't got much, but I could throw on some fries or chicken fingers or something."

"No, thanks," I smile, snapping myself out of the trance the key had put me in as I shove it into my pocket.

"Com'mon, you've gotta be hungry. Look at you, sure, you're all skin and bones."

I snort, then shake my head again. "Really, I'm fine."

He shrugs, then leans back so that he can see under

the counter. "How about a drink then? Got some tequila down here... there might even be a little bit of Snapps if we're lucky."

That sounds tempting, I'll admit. I haven't had a smoke or a coffee or a good drink for longer than I'd care to think about. For some reason that bothers me more than the way my stomach is churning, begging me for those promised chicken strips. But my teeth are still set on edge and I can't shake that weird, uneasy feeling in my gut that has nothing to do with hunger. He's looking at me expectantly, waiting for my answer and trying not to make it look like he's waiting. I force a smile onto my face. "No thanks. Been on the road a while, like to just get some rest."

Jay nods, then claps his hands together. "Fine enough. Guess I'll see you in the morning."

I nod once, then turn around and leave the way I came in.

⋏⋎⋏

There's a place you have to go to in order to deal with things. A kind of hollow place inside yourself that you don't even realize is there until you're in it. Like a hole in your chest that you crawl into and feel sad and safe and secure. If your significant other leaves you, you'll probably go there for at least a month or two unless you're totally devoid of emotion or were just fucking them. If someone close to you dies you'll go there for half a year or more, depending on who they were and how much a part of your daily routine they were. Run someone over with your car and you'll go there for years. You'll probably need a priest or a therapist to help dig you out.

When it comes to what I've done... that's a whole 'nother place. Like a secret hole within a hole that nobody knows about except me. Well, maybe not just me... but I can't imagine there are too many other people who've gone through what I'm going through. One of the first things I tried to make peace with when I started out onto the road was that I was going to live in my hole. You don't ever get out after this. It's like a body's natural reaction to the influences on your mind. It finds a state of being for you to default to and sticks you there so that you can cope with what your life has become. After that, all that matters is pressing forward.

The room is sparse, but I can't say I expected much. There's another fern but it's plastic and tacky. There's a ten-inch television on a rickety old table across from the foot of a double bed with visibly loose springs. There's no night-stand, but there is a lamp bolted to the wall on either side of the bed with a little articulated neck so you can put it where it suits you best. There's a bathroom almost immediately to my left when I walk into the room with just enough space in it for the toilet and a stand-up shower. There's no sink, but I suppose the argument could be made that the faucet in the shower could be used as one. All in all, the whole place could've fit into my kitchen back home.

Turn a blacklight on the average motel room in America and you'll find more than enough to make you re-think the pros and cons of sleeping in your car. Urine stains, vomit, old pizza, semen stains, lubricant, formula... the list is never ending. Anything that can fit through the front door and secrete probably has and did at one point or another. I'll say this: the room might be small, but it's immaculate. No dust, no dirt, no stains. No scent of cleaner either, means Jay didn't take any shortcuts and actually washed the sheets instead of just spraying them down with Febreeze.

"Not allergic to work anyway," I grin to myself before I peel out of my shirt. I wince as the sticky, sweaty fabric passes over my ribs and onto the floor, hissing through my teeth when I'd rather be howling. When I look down I see that there's still a fairly large chunk of skin missing about two inches below my armpit. The muscle underneath is pink and stringy and wet but it's not bleeding anymore so there's not much I can do but give it time. I'm sure that if I slept it'd get better but that's even less and option now than when I was on the road.

I swallow, unbutton my jeans, and let them fall to the floor. My hips and legs don't offer much resistance to them on the way down. I think I've lost twenty pounds since I started on the road. My underwear go next, the elastic snapping in places as I pull them around each ankle and toss them to the foot of the bed. When I look down at my naked form I barely even recognize it. There's tone there that never was before, and the lack of fat has reached an unhealthy level. Almost all the bones of my torso are clearly identifiable and my kneecaps look like swollen bulbs in the middle of my legs. I don't pay it much attention before turning into the bathroom.

I don't bother to close the door. I don't bother to smell the soap or the complementary bottle of shampoo that looks like it was stolen from a Holiday Inn. I don't look at myself in the mirror to see if my face has changed as well. I just turn the hot water on blast and leave the cold where it is.

The pressure's amazing. Almost blows me back, but I don't care. The second the water hits my flesh it turns bright red, steam rising up into my nostrils as the spray beats two or three layers of dead, putrid flesh off me that should have come off days ago. My side kills me, but I don't care.

After a moment I step forward until the water pours over my face, running through my hair and down the back of my neck. The chlorine stings at my eyes and leaves a foul taste in my mouth as I spit it out between my feet, but there's a happiness to it I can't even begin to describe. There's something deeply instinctual that is immensely satisfied by simply being warm and wet, preferably at the same time.

For the first ten minutes I don't even bother with soap. Just the water on me is enough. After that I grab the tiny, square plastic-wrapped bar of soap from the shelf and start to lather up. It's worn down to a sliver by the time I'm through with it, and part of me wants to keep going. The lather it makes is pink and carries a rosy smell on it, a welcome change from how I smelled right before. I scrub past the point that any person really should, to the point that I think I almost feel the electric charge that comes when my body starts to heal. I stay in for about thirty minutes even after that, just soaking and feeling the water trickle along every last part of me. When I get out I'm a bright shade of red and the air on me feels like ice in comparison, makes me feel alive.

Sometimes you don't know how dirty you were until you feel clean again.

For a moment I debate putting some clothes back on, but I can smell them for what they really are now and decide to put it off, laying down on the bed just like I was and turning on the television.

斺

The next thing I hear aside from the mechanical sound of canned laughter and the drone of badly-written scripts comes about four hours later. It sounds like a wet mound of ground beef being tossed onto the kitchen counter by my mother, though instead of being followed by the sick, slimy sound of her fingers pressing inside, the sound just repeats itself over and again like a broken record. For a minute or so I don't really register what I'm hearing. I can't sleep, but I've been lolling about in that weird area somewhere between sleep and awake for too long, watching old reruns of Fresh Prince.

All at once I sit up on the bed and turn over the side, facing the light coming in through the window. I can't see anything at first, and then shadows move in front of the light, so fast that if I blink I would have missed it. First up, then down, then the tell-tale sound of meat getting tossed around again.

I get up, still naked as the day I was born, and walk over to the window. I put my hand on the plastic blinds and wait a moment. There's dread building in me that knows what I'll see when I pull them aside. Part of me wants to just turn up the volume on the television and pretend I don't hear anything, but I can't do that. Call it curiosity or heroism or just plain stupidity, for whatever reason that blind was moving aside the second I heard even the slightest thing.

I pull them a fraction of an inch and I can see enough to know what's going on. There's a big guy not five feet in front of the window raising his hands again, blocking out the sun with the massive mounds of flesh he calls fists. They look like they could just tear me apart the way a kid takes the wings off a fly... not something I say every day, either. Knuckles are hairy and full of abrasions. I mean full. They're basically hair growing out of scabs.

He brings down those hammers and I hear them connect with something soft and wet. I don't wince outwardly as the sound reaches me, but something inside me shutters. I know that feeling. I don't envy the guy taking the beating.

I turn my head to the side to see who it is. I'm almost relieved that it's nobody I know. That's another thing about my luck: if some guy is nice enough to give me a ride, later that day I will be put into a situation to save his hide. That's just how my life tends to work, much as I wish it didn't. There's no such thing as a free favor, even if the person giving it meant for it to be.

The guy getting the snot beat out of him looks older, maybe forty. Well kept, though. Bit of salt-and-pepper hair that's cut close and looks like it had been styled neatly before Brutus started knocking him around. Thin little square glasses over a well-shaved, well-cleaned face and a striped blue shirt that looked like it cost more than everything in my wardrobe. Combined.

I watch for another second, give my balls a good

scratch and finally remember I'm still naked. Frowning, I turn away from the window and let the blinds snap back into place.

Now, I know what you're thinking, incidentally. Why aren't I helping? First off: not my problem. Can't count the number of times I've been down and out with way worse odds than one-on-one and nobody came to help me. If the rest of the world can turn their cheek, so can I. Second, I have no idea what the score is out there. Sure, the guy's getting beat to crap. But I should assume just because he's the underdog that I should be on his side? Fuck no. Brutus out there could be a parent and the well-dressed little prick could be a child molester. Or a rapist. Or they could just have gotten into a bar-room brawl. Shit, I don't know. But there's plenty of possibilities on how this could have made it to my doorstep without it being the big guy's fault and me jumping in will only make things worse.

And yes, I'm putting on my pants.

I hate the feeling of dirty clothes on clean skin. It makes me feel all gross again, like I never showered at all. It also puts me in a damn bad mood, one I'm getting more and more inclined to share.

"What the hell is this?"

I turn toward the window again. The shadows have stopped dead in their tracks. Dammit. Someone else stumbled upon the little party, and I can guess who. The voice is high from stress and surprise, but it's definitely Jay. I don't even have to look outside to see that.

I finish zipping up and head for the door. Not even gonna bother with a shirt, it'll take time and just get in the way. Find the topless look helps with the intimidation factor anyway, especially when the fists start flying.

When I open up the door I see a third guy I hadn't noticed before. Tall bastard, looks damn close to six and a half feet. He's wearing denim... everything. Denim shirt, denim jeans, denim jacket... guy's a Calvin Klein ad waiting to happen. Would be, anyway, if not for the mask. Didn't notice before, but both Denim and Brutus have old-school wool masks pulled down over their mugs. I know that doesn't actually mean much really, but for a kid raised on comic books and super heroes, guys in ski-masks helps you make your choice about who the bad guys are. Also means that the odds aren't one-on-one, like I thought first.

Also doesn't hurt that Denim's holding a gun.

Cheap frigging handgun, like the kind I've seen a hundred times before. The Tees used to use them all the time. Shoot them once, throw them away. Make it so they can't be traced back to you. Makes perfect sense in a country where guns are cheaper than milk.

I can see it all now, even the bits I missed out the window. The reason the well-dressed gent wasn't squirming or screaming or trying to fight back: when there's a gun pointed at you, you tend to let the guy with the fists do all the pounding he pleases. That changes my mind more than anything. The guns and the masks make this a plan, far as I'm concerned. Could still be wrong, this is still Utah after all... but I don't think I am.

Then there's Jay, kicking up dirt as he runs over from the main building. Guy's looking to get himself killed, making a target out of himself like that, yelling and screaming.

Not that I can say much.

Denim's already ignoring Jay when he hears my door open, he's spinning the gun around and pointing it at me, teeth grinding beneath that ugly ski-mask.

Right away I notice a few things. The guy is holding his piece with both hands and it's pointed straight at me, out as far in front of him as it can be. That's the way it should be done, not like the assholes you see in the movies, holding the gun with one hand tilted to the side. I've been shot at like that before. You don't need to heal fast if the bullets don't connect. Also, his hands are like a rock. Typically, you give some tech-support dweeb who thinks he's a vigilante a gun, he thinks he's the top of the food chain... until he goes to shoot it. Then his nerves go straight to hell and he's shaking like an epileptic. Not this guy. He's definitely pointed a gun at something living before, probably a human from the level of cockiness in his stance. I'm not good enough to tell based on body language whether or not he's shot or killed a man... but my gut says yes.

"Really wouldn't," I say, and my voice still sounds hoarse and aged. Probably makes me seem older than I am, which I'm fine with at this point.

His eyes fall down over me and I see his mouth lose the steely resolve it had a second ago. It takes me a minute to realize that he's probably just noticed that chunk missing out of my side. Never did clean or examine it, imagine it looks pretty gnarly right about now. Seems like it helps my cause though. Even though Denim's hands are still solid, his feet are shuffling ever so slightly now. That's all I need, really.

"Fuck're you?" Brutus asks. I can see the rest of him now, and the name I gave was well deserved. Motherfucker is big. Looks like a lot of it's fat but still, that much weight to throw around doesn't mean anything good. If I needed proof of that, all I had to do was check out the well-dressed gent's face. Looks like I wasn't as far off as I thought with my ground beef analogy.

"I don't want any trouble," I say, and it's true. "Just let the guy go and we can all have us a good day."

Denim's still pointing that god-damned gun at me. I bloody hate guns. More than anything else in this world, I hate guns. He glances over at Brutus and cocks his head in my direction. Brutus lets the guy fall to the ground and then starts to lumber toward me. Jay's still standing back, his feet shuffling back and forth, not really knowing what to do.

I can see they're trying to use the same plan on me. One guy points the gun while the other beats the living piss out of me, maybe even kills me. It's not a bad plan, as plan's go. Except...

Brutus puts one of those massive bear paws of his on my shoulder and is drawing back the other hand. Before he can even think about what's happening my hand is inside his arm. Brought out the claws as I moved and slid right into the guy's wrist, can feel all the blubbery fat around my fingers as I grab a big chunk of meat and bone and pull.

One thing about big guys, I don't mind taking chunks out of them as much. I didn't touch anything vital and he'll be in pain for weeks... but most importantly, he'll never think the same way about a guy my size again. I think that's important.

Brutus screams and falls back, putting me back in Denim's sights. I've gotta give the guy credit, he still wasn't shaking. But he was sweating. I would be too, if my odds just went from two-on-one for to three-on-one against in less than thirty seconds.

"Why don't you just leave me alone?" Jay yells, getting brave again now. "Why can't you just leave me the fuck alone?"

Denim turns his head just enough to see Jay for a moment, then does something I never would have expected. He holsters his gun. Now that's a bold move, especially having just seen what I did to his buddy. I don't know if it's supposed to be a bluff or a surrender, but either way he gets his point across: I'm scaring nobody.

Right then and there, I decide that's one thing that has to change.

He walks over and helps Brutus to his feet, glaring at me the whole time with these two sea-green eyes like I've never seen before. I file that away. I'm filing a lot of things away. I think of a million things to say to him as he helps his partner away, from threats to bolstering to snappy retorts. I say none of them. This isn't high-school anymore. I just watch as they pile into an old pickup and start the engine, then pull away.

They're out of the driveway before Jay dares to even move. When he does, he goes right for the vic.

"Joey!" he says, panic finally making its way back into his voice.

I stay on the steps right where I am. I don't wanna get any further into this than I have too. If Jay has it from here, he can take it. But I don't go back inside, much as I want to... just in case I'm needed.

Jay picks up one of Joey's arms and drapes it around his shoulder, hoisting him up by the waist. They both grunt, one out of exertion and the other out of pain. Joey's ribs're broken and sprained I can tell from here, the way Jay's carrying him they're all be that way by the time they reach the main office.

"Need a hand?" I say, facing away from them still.

Jay stops and looks up at me. He's strangely not as welcoming as he was before, even though you'd think he'd be more so. I'm not surprised. There's a look in his eyes that I've seen before. Mr. Miles showed us old newsreels in history class once of the American troops rescuing Jews from the concentration camps. Even though they knew they were being saved, they still looked at the soldiers with such suspicion. Mike always said his grandfather had that look until the day he died.

"Sure," Jay says finally.

I swallow back. "Lay him back. Go get your caddy. It's only a few meters, but it'll make all the difference to him. Trust me."

Jay nods, laying Joey back down and running back toward the main office.

I watch him go, then turn back toward the vic. Joey, I guess I should call him. I just stare at him for a second, all blood and mucus and puss. That uncomfortable feeling is back again, though I can't say why. It's not like I'm not used to gore. Shit, I'm pretty sure if I looked down I'd be able to see one of my ribs. After a second I force away whatever the hell my issue is and walk over to him.

He tries to lift his head when he hears me getting close. He opens his mouth to speak, and when his lips part they make a sick, sucking sound like a wound reopening. "Than- -"

"Save your strength," I say, cutting him off. I actually just don't want to hear it. I mean, vehemently do not want to hear it.

He lays his head back down and looks up at me with his one good eye, the other swollen shut. There's blood coming out of every natural hole in his face and a few extra that Brutus must have put there, including a not-too-friendly looking gash under his right eye that makes me cringe every time he takes a breath. I can see the skin flapping against it as he lets out air, like drapes caught in the wind. It's disturbing as all sweet hell.

I hear the rev of Jay's caddy and turn to watch it lumber across the parking lot, sinking down into every pothole along the way as it does. Jay's hands are shaking so bad he can barely grip the wheel. It's the adrenaline. Too much of it pumping through with nowhere to go. He'll be over it in a minute, then the bitterness'll really set in. I've been there.

He pulls up and leans over to the passenger side door, pulls the latch and then gives it a hard shove. I bend over and pick up Joey myself, one hand under the neck and the other under his legs. Jay was about to get out of the car and just stops... just stops and watches me as I load Joe into the passenger seat. Slowly he lowers himself back into the driver's seat and closes the door behind him, but continues to just stare at me.

"Com'on," I say, snapping him out of that stupid-faced trance he'd gotten himself into. "Drive."

Jay slams the car back into gear and backs up, spinning around until he's facing the main building again. I wince as I see how the speed of the turn makes Joey slump over, then start jogging toward the main room myself. I make it about twenty feet before the caddy overtakes me. By the time I step in through the door and get another whiff of all those plants, Jay's already got Joey laid out on the couch in the corner.

"Sons of bitches," Jay curses under his breath, pushing the sweaty hair out of his friend's eyes.

Joey struggles for breath as Jay tries to make him more comfortable, the sides of his torso shaking every time he inhales. My heart goes out to the guy, it really does. I've felt that way no less than a dozen times before. The first few I thought I was dying it was so hard to get my breath. If you've never experienced it, there's no way I can properly relay the terror you feel when your body stops doing what it's done naturally all its life.

I almost want to ask what this was all about, but don't. The less I know, the better. I haven't been in Indigo six hours and already it's my least favorite spot I've been to yet. I'm cursing myself for taking the ride as I say: "You should call in a police report."

Jay turns back toward me with a what-are-you-retarded? look on his face, which quickly softens into something passing for acknowledgment.

"Uno," Joey grunts, barely conscious.

Jay sighs, looking back to his friend without giving me another look. "No cops."

Fine, I think, stepping back a pace. What do I care

anyway? For all I know this is a bad coke deal. That, and I can't even begin to imagine how I'd explain my presence to the police. Already told Jay my name, not like I could make up a fake one on the fly and not have him notice. "You got a first-aid kit? Or a bathroom? Can make most of what we need if you got a bathroom."

He doesn't even hear me. He's too transfixed by his friend's pain to take in anything else. He doesn't cry, he doesn't sob and he doesn't yell. He simply can't process anything outside of Joey's blood-soaked face. As far as he's concerned they're the only two people in the world, let alone the room.

I been there too, so I find the bathroom myself.

Towels are necessary, lots and lots of towels. Guy's leaking blood like nobody's business, and not everyone's as gifted as I am in that regard. Hydrogen Peroxide's a good find, too, but iodine isn't something Jay keeps on hand, and it's what I prefer. I take what I can find and head out to the main lobby again.

Jay's clutching Joey's hand now, and it doesn't look good. They're staring at each other without so much as saying one word, and I see that ferocity in Jay's eyes as he wills his friend to stay with him. His free hand is in his friend's hair, stroking it gently though his fingers and not caring at all about the blood.

That uncomfortable feeling comes racing back. I'd almost forgot about it in the commotion, but now it's all I can think of.

It's right in the center of my chest now, like a bundle of electricity that just wants to get out, making me fidgety all over.

Jay takes a large towel from me and starts to dab off Joey's face. My head yells at me to let him know how bad an idea that is... all that loose skin could stick to the towel and come right off. But I'm still in a weird state of shock and I don't say a word. Just as well, the towel works fine, wipes the blood off and shows the bruised tissue underneath.

"Jesus Christ," Jay curses as he dabbs most of the blood away. Some of it stays though, the vessels having ruptured under the skin without actually breaking the surface. He might actually need me to slice him if the pressure builds too much, but that's nothing he needs to know now. Jay holds his hand so tight that I'm worried he might break it. It's sad to watch, even worse given the memories it dredges up. He stops with the towel again for a moment, running his fingers over Joey's hair and down his face. "God, I'm so sorry I wasn't there."

I raise an eyebrow as I watch the scene playing out before me and wonder something for the first time. Something that should have probably occurred to me quite some time ago.

All at once the Womb drives all its energy toward my sense of smell as if of its own will, confirming what I just asked myself. I can smell them all over each other. It's like they bathed in one another's pheromones, in a way not even the amount of Joey's blood on Jay's hands would account for. Nothing could account for that amount of sweat and bile and several other things I'd prefer not to mention.

Joey coughs a sickly sound and leans in close to Jay. Jay leans in a little too, then turns back to me.

"We can't thank you enough," he says under his breath, and it's almost backhanded but not quite.

His voice drives it over the edge. I'm officially more uncomfortable than I've ever been in my entire life, and it's not going away. Not going to go away. "No problem. Really, it's no problem... you really should get him to a hospital."

"I'm fine," Joey says, at least that's what he meant to say. What he actually said were sounds I didn't think the human tongue was capable of.

"Really, yes, thank you," Jay says again as he picks up the towel. "We've bothered you enough..."

"I'll just go to my room then," I say, only because I can't think of anything else. I realize not long after that the drama of that afternoon was more than reason enough for me to get the Holy Hannah out of there, but it was too late. I was already out the door and walking through the dirt toward my room.

I feel like I should clarify.

I mean, I don't want to, but I feel like I should. I'd love nothing more than to never talk about any of this again and pretend I didn't just figure out what I figured out, but here we go.

It's not that I have a problem with gays in general, it's just that I don't quite know what to make of them. Makes me damn uncomfortable. In fact, right about now I think I'm more uncomfortable than I've ever been in my life. Just about everything makes me uncomfortable in one way or another, until I find a place for it. Those guys attacking Joe made me damn uncomfortable, until I realized what was going on. As soon as they were in their box, I was fine. I packed them away in the storage closet of my head and wrote 'bad guys' on it with a big fat sharpie.

This, though. Ugh. Even when I realize what it is, even when I see the situation for what it truly is, I still don't know where to put it. There's no box for this, no spot in my subconscious for this to go in a carefully labeled container.

I'm laying on the bed in my room again now. Even though it's just as comfortable as it was a few hours before, I'm not. Nowhere near. My senses are playing tricks on me in ways they haven't since I was ten and still afraid of the dark, creating things that aren't really there. Hearing things that aren't really there, or even if they are, don't mean what I think they mean.

I hear the soft drone of conversation when heard through several layers of drywall, unable to pick out what was really said, sounding like the adults on Charlie Brown. That soft, slow mumble; just loud enough that you can't ignore it but not loud enough that you can pick out a single word.

I picture things to go along with the sounds, the same way I used to picture flying saucers to accompany the whirr of the air conditioner in my parents' home; or that the creek of the floorboards was something coming up the stairs for me. I picture Jay and Joey laying next to each other in bed, bare chested with a sheet draped over them as they both talk the night away, unable to sleep. There's a low tone to one of the voices, that's Jay. He's trying to sooth his partner, I imagine. Trying to provide some comfort or feeling of hope. That's a hard thing to do when you don't feel it yourself, and it's never quite convincing.

I hear the creek of pressure on old wood, followed by a long squeak. I try not to let my mind think of what that could be, but that's the thing about an overactive imagination: it does things whether you want it to or not. Actually, in my experience it does things especially when you don't want it to.

When daylight breaks they're still talking. A few times voices got louder; a few times voices got softer... a few times the voices stopped altogether for several minutes, but those times were few and far between. My head is splitting and I'd kill to sleep. Not that I would've been able to anyway, but I'm really noticing it now.

My eyes shoot open and I sit up in bed as fast as I can. For the second time, I realize something that should have been right in front of my face from minute one.

I have to get the fuck out of here.

Beyond my misgivings about the situation, I need out of Indigo. I'm exhausted beyond the comprehension of it, but the second I go to sleep, I'll become the Womb. The beast inside me will wake up and act on my feelings, my emotions... my prejudices. Its killed before based on my own feelings, positive and negative. Anything intense. Schneider, the Tees... too many to count. If anything happens here... if it gets out here... I'll have saved Jay and Joey only to pit them against something much, much worse.

I'm up before my train of thought even really finishes. My shirt still smells like I pulled it out of the stomach of a dead whale, but I couldn't care less. Just want the fuck out of here, for a variety of very good reasons. I grab my stuff, double check that I've got it all, then open the door and head back out on the road toward Salt Lake City.

I'm half way through town when I meet my first human soul. The sun's still only poking its head over the horizon so that's not entirely unusual, especially for a small town. Nothing's twenty-four hours here, and anyone that's up are probably just getting ready for a commute.

Or police.

And of course, it's the latter. It's a beaten up police truck with the lights inside the grill that looks to have been commissioned because most of the drivers they pull over here are ATVs. It's parked just off the side of the road on the business end of a blind hill right after the speed limit drops dramatically, probably waiting to catch people in a speed trap.

There are two officers inside that are both a little chubby around the jaws. The first isn't particularly out of shape, just round in the face. The other is a mammoth of a man. They think I can't see them from behind that tinted glass, but I can. I watch as their eyes follow me as I walk in the dirt along the side of the road, cross it, then slowly round the turn on the inside track and disappear from sight. I swear, even after I'm away I can still feel their eyes on me.

I'm almost back on the highway when I see a diner a realize that at some point during the night, my side healed itself. Not really sure when, but there was actual skin protecting my rib cage now. It brings my appetite back and suddenly I want two things: something sweet and something smoking.

A take out magically appears there in front of me. I'm not kidding, it was not there until I discovered I was hungry. You can say I didn't notice it all you want, I stand by my analysis of the situation. I go in and sit down at the booth and a spring sticks in me but it's still heavenly, all the smells of baking and frying coming at me all at once. I'm waiting less than a minute when a waiter comes up to me and asks me what I'll have.

"How much is coffee?" I ask, remembering how empty my wallet has gotten these past few weeks.

He grins. "It's free on Sundays."

I stare at him for a long time. To my knowledge my face was expressionless, so I don't think he understood how happy he made me. Still, my mind wouldn't allow that to click in. "What day is today?" I ask, perhaps a little too eagerly.

"Sunday," he drawled, smiling wide.

I smile. "Coffee," I say. "You may wanna put on another pot."

I'm on my third cup when the police truck pulls up to the diner, and immediately curse myself for not getting the fuck out of dodge when I had the chance.

The two cops open their doors almost simultaneously, then slam them shut. The big one comes around the side of the vehicle and claps the other on the back, and immediately I relax. They're smiling, big and broad. And laughing, they're laughing too. No matter how much they like their job, I have serious doubts that they'd be that happy coming into pick up little old me. Especially not knowing what they were getting into.

Regardless, there's something about the happiness that I don't like.

I can't be coming off very well at this point. You must think I'm some homophobic narcissist with a hate on for authority figures. I don't think that's true. It might be true, but I've never once gone looking for trouble. I'm actually trying to get out of town to avoid trouble.

Still, I'm relieved for the moment that they seem to just be getting breakfast rather than playing cowboy with the new kid in town. They come in through the front door and give the waiter a little salute before sitting down at the counter on adjacent stools, the bigger one looking like he would break his.

The small one starts chatting up the cook in the back and I relax. I take a sip of my coffee.

Jinxed it.

The big one's bored and turns over his shoulder to look around and almost immediately locks eyes with me. I stop slurping my coffee and just sit there for what feels like forever, the cup up to my face and our eyes locked. I curse about eight thousand times in my head in those few seconds.

He turns away first, tapping his partner on the arm lightly. His partner turns, they have a brief exchange I don't need to hear to understand, and then they both turn toward me.

Nothing like discretion.

They stare at me again for what feels like forever and

I'm torn as to what to do. I haven't ordered anything I'd have to pay for yet, so I could just get up and leave. I could just turn away, but would that look more I was trying to avoid them or that I hadn't noticed them? Something catches my eye and makes the decision for me.

There's a person in the back seat of the police truck.

The tinted windows in the back seat work wonders better than the ones up front. I can't see the person in the back, but I know who it is all the same. The sun's coming up behind him and casting his shadow on the glass as though it were burned there, with the short hair and the small ears that stuck off from his head regardless. It was Jay.

Fuck fuck fuckity fuck fuck.

Why oh why oh what the fuck? Doesn't make any sense. Did Denim and Brutus call the police after I handed their ass to me? That was possible. Given the amount of times I use my fists instead of my mouth to solve problems, I'm actually surprised it doesn't happen more often. Was I wrong about the situation from the get go? Was there something more to Jay besides just being the "special friend" of some random victim of violence? Of course it wasn't a random act of violence. It was a hate crime, I've seen them before. Really, I should have recognized it from the second I saw Joey's face.

They're still staring at me. I look back toward them and my eyes meet the big guy's; and I know I'm screwed. Can't explain it; it's just another one of those feelings. That uncomfortable anxious electricity in the center of my chest that makes it hard to breathe. I turn my gaze from the big cop to the smaller one (who's still a fair size bigger than me), and the feeling goes away. Something clicks into place, like the insane filing system that's in my head starts spinning its rolodex to find something for me.

He has green eyes.

Deep, intoxicating sea green eyes. The type of eyes that if they were on a woman would throw me for a loop. The same type of eyes that Jay had.

"Denim," I say finally, looking the man over. I try to picture him with a ski mask and jeans on, and it fits. More than that, I now have no idea now I didn't recognize the big guy next to him as Brutus almost immediately. They watched me walk out the road and realized that Jay and Joey's guardian angel was gone, went right back to finish what they started. There is no doubt in my mind right now that while I was sitting here, slurping coffee like an idiot, Joey was dying. Poor guy wasn't terribly far from death's door when I left him last night. At least now I know why they didn't want any police.

There's also very little doubt in my mind that Officer Denim is also Jay's father.

I lay down the cup and wipe my face with my hand, trying to look as casual as possible. I get up and turn around in one smooth motion, walking between the booths and tables toward the bathroom. I don't need to ask where it is, I've been trying to ignore its stench since I came in. Their eyes burrow a hole in the back of my head the whole walk down and even after I disappear into the stall.

There's a window. It's small, just small enough for me to fit through. I rip up my side again doing it, but that's fine. I'm willing to bet real money that what Officer Brutus had in mind for me was much, much worse.

The foundation of the takeout was on a slant, so even though I'm on the first floor I fall a good twenty feet into the vacant lot below. My back is killing me as I scramble to my feet and hurry around the edge of the diner, hopping a fence and sneaking around the side of the police truck.

Jay's crying.

Any lingering doubt as to Joey's fate is gone when I see his face. I've seen that look before, way too many times. It's not grief... they actually haven't come up with the right word for it. It's as different from grief as anger is from fury. It's on such an extreme level that the word doesn't do it justice. For an instant I almost want to leave him, the danger of the situation almost outweighed by his simple human need to be left in peace to grieve. I shake it off and rap on the window.

He jumps out of his skin, then turns toward me. There's hate in his eyes that fades a little when he recognizes me, and I feel like the world's biggest dick. And no, that wasn't meant to be any sort of pun.

"What're you doing here?" he yells, and I barely hear him through the glass.

"Shut up," I respond, unsheathing a single talon and bringing it down to the lock.

"They're going to kill you!"

"Yeah, probably," I sigh, opening up the door.

He steps out and immediately turns toward the takeout, his eyes scanning and then finding his father and Brutus. Self preservation takes over and for the briefest of moments he doesn't remember Joey; he's filled with fear and stuck in fight or flight mode.

Flight, man. Flight.

"We gotta get out of here," I remind him, tugging on his arm.

"No, no. You don't understand."

"He's your Dad. He's a bigot. He's a cop. Three things that aren't working out too well for you right now. Either way, we gotta get out of here."

He shoots me a how-the-hell-do-you-know-all-this? look, then starts jogging over the road with me toward the highway. I have no plan. I mean, I never have any real plan; but this time I've got nothing. I've got: run. Get the gay guy out of the backward town and get the fuck out of dodge and try not to let anything freak out the Womb into doing the bigots' job for them.

Actually, it wasn't a bad plan.

You know what they say about the best laid plans of mice and men.

I feel the bullet in my back a half second before I hear the unmistakable crack of gunpowder. Can almost hear my left lung deflate as the bullet comes out my front and digs itself into a tree.

I don't fall, the ground comes up and smacks me in the face. My head hits off the gravel and grinds in, and for a very brief moment that's my top concern. Then the shock wears off, happens faster and faster it seems, and I feel what's going on in my torso. There's a pressure in my chest that builds that has nothing to do with being uncomfortable and everything to do with the air forcing its way from my lungs into my chest.

I don't really realize I'm rolling until I stop, my back slamming against a guardrail on the side of the road. It makes a horrible sound like a gong, but I barely notice it. My ears are already half filled with blood.

For all the talk about my vaunted healing ability, I think I bleed easier than most. Sometimes I think it's a coincidence; that maybe Engen scientists didn't realize their precious baby boy was anemic or something... other times, I think it's something the Womb did since this whole mess started. Like on some purely genetic level it knows that the sooner I bleed out, the sooner it gets to play.

The blood that's coming out of my chest looks like some rich prospector just struck oil. Its shooting up like its propelled by a hose screwed into my back, bubbling over and splashing back down on me.

No matter how many times this happens, it's always terrifying.

The blackness wraps itself around me and squeezes. It's like being squeezed by a boa constrictor. Every breath becomes agonizing, every heartbeat becomes harder and harder, faster and faster. Everything hurts, like my body is at war with itself. Systems shut down as the Womb's take over, flushing throughout me inch by inch until I'm gone. Until there's so little of me left that I don't even recognize me.

There's a feeling like going to sleep that I can't fight no matter how hard I try. Like being put under the needle or drowning, your brain just starts ignoring your orders to stay the fuck awake. Vision starts to go black around the edges and I see Jay rush over to me, grabbing me by both shoulders. He's yelling in my face, but I can't hear him. I'm almost completely gone now, can't even move my hands. Feels like I'm tied down, and I might as well be for all the good I'm capable of right now.

As all my normal functions slow down, everything gets tingly and painful, like pins and needles when your foot falls asleep. Then the Womb kicks in and it burns. Doesn't really burn I know, but that's the best I can describe it. It feels like its burning. Every time it occurs to my sleep and oxygen deprived brain that maybe, just maybe, this time I'm not transforming. Maybe someone finally taxed the Womb too much and the burning isn't the transformation.

Maybe this time I'm really dead, and that fire means something very different. The road I've been on, wouldn't surprise me.

I finally pass out. Last thing I see is Jay leaning over me, looks like he's grabbing my face and trying to get me to wake up. I'm almost glad I won't get to see what happens next.

ʌ〈ʌ

I wake up standing, my claws still out. My clothes are soaked but mercifully still on as the tar floods off of me into a puddle on the ground. I'm breathing so hard I think my lungs are going to pop, but it's better than the way they were feeling a minute ago.

It's an odd thing to be aware you lost time. It's like falling asleep, but not really. There are no dreams, and it's like someone stops the clock in my head. In my mind I instantly go from watching Jay lean over me to here, and the effect is unimaginably jarring. Like having frames of a movie cut out, or whole scenes. What's worse is the knowledge that you've missed time. Your brain tries on its own to find what its lost and can't, and no matter how many times you tell it not too, it keeps trying. Like it laid something down and then forgot where it was, it'll just keep searching for those memories. I'm nowhere near pretensions enough to say that this is what it feels like to have Alzheimer's or the like... but it's scary enough that I'll always respect the people actually battling the disease.

I reach up and peel that thin, slimy layer of coagulated; goopy blood from may face and open my eyes.

There's blood... oh lord, there's so much blood. I'm not terribly far from the guardrail where I passed out, just a few meters into the trees beyond it. I can still see it out of the corner of my eye. I'm kind of standing in the middle of a bush, twigs and thorns sticking me from all sides as I'm surrounded by evergreens and bare trees. There's very little green and brown, despite that. It's red. The trees, the ground, everything's red. You wouldn't think the human body could hold that much blood, but it sure can. You ever spill a quart of milk? Watch how it gets everywhere? There's four quarts of blood in an adult human.

Yeah.

What nobody expects is the color. The red's dominant, everyone expects that... but when the Womb gets into a full, all out fury; it's never just blood. They're never just dead. There's yellow hanging from a nearby branch from an intestine. There's all sorts of brown from feces that hadn't been excreted yet. There's green undigested food and there's purple from god knows what. Lung I think.

There's pieces everywhere, it takes me a moment to find something recognizable.

Brutus is leaned against a tree about five meters to my

right. His arms are wrapped around it, hugging on for dear life, his mouth turned downward and frozen there. The way he spent his last moments are painfully clear. If his position and expression weren't enough, he's been hollowed out pretty good. There's a rudimentary circle from the bottom of his chest right down to his naval where I ripped out his stomach. Should be able to see lots of fun stuff with a hole that big... but all I see is spine. Lungs, liver, kidneys, intestines, stomach... all gone. It's probably what's decorating the trees.

Denim's not far away. Neither of them made it very far once I turned. His face got most of the work... eyes specifically. I think that's some kind of suggestion I put in there when I noticed how green they were, but there's no way of knowing. In any event, there's at least thirty gashes across his eyes that go right down to the retinas. Eyelids are long gone. Happened before any killing blows, too. You can tell from the blood. Looks like the final cut was one right down the center of the neck, probably with the talons on my feet. Again, I'm speculating.

Then I see Jay. He's covered in blood and bile, lodged against a large rock about three feet to my left.

He's also alive.

Shivering with fear and covered in his own vomit, unable to take his eyes off me... but very much alive. In fact there's not a scratch on him, or at least, no more than there were when I took him out of the police cruiser. He's much paler now... but then, that's to be expected.

I get out of there about at fast as I can.

I'm back on that same stretch of highway later that same day.

Sometimes I get uncomfortable. Sometimes for no reason at all other than I am. This isn't one of those times. This time, I know exactly what's wrong with me. I'm full of thoughts I don't have the answers to, none of which I like very much.

I hate that I was uncomfortable around Jay. Hate that I was paranoid and backward and afraid when I realized the truth of the situation. Hate that on some level I had more in common with Brutus and Denim than I did with Jay and Joey... but as much as I hate myself for it, it doesn't change that it's true. At least I'm aware of it now, can do my best to make sure it doesn't color my judgment... even though on some level I guess it always will.

What's really terrifying is that for once, the Womb had it right where I failed. It was Jekyll and I was Hyde, somehow.

I was so convinced that the Womb would act on my own feelings toward Jay... but it didn't. You could make the argument that it went after the sons of bitches shooting at it... but there's no reason it wouldn't have done Jay as well.

I could just be attaching meaning to nothing. Could be making mountains out of mole hills. But the thing is... I'm just not sure anymore.

Got a lot to think about.

Glad this road is a long one.

REPRISE

I guess I'm not really sure where to begin.

Hmm? Yeah no, it's really good. Blue Mountain? Ethiopian, wow. Do you have any cream? No, no sugar thanks... no.

So like I said, I don't really know where to start. At the beginning seems like a safe bet, but there are two beginnings to this story. I mean it really began years and years ago, before I was born, but that's getting a little out there I can tell. Yeah no, sorry about that. The more epic the story gets made, the more blame there is to spread around, the less there is for me. I think that's become my way of dealing with it. No, let's start this story off right.

It started when Jamie Dawkins was killed.

I'd been living in this weird world up until then. Things just happened and they didn't really matter. Everything seemed so important -- what Mike and Cathy were doing at lunch, if I was walking Sara home, who she was dating -- and yet none of it had any lasting impact. Life was like one of those sitcoms where at the end of every episode things have to be reset to status quo so they'll make sense in syndication.

That's when they repeat the episodes, but not always in the right order. TBS Superstation style.

Everything seemed so big, and yet nothing really mattered. Not only that, but we didn't notice things. Like the Tees and the Omegas. These are two major, major gangs. This is a small town, you'd think a bunch of idiots walking around like this would attract some attention, but nobody really talked about it before Jamie Dawkins died. But that's the way of the world I guess. The second the good looking football player gets killed, everyone stands up and takes a look around. I sound bitter. I shouldn't. I'm sorry.

That whole time was confusing. There was so much death, Jamie was just the start of it. A lot of people died and a lot of things happened that really shouldn't have, and in the end it all got pinned on one guy: Adam Genblade. There's a lot messed up around all of this and it only gets more messed up the more layers you peel off, like an onion wrapped around a pile of shit, pardon my language. They arrested him up at this crazy building in the woods, and there was so little done about that building. It's still up there, half blown to hell and its walls opened up like a wound, but nothings done about it. Anyway, the story after he was arrested was that Genblade killed all those kids and kidnapped me, because I was there when they caught him, up in that building. Shaking like a leaf and crying and just plain looking the fool. People gloss over that, part of me thinks they're being kind. Another part thinks this town gets amnesia when it wants to.

So that was that, Genblade killed all those kids and he was going to be set to death for it. Everything was wrapped up in this nice little bow, until the murders started again, with Genblade behind bars. So you've got Genblade in jail claiming he killed all those people, all the while the real killer is apparently still out there killing kids, and you've got me: just me, sitting at home with a gun to my head.

Don't look at me like that.

Yeah, I'll have another cup.

The whole thing had me ready to just end it. I just didn't know what to do anymore. I didn't of course... what with me being here and all, I assume you guessed that. Most of the props for that go to Cathy. Every time I'm at my weakest, she's the one who's there to pick me up and dust me off and get me trying again.

It comes out that Genblade was just covering for the real killer, something I had no small part in figuring out, although Cathy gets most of the credit there. I'm fine with that though, really. The real killer was just some kid our own age, someone I thought of as a friend even, guy named Derek Smith. So now both he and Genblade are behind bars and you'd think -- think -- that that would be the end of that, but it's not. Because it's like we were sitting on this giant powder-keg and those two just lit the match.

Violence breeds more violence. The Tees, already violent enough as it is, went militia after the Genblade Derek thing. People were scared. They were scared of this powerhouse serial killer from the weird building nobody went near, and they were also scared of their own kids sitting alone in their rooms and listening to Alt Nation on XM Radio. People were scared of the big unknown outside and the things right there in their own home and that was just bad news, scared all the time. Combine that with the violence of the Tees and you had the recipe for real trouble. But they didn't go after Genblade or their own kids or anything like that. Like most people they took that fear and went after things they didn't really know, but they didn't know anything, so they just lashed out. First targets were old rivals from across the highway, and they killed friends of mine doing it: Sud Windsor and, eventually, Mandy Peterson.

I'm sorry, I know that wasn't easy for you either.

And then even after all the Tees had run off or were arrested or just plain disappeared,   things still didn't calm down. Derek Smith escaped, and he's still out there somewhere. And the Tees started to get killed off, and the graveyard got broken into... and all of that's linked.

No, I don't mean that the way you would. I don't mean in some great plan it's all linked. I mean that in a much more concrete, tangible way.

It's all linked through me.

I said all this started years ago. From what I know, it started in that building with the hole blown in it out in the woods, and it wasn't with Genblade... it was with me. I'm not going to pretend to know what they thought they were doing. They were just the sort of nuts that thought religion was science and science was religion and used either to justify everything, but what came out of it, was me. I've got something inside me because of them, they called it the Black Womb. It makes me stronger and faster and better but it also takes away... everything that makes me, me. Although that's not quite right either. Sometimes it's like an animal, but then sometimes it can show real thought. It's never the same thing twice, always changing and adapting.

It's been there from the start:

Black Womb touched down against the rooftop of the Factory, a long growl humming out of its throat. Its entire body was made up of oily black scales that clacked this way and that as though they were alive, except for its eyes and mouth. And its claws, too. Four of them on each hand, the color of bone and transparent. Its eyes were an aquatic green-blue, and though they were devoid of pupils, they scanned the night air just the same, as if fascinated with everything it saw with a child's curiosity. It had not been alive long, it knew that. Or at least, it had not been conscious long. Even though many of the things it saw and smelled and touched were new to it, they still twanged in its memory, just out of its reach. It was like the memory was there, but when the creature went to reach for it, something stopped it. Like a song one remembers the tune of but none of the lyrics. It was incredibly frustrating.

Even this place, it knew somehow. This large dwelling with brightly colored lights and the dim thump of bass music, which it now felt against the soles of its feet and their reverberations up through its body. The ceiling was wet and warm, its tar sticking to the Womb no matter what it touched. Its enhanced hearing picked up the sound of squeaking hinges, although it had no idea what that sound was yet, and the rhythm seemed to get louder, and there were words now that it did not understand.

Cautiously, it lay its hands down on the edge of the roof and peered over, digging its claws in for support just in case. He watched a tall boy with dark hair and large muscles covered with a sports jacket close the door to The Factory, and the music went back to the dull thud it had started out as.

As the Womb watched, Jamie Dawkins started to walk down the street. It was getting dark, the sun having finally disappeared behind the horizon about twenty minutes ago, the sky still holding onto its glow with pale pinks and oranges. He lit a cigarette and took a long draw. He stopped and finished the smoke on the corner under a street lamp and threw the smoldering butt down onto the sidewalk.

Across the street, Derek Smith noticed him as he was walking toward home. Jamie was hard to miss, the street lamp acting as a giant spotlight for him. Derek's eyes narrowed as his face became livid and hot, thinking back to his argument earlier that day with Theresa over their affair and the pregnancy test she had told Jamie about. He clenched his fists and took a step toward Jamie, still concealed in shadows, then stopped. There was someone else behind Jamie. Fearing the odds of two against one, he waited to see what the second person would do.

Jamie heard something behind him, like a sound of something metal hitting the pavement, then started walking again. He zipped his jacket to protect against the harsh cold of night. He could see his own breath as it swirled up around his head like a wreath.

Eve Spider stepped out of the shadows behind him and stepped in time with Jamie, squishing the cigarette beneath her heavy feet. As she walked, her red robes and long black hair twirled in the wind and made it impossible to get a clear view of her features, but from the other side of the street Derek thought he could clearly see that she was Asian, and remarkably beautiful. What he really saw though was the long blade that draped down by her side, with a spider emblem etched in jewels along its handle. She was making no effort to hide her presence, in fact it seemed as though she were deliberately clacking her heels against the sidewalk in time with Jamie's loud enough so that he could hear.

Jamie heard it now, he was sure of it. The footsteps getting closer and closer to him. He started to pick up his pace, and so did she. He broke into an all out run and heard the second set of footfalls do the same. He got to the end of the block and made a sharp turn, beads of sweat already forming on his forehead. He got to the end of the next block and bent over in pain from a stitch in his side. His lungs heaved, each breath bringing agony, and he grunted from the pain.

On the rooftops above, the Womb had been following the encounter as much as it could, its attention rapt with the thrill of the chase, its heart beating in a way it never had before deep within its gut. It was excited, and it wanted to see what happened next, a want that bordered on all-out need. When Jamie had fallen over in pain, it too had felt it in its side -- in its heart. It was the first real pain it had experienced since its birth, and the creature wanted to howl in defilement, but held its tongue for fear of giving itself away as it continued to watch.

Jamie turned around to face his attacker for the first time.

There was nobody there. He searched the streets and

doorways around him, seeing nothing. Suddenly, he started to laugh. He stomped his foot down onto the black pavement and listened to the echo of the sound returning to him. "You're losing it," he whispered softly to himself.

He turned the corner and immediately bumped into a Adam Genblade. He was covered in a trench coat and seemed to be made out of shadows rather than any tangible material. His eyes burned bright with hatred as he made a menacing move toward Jamie, who screamed loudly and took off in the other direction.

His stitch got the better of him again, this time right away. Genblade grabbed him and pulled him into the darkness. He took a dagger from his coat and jabbed it into Jamie's right side. Blood gushed immediately from the treads etched into the sides of the blade, spattering onto the street with a sickening sloshing sound.

As Jamie's vision because hazy and he realized it was over, he stopped struggling against the man's iron grip. He fell to the ground and struggled for breath as the life ebbed out of his, faster than he would have ever expected. Faster than it ever did in the movies, at any rate. He got out three struggled breaths, and then stopped.

Spider came around the corner, walking into Genblade's arms and giving him a lover's squeeze. "That was almost too easy," she said, and her voice whined a little, as if disappointed.

Genblade smiled at her as he put away his blade, showing off row upon row of jagged teeth. He brought her in tight to him, her thin body warm against his own, and kissed her passionately, stroking his thumb along her cheek as he did and leaving a dark red smear behind. "It served its purpose," he said softly, then turned toward the darkness at the end of the alley. "You can come out now, you know."

At first, there was nothing. Then, all at once, two aquatic green eyes opened in the darkness. The rest of it became visible quickly, its outline painted by the twilight and its body just as black as the shadows that surrounded it.

"It's okay," Genblade said, motioning toward the body of Jamie Dawkins. "Go ahead, take a look."

The creature tilted its head quizzically, not quite understanding the words but at least comprehending their meaning. It walked suspiciously toward the corpse, which had already begun to stink as it lost control of its more basic bodily functions. It looked into Jamie's eyes, which were still for the most part the same, but a little bit dimmer, and that same sense of recollection came upon it, but it was clearer now. It still had no idea how it had known this boy, but there were feelings and emotions... sensations, really... attached to the sight of him within its own head. Anger, betrayal, and... pain. This person had hurt him somehow, the creature was sure of it. It felt it as clearly as it had ever felt anything.

All at once, the monster let out a thunderous roar, bringing back its right hand and quickly slashing the boy across the face. One of its talons punctured the Jamie's left eye, sending gelatinous fluid streaming down his cheek and mixing with the blood that slowly dribbled out of the fresh cuts.

The creature looked down at the jacket, and more sensations filled it. More pain, lots of times now. Physical pain, as well as many others. All others. For the briefest of moments, the creature gained access to its memory and found that there was nothing there... except pain. Then the door shut closed again, and before it knew what it was doing, it was ripping at the jacket with its claws... and the tender flesh underneath, until it was not even possible to tell where Genblade had made his incision. There was some manner of symbol on the jacket that the creature was unfamiliar with. It looked like the left half of a circle, and it ripped into that as well, sending blood smearing across the alley walls.

Behind them, Adam and Eve watched, smiling as proud parents would smile when watching their child walk for the first time. "That's a good little Black Womb," Genblade sneered, chuckling to himself.

The creature turned, blood dripping from its mouth and hands. It had never heard those words before; if fact had heard very few words in its short life, but it recognized them somehow as being in reference to itself. "Black Womb lives!" it bellowed, rocking its head skyward like a wolf baying at the moon. It coiled its lean, muscular legs and leapt skyward, ricocheting from one brick wall of the alley to the other until it was again atop the buildings and out of sight.

Genblade and Spider watched it as it went. "Black Womb lives," Spider smiled, almost warmly, in a voice that sounded warm and cool at once -- like a spring breeze.

Genblade took out his knife again and stepped toward Jamie, cutting away a rib that the newly-named Black Womb had left untouched and discarding it against the alley floor with a wet click. For the next ten minutes, he and Spider rummaged through Jamie's organs, taking what was useful and healthy. One small slice into the right lung revealed that its innards were black and tarry and best left alone. When they were done, they took their prizes in a container that their master had left for them and turned to leave... when Spider stopped, grinning mischievously to herself. She reached into Dawkins for a moment, and when her hand retracted it was covered in blood. Grinning like a child with a set of finger-paints, she scrawled the words Black Womb Lives! in red on the wall behind Jamie, the turned and left with Adam.

Aside from Jamie Dawkins, their presence was marked by almost no one.

Almost.

Derek Smith stepped into the mouth of the alley after a moment, looking at the mutilated body. He thought he should be filled with horror... but wasn't. He was aware that he sound have been, but his nerves were calm and there was no urge to scream or vomit or run. Taking one cautious step at a time, he walked toward to body, slowly stretching out his hand until it touched the boy's insides, which were now on the outside. They already seemed cold. When he took back his hand and saw that it was covered in the red liquid, he finally identified the feeling that had been growing inside him... it was relief. And excitement. And... pleasure. It was a warm, tingly feeling, the likes of which Theresa had never given him, despite her best efforts. Smiling, he picked up the chunk of rib that Genblade had discarded and placed it in the pocket of his jacket, and walked out of the ally, thinking of what this might do for his father's career.

Right from the start. I'm sorry.

And the Womb was the real thing the Tee's were afraid of, why they were so up in arms. But worse than that, remember that building in the woods? Well there were more guys from a different building who decided they wanted in on all this too, and one of them was Warren O'Toole. You remember him. He pretended to be the councillor at our school for some time, trying to figure out what was going on and report back. When he started to have trouble, he started poking the bear... he's the one who unleashed the Tees on the school and caused all that trouble, and in the meantime he'd been drugging me, making me think I was in control when I really wasn't.

When he died, without that drug I started to go off the deep end again, go feral. It was me that killed the Tees in one of those states, and me that ripped up the graveyard, that desecrated Sara's grave. Not that I was aware it was me at the time, or that I even really remember it... but there it is.

So Mike and Cathy started chaining me up in the old church, the one that this one replaced. Right up at the altar they'd chain me up every night, and in the day I tried so hard to do some good. Tried to be proactive about the things I was doing and how I was doing them. I helped you out, even, with that business with the boy-who-cried-wolf.

Anyway, I'm not looking for points. Just saying.

So this whole time I'm trying to get a handle on the Womb, trying to stop it from coming out every night. I figure that if it can be halted by drugs it can be halted in general. Just because I don't have access to the drug doesn't mean I can't stop it on my own.

Then what happened today happened.

"All for you, babe," I said as I leaned back against my locker and had the first natural smile I'd had in weeks, holding a photograph of a girl wearing a blue prom dress. It had ridiculously large, puffy arms. She had blonde hair up in a beehive that had been preened to perfection for hours in front of the mirror. She was blowing the camera a kiss. Objectively I knew it was the camera, but every time I looked at the picture she was blowing it to me.

I placed the picture carefully back inside the inside breast pocket of my leather jacket.

I could hear Cathy coming before she spoke, clacking toward me at a steady brisk pace as though she wanted to run faster but couldn't. "Hey," she said when she thought I hadn't heard her. When I turned she embraced me. Her long black hair danced around her. She was wearing heels and was a little taller than me because of them. I hated that. Her eyes were big and brown. She thrust her arms around me and planted a big kiss on my cheek, producing a loud smacking sound. She asked me if I'd done it, twice in a row, like some excited rabbit in a cartoon.

Mike told her to calm down as he walked up to join the us. Cathy released her hold on me. He stared at me for a solid ten seconds, then asked me if I'd done it too.

What they're excited about is that I've gone three days without turning into the Womb at all, even at night. They still chained me up in case, but I'd managed to force it off for a full seventy-two hours. I know that doesn't sound like a lot, but I figured it was like smoking -- getting over that three-day hump was the hardest. Either way I didn't figure I was done, I was still taking it a day at a time, but it felt like a big milestone all the same.

There was a moment when I tried to hide it from them, but my smile crept up like a stalker in the night and before I knew it I was grinning. I reached out and pulled Cathy into another hug. "Yeah, yeah I did it."

"All right," Mike grinned. He held up his hand and I slapped it. It seemed like an empty gesture, but somehow it felt good all the same.

"That's the longest, right?" Cathy asked, excited into talking fast and in a much higher tone than usual again. She brushed her hair back behind her ear and stood. "I mean, since the O'Toole thing... that's been the longest yet, right?"

My face was hot. It had been a long time since I'd gotten this much positive attention. It made me uncomfortable.

"So not since Gallagher," Mike said.

I nodded.

Cathy put a hand on my shoulder and told me she was proud of me. Actually I think she said they were proud of me, speaking with that kind of royal we that people did when they'd been together a long time. I told her I still had a long way to go as we watched Mike sort through the trash in his locker for his geometry textbook. After a moment with her hand on my shoulder I added: "But every day's a new record now, and that's something. Maybe I really can force it back. No hypnosis, no drugs... just me."

"We should celebrate," Cathy grinned as she squeezed my arm. She suggested my coming with her and Mike to The Factory tonight, it was finally closing its doors for good. "Mike and I are going to the Factory tonight for the closing.

I said I would, that it would be like old times.

"Mmm," Mike said, a wry grin spreading over his lips. "I heard they were going to raffle off the X-Men / Street Fighter game."

My eyes may have bulged out of my head. "Dude... you can't be serious?"

"Swear to God. Pulling names out of a hat or something."

"Okay, I have to go now."

"No drinking," Cathy reminded me, pointing an accusing finger in my direction.

"I don't drink," I corrected, shooting her a sly smile.

"What about in that bar across town?"

I lowered his head and scuffled my feet. "That's different."

"Why?"

"Because I didn't know you knew about it."

She snickered and ruffled my bangs with her fingers. "You can't keep anything from me."

We started to walk to class, when that thing deep down in my gut shivered and twitched and my nostrils flared from some unknown signal from it. I stopped mid-stride.

"What was that about?" Mike asked, his face growing grim. "Your little buddy acting up?"

"You're one to talk."

"Huh?"

"The scents all over. When were you guys planning on telling me you were being physical again?"

They both stopped dead in their tracks, and Cathy

began to blush.

We head off to gym. It wasn't my class but I went anyway. The coach rarely paid that much attention to who came on what period, and more that everyone came at least once a day. Cathy sat on the stage and watched Mike as he caught the basketball in mid-air then passed it to me without looking, before he slammed shoulder first into the rubber floor of the gym. She cringed and smiled all at once and watched him wipe his sweat-soaked hair out of his eyes then get back up and into the game.

He was the master of the no-look pass. I'm getting distracted, I'm sorry.

I dribble the ball up toward center court, feint to avoid Tommy from knocking the it out of his hands, the basket is getting closer and closer. I stop at the three point mark as Ivan Gumm and Trevor Pilgrim run up behind me on either side, they were going to knock the ball out of the air as I threw it. I let the ball roll backward off his fingers, and it bounces twice before Mike catches it, making his way to the left where nobody was guarding. He drew back and let the ball fly from his fingertips. It bounced once off the backboard, then into the net. That swish sound, there's nothing like it.

I jog over to him and give him a high five as he tries to catch his breath. He asked me how I knew he was back there, and I smirk and tap my nose. Using the Womb to cheat at sports might not have been dignified, but it wasn't like I could just turn them off either. I nod to Cathy and head back into the center, where the coach is again raising the ball into the air. Mike chuckled at his friend, then walked back to his position at the left.

Cathy watches as the coach tosses the ball upward and both Tommy and Kevin Jeffers leaped for it. Tommy's fingers touch the bottom lightly and motion it toward Ivan, who immediately grabs it and starts toward the other net. I chase after him.

This is going somewhere, I swear.

I can hear Cathy take a long sip of her Coke as I bat the ball away from Ivan and back toward Tommy, only to have Mike grab it before he could and throw it back to Kevin, who immediately bolts back toward their net with it. Tommy shoots me this annoyed look like I did that on purpose or something before grabs his water bottle and squirts some over his face and heads back to the game. Cathy's watching him and his scowl too, I see her out of the corner of my eye. She also sees as he starts to smile afterward, she says, and was glad that he wasn't going to start something.

I didn't see that part.

"I know why I'm not out there," comes this from beside her, and I pick it up as though I'm sitting right between them. "Why aren't you?"

The guy's name is Lawrence Hogan. When I look over he's got one hand relaxed at his side and the other in his pocket as he is grinned down at her. His face was unshaven and patchy, apparently nobody had bothered to tell him that he wasn't able to grow a beard yet. He's thin and lanky and wearing a baggy t-shirt and jeans over his body. His shoulders look muscular but the rest of him seemed to lack something, although I can't quite put my finger on what. His hair was long a wild, black hair curling in all directions and brown eyes that lit up when he smiled. At first I'm confused by what he means by why he wasn't out there, and I can tell Cathy is too, then I notice that cast over his right foot, almost hidden by his baggy clothes, and I see the crutches leaned against a chair a few feet away. I get all of this in less than a second as my eyes scan over the court during the game. It takes me longer to process then it does to see, that's just the way it works. The Womb catches everything, and sometimes I've got to filter out the bullshit to figure out what's relevant.

Cathy smirks at him and brushes her hair back behind her ear. "I'm using my monthly cycle as an excuse," she said, then grinned and told him she did it about once a week.

He laughs at this and motions toward the empty spot on the stage next to her. She nods and he sits down then drags his crutches a little bit closer. I take note of where he sits with squinted eyes. There was a good two feet between them, marked by her Coke. Enough room for Jesus, as my grandfather might have said.

Lawrence took out a Power-Aide and opened it. He took a drink then laid it next to hers and made some kind of comment like: "Just watching them makes you thirsty, huh?" That wouldn't have impressed me and clearly didn't impress Cathy, but I was getting the impression that he wasn't trying to.

She nods as she watches Mike get an elbow to the gut from me. It was an accident. We were both reaching for the ball and I was paying too much attention to her and not enough to where the other players were. There's a metaphor there, somewhere. He bitched for a second but recovered quickly. Cathy smiled at him without him knowing and took another sip of her drink, as though confirming what Lawrence had said. After a moment it was like she realized that Lawrence wasn't watching the game and that the both of them were alone on the stage, and I guess she started to feel like she was being antisocial, so she asked him if he was seeing anyone lately.

He smiled and his curls bob a little. He tells he he's seeing Kendra Ellah, who's a year younger than the rest of us. She had cute freckles, dark hair, and was captain of the cheerleading squad -- at least according to Cathy. The description made Lawrence blush and look down at his feet. She asked him if it was "anything serious," which I don't think is code for sex yet but it will be soon enough. I'm sorry, I know you don't want to hear that, but it's true.

He said no with his eyes still glued to the floor, but it comes out as "Naw" with that battered New England accent. They'd met two weeks ago, he said, right after he'd broken his leg. He hadn't figured out the crutches yet and was trying to get over the stairs. "I Prob'ly would've broken the other leg if she hadn't helped. She broke her ankle on the squad once, so she knew what it was like," he said. It sounded like a sweet story, and Cathy said as much. After some badgering she starts telling him how she and Mike got together which, funny story, was a set-up by me and Sara. I take no credit.

On the court, Tommy finally gets his hands on the ball and starts running toward the net as fast as he can. He's slamming the ball rather than dribbling it. Mike races after him, but he's pumped with adrenaline now, and the only thing that stands between him and the net is me.

Tommy jumps for the basket, trying to use his height to dunk it. At the same time, I jump upward to block. I reach up to tap the ball over to Mike, and both our arms are in the air. I catch the ball in my palm and yank it downward, elbowing Tommy in the face in the process, right as Cathy is explaining how I set them up to Lawrence. She's turning to point me out to him just as I do it.

Tommy and I both hit the floor at the same time, me on my feet and Tommy on his side. He slammed down hard. I was about to toss the ball to Mike when I turned and saw what I'd done. I drop the ball as soon as I do and I rush toward Tommy. It really was an accident. I take two steps toward Tommy and stop mid-pace. I get this coppery taste in my nose and mouth. It's overpowering. I'm salivating, and I think I might be bleeding. I'm not.

When Tommy turns around to face me I see that it's him that's bleeding. There's blood gushed from his nose onto the floor and he's glaring up at me with this hatred burning in his eyes. He kept trying to wipe the blood away so that he could breathe but it just kept coming.

I ask him if he's alright. I keep having to swallow because my mouth kept producing moisture, so much so that it made it hard to speak. My nostrils were flaring and taking in all that coppery blood and my heart starts beating overtime, both of them.

Tommy mumbles something under his breath as he crawls to his feet, still trying to make the blood go away.

"What was that?" I ask, my eyes narrowing even as Mike and Cathy came up behind me. There are others crowding around as well. Lawrence watched from the stage, unable to get down without help. I had heard what he'd said, but wanted him to take it back.

Tommy chuckled a little, then turned to look me in the eye. "I said: 'Yeah, right.'"

"Dude, it was an accident," Mike offers from behind me. He was trying hard to diffuse the situation. Both Tommy and I have tempers that are known all around the school. Tommy especially has a history of running off at the mouth and getting into trouble. He still had the shadow of a black eye from the last time that it happened.

"Bull-shit," Tommy spits, small pellets of blood spraying onto my shirt. The Womb surges and thrusts within my gut. He says I tried it while he looks me up and down and scoffs. "Always got to be the big man, huh?"

I wave the half-hearted insult aside and say something stupid like "says you." Tommy's attitude was making my blood boil, but I had to walk away.

And I could have, if it had been left there, I think.

"Naw," Tommy sneers, his teeth red with the blood that had gotten on them. "Says Julie."

I turn back toward him with wide eyes, and before Mike or Cathy could stop me I was on Tommy, slamming him back into the floor. "You son of a bitch!" I scream, and I draw back and plow it into Tommy's jaw. Blood spurts in all directions. Mike and Cathy both reach out and try to haul me off, one on each arm, but it's too far gone now. The coach starts to jog over from the other side of the court. There are cheers from the others boys for me or Tommy, or just for the fight in general.

I feel a long ache in my mouth accompanied by what actually was my blood this time, a sensation I know all too well. A second row of teeth was slowly coming down from my gums from behind the first, ripping fresh holes in the tender flesh the way they had many times before. The skin on the end of each of my fingers began to stretch taunt as the talon at the end of each pierced the skin and poked out after days without use. I'd almost forgotten the rush that came with this part of the transformation, but not quite, as my muscles soak in the black blood coursing through my veins and grew larger, making my second and third strikes to Tommy's face much more feral, much more violent... and much more satisfying. "I've had just about enough of you!" I bellow, and one or two words came out in a voice not mine, a voice that was rough and scratchy. It's almost inhuman, like an animal trying to talk; each word in that voice was vomited out, rather than simply spoken.

"Xander!" Mike calls as he gives up on trying to pull me back by the arms and wraps his around my neck instead.

I yell and backhand both Mike and Cathy. Mike slams into the coach but doesn't fall, but Cathy was pushed backward several steps, then tripped and fell and slammed the back of her head against the floor. If it had been anything other than rubber, she would have had to go to the emergency room. Even as it was, she was going to have a nasty bump.

I stop immediately, my muscles relaxing. My black eyes begin to dilate and become more normal, the snarl fading from my face and being replaced by a look I can only imagine was deep, profound regret. As the coach and a few others see to Tommy, who was still talking and seemed as though he would be all right, I take a few cautious steps toward Cathy, who was already rising and rubbing the back of her head.

Mike steps between us and glares at me. I stop moving forward and look down at the blood spattered floor. I feel like a child who's just been scolded, and do not make another move toward Cathy. Mike turns to her and helps her up. He whispers something into her ear and I force my senses not to pick up what it was, knowing I wasn't meant to hear. It didn't matter. Like I said, it wasn't something I could turn on and off.

He's asked if she was okay. She nods and checks her hand for blood as she withdrew it from her scalp, finding none.

"If you want me too, I'll end him," he smiled. He was only half joking and I know it, though she doesn't.

She laughs, then leans in and kisses him... then she turns toward me with eyes filled with hurt. "What the hell was that?" she demands, in a voice I've never heard her use before in all our years of friendship. I realize I deserve it. I say nothing for a long moment, refusing even to meet her glare.

"You almost - -" Mike starts, then looks around to make sure the crowd is far enough away. He lowers his voice. "You almost Wombed out. At Tommy, in front of everyone... for nothing!"

Again, I say nothing.

"Maybe trying not to transform isn't such a great idea," she frowns, her voice more normal and sympathetic now that the dull throb in her head was subsiding. "Maybe it's like anger, and if you bottle it all up, eventually you'll explode at somebody for no good reason."

Finally I look up, my eyes wet with tears and a few dribbles of blood coming from each corner of my mouth. The sharp womb-teeth are still trying to force their way down. "I think I need to talk to someone..." I said. At the sight of his tears, Cathy forgives me without saying a word a takes his head onto her shoulder. She rubs my back until I compose myself. Mike watches. After what must be ten minutes he interrupts us, and we all walk outside together to get some fresh air.

So that was when I decided I had to talk to someone. And you were the only person I could think of.

Xander looked down at the floor, then up again at Reverend Robert Gallagher.

Gallagher was staring at him with wide-eyed fear, his hand covering his mouth. With his free hand shaking, he reached for the coffee mug in front of him and tried to take a sip, then realized it was empty and got up. He walked towards the percolator without making so much as a sound.

"I've spent the three days since trying to figure out the line between good and evil. Is it okay to do a horrible thing to justify something good? Cathy's been talking about that a lot. So, I've been trying not to transform at all, then today I almost did it right in front of everybody. I almost killed a friend, for no good reason.

"I need to know what to do, Father. I need to know if I can do this. I need to know who I am and what my path is. So, I came to you... and here I am."

Xander looked at Gallagher expectantly, but the man's back was turned to him. He finished pouring his coffee, the pot still in his hand as he took a long glug of it past his lips, his hand finally slowing its steady shake.

"You..." he said, turning just enough that Xander could see the tears in the man's eyes. More than that, he could see the hate. "... Are a devil," he spat, then drew back the coffee pot and slammed it into the left side of Xander's face, sending him toppling off his chair and onto the floor.

"Father?" Xander whispered, his voice harsh and shocked, as he withdrew his hand from the side of his face and found blood on it as papers from the desk scattered all around him. "What are you doing?"

"I will put an end to you, you monster!" he bellowed as he raised the pot high. He stood over Xander and slammed it down onto his face. And then again. And again.

"Father, no!" Xander yelled, raising his hand not to harm the man, but to try and defend himself.

"I will do what you cannot, my son. I will stop your evil here, before it hurts any other." He raised the pot again, as high as he could. "I shall smite the wicked and plunge you into the fiery pit!"

"Father!"

Gallagher brought the glass pot down, still spraying dark brown liquid in all directions as he thrust it forward, connecting with Xander's lower jaw... and this time shattering. Four large pieces of sharp glass ripped into Xander's face and neck, the blood that had started a few moments ago flowing even more. It pumped and gurgled its way out in sickening gasps, finding its way through his mouth and nose as well.

He felt the blood fill his throat and lungs. He tried to cry out, tried to make his friend see reason... but no words would come, only spouts of red liquid and bile.

Then he felt something else, deep inside him.

He felt the familiar pump from deep within in his side. Something that recognized the coppery taste of blood -- and liked it. Something that yearned for it, and demanded more. Xander's eyes went wide, as he felt the blood and the fear and pain take him over, the way it had many times before. He raised his hands to try and stop Gallagher, but he could already see the veins on the backs of his hands swelling up with pressure, turning black.

Gallagher slammed the shattered remains of the glass coffee pot one last time, his thrust taking him forward toward the boy as he connected. Before he would have pulled back for another blow, his eyes went wide and his mouth slack. He heard a sound that reminded him of the raw hamburger meat when his mother would sink her hands down into it, a kind of wet sucking sound. He looked down, and from his point of view, Xander's hand was missing. The boy's arm was stretched out toward his stomach, but stopped at the wrist, pressed against him. It wasn't until he saw the blood or felt the vibrations of the boy's fingers inside him that he realized the truth.

He opened his mouth to speak, but it was now Gallagher's turn to be unable to do so, as blood started to stream out of it. He looked forward into Xander's eyes, and they were as black as coals -- and then he slumped forward.

The redness that had bathed Xander's throat and shoulders a few moments ago was gone now, replaced by a dark liquid gel that spewed out onto his body. It overtook his flesh as if it had a mind of its own, twirling and jolting about, like some mad god with a silk brush had decided to paint him black with great sweeping strokes. Gallagher fell to one side, still fighting for each shallow breath as he watched the blackness overtake Xander. It looked wretched and painful, each and every one of the boy's muscles twitching and convulsing uncontrollably, helping the liquid along until finally there was nothing left but an animate shadow where Xander had once lay.

Suddenly, aqua-green eyes appeared, as if they had been sliced there. Large, cat-like, triangular eyes. And then a mouth. It turned towards Gallagher, and all the man could do was lay there and watch as the Black Womb raised its talons high and then plunged them into his eyes.

He had just enough air left in his lungs to make a muffled scream, before even that was gone.

The last words he heard before he saw what awaited him in the next world were: "Black Womb lives!"

. . .

Mike and Cathy walked down the streets without a care in the world.

They were two people more in love with every passing moment. Cathy walked slightly ahead of Mike, and he jogged to catch up with her, tickling her sides gently, playfully. She laughed, her auburn her flowing like a summer breeze as she did. He took her by the hips and pulled her close, then pushed her hair back behind her ear.

He kissed her.

It was gentle at first, but then he couldn't help but

press into her. Her lips were soft. Her hair smelled like strawberries. He loved that smell. She brought her hand up to his face and touched it gently, then pushed back smoothly to break off the kiss. They looked at each other, then leaned in again for a short, light kiss.

She took him by the hand as they started walking toward her home. "Where do you think Xander went?" she asked, her voice sounding like the hummed tune of some wonderful song with no words.

He stopped, looking back the way they'd come. Xander's house wasn't far behind them, and it didn't look like any of the lights were on. "Do you think we should go check on him?"

Cathy smiled coyly and gestured him towards her with one finger, then started to walk away again. He chuckled as he smiled and followed, his hair still messy from the kiss they'd shared at The Factory.

Somewhere, deep inside, Cathy knew they'd make it. All of them together, they would make it. Derek was gone now, and even though he didn't think so, she knew Xander was close to getting control over the Black Womb. That he really could help the innocent, the hurt, and the terrified. Mike knew it too, although she knew he would never say it out loud.

Cathy skipped along in front of Mike, stringing him along by his hand. He laughed at her, then pulled her close and kissed her again. She brought her finger to his lips and smiled. "Save it for later, lover."

He nodded eagerly and walked up the sidewalk after her. They passed the old Deli and looked through its windows, smiling at the memories they couldn't help but see there. They'd had their first date in that Deli.

Her lips were like silk against his. She was in front of him, her back to him. His arms were around her. He loved the way she seemed to fit perfectly into his arms. He loved the way she kissed. He loved they way she brushed her hair. The way she hit him and expected it to hurt. The way she apologized when it did hurt. "I love you," he said. She pulled his face in for another kiss, even more delectable then the first. Oh yes, he thought privately. I almost forgot. I love the way she kisses right after I tell her I love her. He closed his eyes and savoured the moment. His every sense perked and took in everything. He could taste her cherry lipstick. Smell the strawberry shampoo she'd used just hours before. He could feel her chest rise and fall next to his. He could see her in his mind's eye, so perfect. He could hear --

Then it happened. It seemed so long ago now, but it was still embedded within him. That deep, primal fear for one's own life. Like Pavlov's dogs drooling at the sight of a can opener, or soldiers that snap to attention at command years after dismissal. This was like that. He didn't think it'd matter how long it was, this would always cause the same reaction. His eyes snapped open. He could hear it.

-click-

Cathy sensed that something was wrong. She knew his eyes were open, even before she opened hers. "Mour nob ooking it we... ware oo?" she said, still caught in the kiss.

He broke off the kiss. "What' d you say?"

She smiled at him. "I said 'you're not looking at me... are you?'"

He didn't smile back, that's how she knew something was really wrong. "Not just then, no." There was a long pause, where she could hear nothing but night air. She wanted to say something. To chide him for not telling her what was wrong. To comfort him. But Cathy Kennessy knew her love well, and she knew when he wanted to talk and when he did not. "Did you hear that?" he said finally.

Her eyes went wide. She remembered the last time she'd heard those words escape from his lips. "Don't scare me like that," she said, all humour gone from her voice.

"Do you honestly think I'd joke about it?"

Sweat beginning to bead on her brow.

As the still air fell between them, she heard it too.

-click-.

She stepped to her boyfriend and held him close.

"Start walking," he said.

She did so.

Mike reminded himself that the Black Womb had never actually chased them. That although he had learned that anxiety-building technique in the heat of battle with Adam Genblade, he'd hadn't been the one to use it on them. He reminded himself that Xander had never hurt them, though Black Womb could. That Derek had done those insane acts, and then spared them each time for no other reason than his insane mind still considered them friends. That Derek was long gone, and hadn't been seen or heard from in weeks. He reminded himself that Xander had sworn to protect, and that Black Womb usually merely manifested what Xander wanted. Mike reminded himself of a lot of things, but the reminder of the cold steel ripping at his flesh after the -click- sound overpowered them all.

He stopped, as did she, under a street lamp. "What - ?" she asked.

He raised a hand for silence. They were both quiet for a long time. The clicking had stopped.

After a long moment of silence, they both breathed a sigh a relief, then turned and laughed at one another. "We've really got to stop being so paranoid," Cathy said as they turned around to head home. As she did, she ate her words.

Before them, bathed in the light from the street light was the Black Womb. It stood straight, its arms close to his sides. Its palms were open and its claws were out, Its aqua-green eyes glaring at their silent forms.

Neither of them knew what to do. They had to remind themselves to breathe.

The creature's thick shoulders moved up and down as it breathed heavily. Blood dripped from its claws. Its mouth was opened slightly, showing rows of sharp teeth, and the redness beyond.

Its just come from a battle, Cathy thought to herself, her heart racing. Maybe it wants our help.

A low growl that emitted from the creature's throat put any and all of those thoughts to rest. It took a step towards them, and they took a step back. It looked at them, its eyes narrowing, the way a cat looked at a canary. Its tongue protruded from its mouth and tasted their scent on the air. It licked the blood from its finger tips. The creature was caught in an incurable blood - lust created by a fight that had most likely ended too soon. It was hungry for blood.

It leaped at them, claws ripping at Mike's jacket.

"Run!" Mike yelled, as he forced Cathy ahead of him. The creature landed on all fours on the sidewalk. His glossy eyes studied their movements, how they ran. The way Mike still veered left after his injury months ago. The way Cathy's right leg still limped a little at its base. They'd both been... damaged. It moved quickly, like a jaguar, leaping to the sidewalk and then onto two legs to pursue them.

"Keep... going..." Mike encouraged Cathy, holding his side. They were almost to her house. But they'd both danced this dance before. He wasn't about to make the same mistakes twice. He cut through an old alley, hoping to run across the back yards of the complex's until reaching her back door. They could see the house now.

"Mike..." Cathy pleaded, grasping at the stitch in her side. "It hurts."

"It's okay!" he said, scooping her up into his arms. "I've got you!"

In front of them, they heard the sound of feet on concrete. "Maybe it's Dad," Cathy whispered. There was no sound for several long moments. Then they saw it. Heard it. The creeping, jagged shadow of Black Womb fell across the ground in front of them, followed by a deep growl. As they backed away slowly, the growl escalated into a roar. It practically poured itself silently in front of them, slowly pursuing them. Terror shot through both their eyes as the thing made headway on them. It inched closer to them, step by step, until it was almost on them. It raised a taloned hand and they began to run, but they were too late. The claws sliced easily through Mike's chest, gnawing at the bone underneath. Mike fell to the ground, his breathing laboured. Cathy went down with him and scrambled, her legs beating at the ground as though she were trying to get away on a bicycle. She struggled to hold his head up. She wanted to plea with the Xander Drew within the creature for mercy, hoping to reach her beloved friend. But all she could do was glare at it.

It brought its hand up again and slashed at her face and neck.

She felt blood trickle down her chest and her back, the way it pushed and oozed out of the open wounds. She could feel herself slip away. The last thing she saw and felt was the Black Womb bending over and ripping at Mike, tearing at his ribs, his legs, his arms. Her last thoughts were of how much she loved Mike -- and Xander. She sobbed and screamed and forced her eyes shut.

Three months later, Catherine Kennessy was let out of the Coral Beach General intensive care unit.

She had a punctured lung that made any physical exertion painfully impossible.

She spent every waking day of those three months crying into her stiff paper pillow, thinking of all that she'd lost. Wondering if she would ever get it back again, or if things would ever be the same.

Xander Drew was nowhere to be found.

THE GAME

The buildings loomed overhead like massive stone dominos, threatening to topple over on her at a moment's notice.

The world around her was as black as pitch, every streetlight within a mile having been beaten out long ago. Every so often she'd stumble upon a stray piece of polarized glass as she limped down the sidewalk.

Her lungs were on fire. She'd moved to Los Angeles for the heat, but now it scorched her inside and out with every laboured breath she took. Her hair clung to her face in bulging, sweaty clumps; it got in her mouth and filled it with sickly salty tang.

Pain shot up from her leg and she clutched at it, leaning briefly against a rail. She ground her teeth so hard they chipped. Colours and light flashed in front of her and for a moment she thought she'd found some reprieve from the darkness, but it faded again as the pain did. When she brought her hand back from her leg, she could feel her fingers stick together and smell the coppery stench of blood and b.o. that wafted into her nostrils. Somehow, enough light came from somewhere that she thought she could see the redness coating each digit, but wasn't sure if it was real or imaginary.

"What's goin' on?" came a small voice from behind her, cracking once as it made the oh sound. Her son stepped into view for the first time since she'd started running, his dark hair and deep brown features highlighted by only the slightest glimmer of light.

"Be quiet, Christopher," she snapped through gritted teeth, grabbing him by the arm. "Keep going."

She started to walk again, her left leg a barely functioning weight hanging from her hip. She took each step as quickly as she could. He watched her intently, pausing every few steps so that he kept pace with her, his eyes moving from her face to her leg and then back again.

"Gails!" came a booming, angry voice from somewhere behind them, the sound ricocheting off the buildings and echoing down everywhere. She paused once but otherwise ignored it.

Christopher turned and looked over his shoulder with wide eyes as two men seemed to step directly out of the shadows at the end of the street. They were both tall and broad, looking like solid square cutouts of the buildings as they turned to face he and his mother. The one on the left held something long and symmetrical in his hand, light shimmering off the silver barrel as he moved it. He turned back around and saw that his mother had gotten a few steps ahead of him and picked up speed to catch up.

The man on the right sighed. He grabbed either side of his shirt and pulled it down to get out all the creases. He was exceptionally tall at almost seven feet and had broad, toned shoulders leading down to massive arms that swung like wrecking balls when he walked. His suit was a deep navy with white pinstripes, offset by a deep red tie that puffed out of his breast and was held down by a shimmering silver clip. His face was oddly angular, a large square jaw plummeting down and almost hiding his neck completely. At first glance, the only thing spherical about him were his eyes, big and brown and catching every shadow around him.

"She's fast," said the man with the gun, running a hand over his bald head getting it drenched with sweat in the process.

"She's an idiot," the larger man barked, not taking his eyes off her as she limped away in the distance. He drew his tongue along his dry gums, then twisted his jaw back and forth in an effort to make it more comfortable and failing. His gaze shifted once from the woman to her child, who jogged along at half pace next to her. He let out a long huff of air, then pulled back the sleeve of his suit and looked at his watch. "I don't have time for this. Take care of it, Roxxon."

"Yessir," he nodded, speaking in clipped words as he raised his gun to eye level and started down the street toward the pair. He ran fast, his legs a dark blur as he fell into the shadows of the sidewalk.

The larger man watched him go, worked up some saliva and swished it around his mouth before he spit it out onto the pavement. He cursed and reached into his breast pocket, and pulled out a cell phone that was dwarfed by his large brutish hands. He pressed and held down a key on the pad then held it up too his ear and waited. "It's me,

I'm going to be late... no, nothing serious." He threw a glance toward the street again, not seeing any movement at all now. "No, nothing like that. Just put it in the oven for me to keep it warm... I'm sure it'll be fine, it always is." He turned and walked away from the street toward the docks where he'd come from, the waves crashing against the bluffs so loudly that they made each of his steps seem perfectly silent.

↑↗

She turned the corner and took another deep breath, sucking the humid air down into her lungs. Her lower lip quivered violently as she tried desperately to remain standing, propping herself against the wall for a second before forcing herself to move on.

Christopher stepped up behind her again, his cheeks flushed and red but he did not stop. "Where're we going?"

"Shh," she hissed again, turning and grabbing him by the hand. "Do you want him to find us? Is that what you want? If he finds us he'll kill us!"

He stopped and did not make a sound, barely even took a breath. Her nails were digging into his arm and making four little crescendoed punctures there, drawing blood to the surface. Still, he did not make a sound.

Somewhere around the corner came the sound of heavy, hurried breathing. A moment later came the sounds of light, uneven footfalls. It sounded more like three men hopping than one man walking, the paces going from slow to quick and then back again at an instants notice.

She cursed and looked around. The building they were

next to was a long, flat wall on concrete that stretched out for the majority of the block, without any alleys or dips in which to hide. Slowly, she turned toward the boy.

He looked up at her, all eyes and quivering, convulsing lip. His chubby cheeks were shaking violently from the force of his breath as he stared up at her, watching as she made a decision and then committed to it. Biting her lip and taking one fearful glance toward the street corner, she bent down on one knee until she was level with him.

"I need you to do something for Momma," she said, her voice turning from harsh to soft and soothing somewhere between sentences. She reached out and touched the side of his head, feeling the contours and grooves underneath his thin hair. "Do you think you can do something for Momma?"

He took a deep breath, let it out, then nodded.

She smiled and fixed his collar. "Okay, I need you to run, sweety." she said, taking him by each shoulder gently and turning him back the way they'd come, past the corner they'd just rounded and to the street beyond. "I need you to run there and I need you to keep running."

"What about you?"

She paused, moving her tongue over her teeth. "I'm going to be okay. I'm going to meet you, but you have to keep going until I come and get you."

"But, you're hurt. How are you going to be able to come get me?"

"Shh, I just will. Trust Momma, now..."

"But--"

"Just do it!" she barked, her cheeks growing livid as she shoved him forward. His legs started to move beneath him, first from the momentum of her arm and then slowly picking up speed and starting all on his own, like a motor that has been jump started. His young legs moved like pistons, carrying his thin frame in great strides across the dark concrete. Without hesitation, he bolted out beyond the safety of the building and into the intersection.

She wasn't watching him, hadn't even seen his first wobbling steps after she'd shoved him. She'd spun around and started down the sidewalk even faster than she had before.

゜゚

Roxxon saw Christopher bolt out from around the corner right in front of him, making him jump. His back had been against the wall and he'd been about to turn and fire when Christopher started his mad dash across the street. He scoffed, then raised his gun until it was level with his eyes and fired.

PANG!

There was an electric spark as the bullet ricocheted off a rail, illuminating the buildings around for one brilliant moment. Christopher ran faster, his legs screaming for relief as he let out a long scream into the night and pumped his arms fiercely.

"Fuck," he spat, stepping out into the middle of the road and bringing the gun back up to aiming level, setting the boy's left shoulder in his sight. He stopped, opened both eyes and spun around, sending the tail of his jacket flapping about.

The woman was just reaching the edge of the building, her limp barely even noticeable now as blood ran through her veins like a train. Without even taking the time to aim he raised the gun and fired, the gunpowder igniting and once again flashing briefly against the walls like lightning. The bullet passed through her back and out through her front in an eruption of blood, spewing out in a magnificent 'v' before her body fell into it, spattering it all over her chin and neck before falling to the pavement.

He turned back around to the road Christopher had been heading toward and found it empty. Cursing, his eyes scanned every creek and crevice for a sign of the boy, then finally turned and strolled over to where his mother lay bleeding.

Her body shook and convulsed violently as she struggled to breathe, her left lung filling with blood more and more every time she exhaled. "Nmm," she hummed, sounding very much like the brief sounds that came between great, heaving sobs. Hot, sticky blood had already pooled all around her in an ever expanding oblong, twisting and flowing into every imperfection in the concrete.

Holding the gun tight in both hands, he nudged her with the toe of his shoe, smearing blood against the otherwise spotless black leather.

"Nmm, hmm," she said again, moving slightly before rolling back onto her stomach and splashing more blood on him.

Scowling, he drew back and kicked her hard in the ribs. The sound the impact made against her saggy flesh reminded him of the sound bread dough made when his mother kneaded it between her fingers over and over again, working out all the lumps until it was perfect.

She turned over onto her back, blood still bubbling up through the gaping hole between her breasts. Her eyes were bloodshot, the pupils darting back and forth wildly. Blood was caked onto her face in massive wet clumps, spewing up through her mouth after every struggled breath. Now that she was on her back, the sound she had been making was much clearer.

She was laughing.

All her pink stained teeth showing in a full fledged smile, her body jittering with each good hearted chuckle as blood and bile and shit came out of every opening in her body.

Roxxon raised a busy eyebrow, then bent down and opened her shirt where the epicenter of the blood-stained hole resided. Pinned to her chest by the strap of her bra was a large ziplock bag packed to the breaking point with a fine white powder that was slowly turning pink as more and more of her blood filtered its way through it. He grabbed it and pulled it back and forth until he finally dislodged it, accidentally twisting her bra until it no longer covered her. He held the bag up and examined it, cocaine tumbling out through the hole in the front and back and billowing away in the hot breeze. He frowned, then put his finger around the trigger of his gun again and fired a shot into the woman's head. Her body jolted from the sudden impact and the laughter stopped. She still smiled though, that twisted grin so big it showed off all her teeth and gums, one nearly indistinguishable from the other after being stained with blood.

He holstered his gun and took out his phone in one smooth motion, pressing the redial button and then bringing it to his ear. "Fields, it's me," he said curtly, taking another quick look around the streets. "Woman's dead. Yeah, kid got away though. They fucking split up, I took priority. Yeah... yeah. I know, I know what you said. Sorry. The product? Damaged but salvageable. I'm bringing it in... don't worry, we'll find him."

He kept talking as he walked back to the intersection and toward the bluffs, scraping the blood off of his shoes in a patch of grass along the way.

Christopher watched from under a porch step, staring intently at the lump of flesh that a few moments ago had been his mother, her breasts still and lifeless as they turned a dusky grey. Blood wasn't coming out of her anymore now, and everything was still in Los Angeles for the first time since they'd come there.

But he didn't cry.

He stayed there until sunrise, then ran. And did not look back.

Two weeks later.

The subway rounded a sharp bend in the tracks that jolted all its passengers to the left. Christopher gripped the vertical handle that came down from the ceiling with his chubby fingers, feeling his stomach lurch up into his throat. He steadied himself in his seat as the car righted itself again, shivering a little and clutching into the bar a little more.

The man across from him was wearing a black denim shirt that was neatly pressed and buttoned all the way to the top. Small, sleek glasses and a sharply receding hairline made his face seem much larger and longer than it actually was. His hair was spiked with gel that turned to a flaky white around the ears and he chewed a large wad of gum while playing with an ID badge that hung from his breast pocket.

Sitting uncomfortably close to him on his left was a pretty, bigger girl with long brown hair that was drawn up in a partial ponytail. She wasn't wearing makeup and had a pierced nostril and lip, as well as barbell ear studs and the kindest eyes he'd seen in weeks. She was wearing a tattered Nirvana tee shirt and a pair of shorts that revealed chubby, smooth legs covered in thin red stretch marks.

Across the hall and to his right was a thin man in dirty, tattered clothes. There was a little scruff on his cheeks, but not much. Large holes had been ripped in both knees of his jeans. He was breathing heavily and leaning back and forth, fidgeting nervously and trying to get comfortable as he surveyed the other passengers. Eventually he locked eyes with Christopher, if only briefly, before moving on. There were bags under his eyes and his cheeks looked pale and hollow. There was a yellowish tint to the man's skin he couldn't identify and he hoped that he wouldn't look his way again.

One seat away to his right was a heavyset man with a shaved head covered by a sideways baseball cap. He had small eyes and a constant grin, hands shoved into the pockets of his kacki shorts. He was wearing a navy blue Toronto Maple Leafs sweater even though it was close to eighty degrees outside. He didn't seem to be sweating as much as he should, except for a thin layer just under the folds in his skin.

Near him was a tall man with broad shoulders. He wore a suit that was tailored to fit him perfectly. His nails were manicured, and his every hair was in place.

Chris shuffled a little, his eyes darting back and forth in his head as he watched buildings zip past. An intercom near the front of the car bonged to life and was followed by a inaudible, droning voice that spoke for several seconds before cutting out again. He sighed, then turned and craned his head to look at the loop of yellow wire dangling a few feet above his head. Frowning, he reached his pudgy fingers toward it.

His uncut nails danced along the edge, not quite close enough to get a grip. He tisked, letting go of the rail for a moment to get more reach.

As if on cue, the train veered to the left again, switching to the other side of the tracks and pulling his tiny body to the right.

He yelped, his hand flailing wildly until he again found the greasy metal pole.

He steadied himself on the seat again and took several deep breaths before turning back toward the yellow chord. He glared at it ruefully, as though it were purposely staying just out of his reach, a bully holding something over his head. He licked his lips and started to stretch out his arm again.

BING!

The "Stop Requested" light sparked to a dim red life at the end of the car.

Chris stopped, turning back toward the narrow hallway between rows of seats. The scruffy man across from him still had his fingers on the chord, staring directly at him from across the way. There was clearly visible grit under his fingernails. He let the cord go, the yellow rubber springing back into place immediately.

Chris squirmed as the train's breaks squealed to a halt, the doors opening with a mechanical, automatic hiss. He swallowed hard and got up out of his seat and shuffled out. Out of the corner of his eye he saw the scruffy man rise up out of his seat as well, scratching his nose twice with the sleeve of his shirt before heading toward the same exit, only a few feet behind.

He stepped out onto the platform and was greeted with a putrid huff of fresh exhaust. He coughed wildly as he sucked in more and more, his lungs aching for oxygen. Picking up pace for a moment he got past the smog and started walking toward the other end of the long stretch of concrete.

Trains whizzed by on the other side, so fast that they were little more than a blur in his peripheral vision, always accompanied by a sudden rush of wind that carried bar wrappers and the stench of rubber on it. He closed his eyes to protect himself from the debris and walked toward the end of the tram.

The building at the end of the walkway was big enough to be at least three stories tall, but only consisted of one. Inside it was only a massive stone staircase ascending the centre, accompanied on either side by escalators. At the top of the stairs, hallways branched out to the left and right that opened up into walkways built above the train tracks and streets, leading to a winding set of stairs on either side that led back down to ground.

He reached the solid glass door of the station and

pulled hard. It opened a inch or so, then slammed back against the wind. He frowned and turned his head slightly to peer over his shoulder.

The scruffy man was still back there, leaning against one of the red rails that separated the tram from most of the tracks. A gust of air had taken his dark hair now, tossing it about as he finished the last few puffs of a cigarette. He turned toward Chris and started walking, his eyes coasting from side to side with each step.

Chris turned back and pulled again, opening the door with one massive pull. He stepped inside before the wind forced it shut again and immediately ran for the escalators and started up despite the way his rubbery legs called out for relief. Stepping past people on cell phones that gave him angry, annoyed looks; he hopped off the elevator at the end and chanced a look over his shoulder.

The man was there again, about halfway up the escalator already. He'd been watching someone going down the stairs the opposite way, then turned and locked eyes with Chris again. There was something about them that sent a rollicking quake down the boy's spine. Something in those eyes that were cold and dead, like the men in the movies that came on late at night that his Mother didn't know he watched.

He spun back around and started for the left overpass, bursting through the doors with ease this time. The wind was worse up here, warm and hard and almost forcing him against the concrete wall. He kept going until he reached the stairwell that would bring him down to the parking lot of the strip mall on the other side, sliding down the rusted rail until he was about halfway down and then hopping off. He landed flat on his soles but kept going, tripping once and falling to his knees against the concrete. He hissed in pain, then turned around to look up and the massive tower he'd just surfed down.

It was empty save for one twenty-something girl with curly blonde hair and a gaudy purple shirt walking up toward the station.

Breathing hard, he scrambled to his feet and bolted across the small null of grass in front of him before landing on the grey pavement of the parking lot. A white Chevy blazed on its horn as it passed right in front of him, forcing him to stop briefly before taking off again. His shoes were old and worn, and every time his feet hit the pavement it felt like tiny stones were cutting at them.

A lanky Asian man on a bicycle brushed past him, nudging his arm with the horn-rimmed handles and almost driving him into the traffic of the lanes. He kept running, dodging a pickup as it backed out of its spot, then finally made it to the sidewalk surrounding the strip.

People flocked in and out of a book store just behind him as he turned around, craning his head around the cars and trucks that drove past. The parking lot was clear, as was the splotch of grass between it and the stairwell.

He stopped, let out a long sigh, then smiled.

He turned to join the crowd around him, walking with the flow of commuters and tourists and transients that stepped to the collective thunder of the city daily. Just past the book store was a video store with flashing lights and towering posters in every window. He glanced at the displays for a moment, then moved on. The next slot was an Asian meat market that had inside-out rabbits hanging in the windows, their pink flesh accented with vibrant strands of red. It smelled like an odd mix of sawdust and kitty litter. There was a balding obese man in the window chopping meat for two patrons that looked on expectantly. Despite the vulgarity of the sight, it still made his mouth salivate.

Then the fourth store caught his eye. It was a fruit and vegetable deli, with a table on either side of the entrance piled high with boxes of carrots, apples, oranges, pears and so many things it made his mind ache to think of them all. Suddenly, his throat felt like the Sahara. He stepped up cautiously, watching people as they filled up thin plastic bags with fruit and then proceeded to a long line of scales, weighing them themselves before proceeding to a man waiting between both desks to pay.

There was a watermelon less than a foot in front of him, glistening with moisture in the mid afternoon light. It was plump and juicy and the stripes on it seemed to hypnotize him, the rest of the world falling by the wayside.

He glanced at cashier. He was thin and lanky, with the exception of a pot belly that stuck out noticeably as though he were eight months pregnant. His apron was stained with juice and sweat, as was the mustache that sat on his upper lip like a morbidly obese earwig. He was taking money from a large man wearing a red and white tee shirt and a goofy grin.

Chris turned back to the watermelon, then glanced down at his hands. He sighed audibly as he compared the sizes, then looked back at the melon in dismay. His vision lolled to the side as he turned to keep walking, catching sight of something that was a slightly lighter shade of green.

It was half squat under the melon and was slightly browned from the pressure. Its stem was broken off and it was still yellow around to stub that remained, but it glistened with dew and looked like the juiciest thing he'd seen in his life at that moment.

It was a pear.

He stared at it, wide eyed and dry lipped as people continued to brush past him with their items in hand. The cashier took fistfuls of cash from each, shoving it into a large pocket on the front of his apron and coming back with change that he counted out with unexpected speed. He turned back to the pear. Before he really knew what he was doing, he reached out and grasped it. It felt so soft that he thought his fingers might break right through the skin. His flesh immediately became moist and sticky with juice, running down over his knuckles and making them feel alive for the first time in weeks.

He brought it to his mouth and bit down slowly, savouring every sensation as his teeth broke the thin green skin and shot citrus onto his throat. His eyes bulged and rolled slightly with that first bite and again with the next three, his smile irrepressible.

He was working on his fourth bite when a heavy hand landed on his shoulder.

"Hope you can pay for that," the cashier said, glowering down at him.

Several customers either glared at him or pretended to ignore him entirely. He swallowed back what was in his mouth without chewing, and might have choked if it had been anything but pear. He looked from the man to the piece of fruit and then back again, only now aware of what he had done.

"I'll take that as a no," he grumbled, grabbing the boy's wrist. The pear fell to the ground and rolled, getting caked in sand and gravel and making what remained of it inedible. Chris watched it sadly for a moment before the man yanked him aside.

"No!" he said finally, trying to pull apart the man's wiry fingers.

The man turned to him, surprised and annoyed by his sudden reaction. "Don't fuss with me today, kid. You're already in enough goddamn trouble, don't make me call yer Mom."

Chris stopped in his tracks, his worn out sneakers skidding against the sidewalk as the man continued to pull him along. His face was expressionless except for his bulging white eyes. Slowly his brow lowered and his lip curled, showing off teeth that were still stained light green from the fruit he'd been enjoying. "Rah!" he barked, no longer pulling back but lunging forward into the pot bellied oaf. He tackled the man's leg, not knocking him over but successfully tipping him back into a table of fruit. The man let go of the boy's hand but instead of running, he started to slam into the man's bulbous stomach with both his tiny fists. He screamed with rage, the sounds he was making too large for a boy his size, as the crowd around watched with a mixture of fright and shock and amusement.

"Kid!" the man yelled, grabbing him by both shoulders and trying to stay out of his reach, no matter how ineffective it was. "Don't make me pop you one, I don't want too!"

"Rah!" Chris yelled again, turning and biting at the man's hairy wrist.

The man reeled back, narrowly evading the child's teeth. He looked shocked, then angry as he brought back his hand.

"That won't be necessary," said a horse voice.

The cashier stopped and looked over his shoulder. Chris did the same, leaning to see around the man's ample waistline.

It was the scruffy man from the train. He stood on the other side of the fruit table. His hair looked even greasier now in the harsh natural light, and there were several splotches on his shirt. He was carrying a knapsack that had sprung several holes and looked to carry some of his items by the most tedious of threads. He'd locked eyes with the cashier and didn't look away, like a cobra. There was a small grin on his face, hidden somewhere between the scruff.

"Who're you?" the cashier asked, letting go of Chris and turning around.

The scruffy man turned and looked at Chris, nodding at him once. "I'm his... brother. Is there some kind of problem?"

Chris looked as though he were going to open his mouth to object, then stopped.

"Your brother is a thief," the cashier said with a matter-of-fact tone, gesturing to the gravelly pear on the ground a few feet away.

The stranger looked from the pear to the man and then back again, raising an eyebrow. "I'm sorry, I told him he could pick up something and that I'd be along to pay you. I didn't think it would be a problem."

The cashier stopped, looking sheepish as customers now stopped watching and continued to go about their business. "I see. If the boy had told me."

"He's a case, I know. How much was it?"

"A dollar thirty-five."

The man raised an eyebrow as he rummaged around his pockets. "And you called him a thief," he mumbled, producing two dollar bills and handing them to the man. A moment later he received his change and put it back in his pocket.

The fruit man turned back to Chris and smiled, ruffling a hand through his hair. "Sorry about that, kid," he said. He reached onto the table behind him and retrieved a fresh pear, handing it to him.

The bitterness almost vanished from Chris's face as he grabbed the fruit, this one ripe and succulent, and immediately began eating.

"Come on, bro," the scruffy man said, stepping around next to him. "Let's get out of here."

The scruffy man waved to the street vendor once more before he turned the corner, a large fake smile pasted across his lips as he disappeared from view. It vanished immediately as he turned the corner, touching Chris on the shoulder and turning him around. "Now what the fuck was that?"

"Un!" the boy grunted angrily, kicking the man in the shin.

He winced, grunting softly and squinting at the youth. "Alright kid, I just spent my last two bucks saving you a lot of trouble and time, but if you wanna be like that, then that's just fucking fine." He turned to walk away, making a dismissive gesture with one hand.

Chris stopped and sighed. He sat down against the side of the building and looked at his pear. It was half gone already, juice trickling down from the ridged marks his teeth had made and then dripping onto his leg. He looked at it, examining its smoothly porous surface, before making another small bite.

ʌ⟨⟩ʌ

Chris sat on the train again, clutching onto the metal bar for dear life with one hand and a plain slice of bread in the other. He was in the back today, leaning against the metal wall made hot from the sun's rays. He pressed as much of his bare flesh against it as he could, staving off the chill from the night before.

Sitting a few seats away from him was a teen with shaggy auburn hair listening to loud music over headphones. He was wearing a plain grey shirt without any symbols or words on it, and immediately seemed boring with his slanted features and dodgy brown eyes.

Near the other side of the train was a bald man wearing a tight, form fitting suit and reading a newspaper. He sifted through the pages aimlessly, grumbling incoherently as he did. He was wearing large black sunglasses that hadn't been in style since long before Chris was born, and they reflected the sunlight right at him so that it seemed to be coming from both sides of the tram.

Across from him was the shaggy man.

He was wearing the same clothes as the day before, the only difference being that the dirt level seemed to have waxed in some regions and waned in others. There was a still scruff on his cheeks. He was staring at Chris intently today, only looking to the side every now and again when someone moved in his peripheral vision or the car went around a turn. Fifteen minutes into the ride he got up, pulled down on his shirt to straighten it, then sat down next to Chris.

Chris shuffled away as far as he could, getting as close as possible to the wall. There was a smell that accompanied the man that was pungent and unpleasant, like b.o. masked by cheap cologne. It wasn't as bad as it should have been based on the way he looked, but it was enough to make his nostrils want to curl in on themselves.

They sat in silence for almost five minutes, the man's hands clasped in front of him as he leaned forward onto his knees. He sighed after a time, then turned slightly to make eye contact with the child. "My name's Xander."

Chris remained silent, not taking his eyes off him.

Xander watched him, twiddling his thumbs and clacking his tongue against the roof of his mouth as he waited for a response. "You want to talk about what happened yesterday?"

Again there was silence, though it was now accompanied by a stern look from the child. He looked as though he might bite again.

Xander sighed, then reached into his backpack and withdrew a chocolate chip granola bar wrapped in cellophane and held it up to the boy. "I've got three left.

I'm willing to part with this one if you'll part with your name."

His eyes darted from the scruffy man named Xander to the bar and then back again. He reached out and grabbed it and started unwrapping it feverishly. "Chris," he said, just before shoving a massive wad of the bar into his face.

"Chris," Xander responded, nodding. "Any chance you want to tell me any more than that?"

Chris glared at him again and stopped chewing even though there was still bar in his mouth.

"Okay," Xander nodded, clasping his hands back together in front of him.

They were silent again for several minutes as Chris ate the remainder of his bar.

Xander licked his lips, then looked down at the smut on his hands, trying to rub it off with the opposing hand. He shifted uncomfortably, looking at the other two passengers. He lingered slightly on the teen, picking up the beat from the song he was listening to and trying to place it, giving up after a moment or two. He turned back to Chris, who wasn't pressed up against the wall anymore, but was still far from inviting.

He sat back up a little, almost allowing physical contact to happen but not quite.

"I lost my mom a while back," Xander said finally, trying to put on a smile. "When I was very young. Made me kinda angry... still makes me kinda angry, sometimes." He paused, noticing as the child sat straight up. "Sometimes when people say things I just go red, you know?"

He didn't speak at first, staring up at him. "How'd you know?"

Xander smiled. "Way you freaked out of that pudgy fruit guy. Reminded me of something I'd've done back in the day."

The boy stopped, then nodded.

"You still hungry?"

"Yes," he said, his voice small and foreign to him.

"Hey, we have speech," he said, waving his arms. He reached up and pulled the chord. The light flashing to life at the end of the car. "Come on, I know a place."

Chris grabbed his cheeseburger so tightly that his fingers dug into the sesame seed bun. Ketchup and mustard peppered with small chunks of processed onion spewed out the other side, slowly seeping out as though it were being spit up from the two breaded lips. His eyes widened with delight and surprise as the beefy taste filled his mouth again, much the way it had the day before with the pear.

Across the booth from him, Xander watched him with an amused grin as he slurped on his cola; hearing the disappointing sound of suction as the straw came up empty. He leaned on the divider between booths with one arm, smiling nonchalantly to the waitress that walked by. She shot him a dirty look at first, but smiled and nodded back by the third time she passed.

"People in this place aren't too used to kindness," Xander observed, almost to himself. "It's like they gotta get used to the idea before giving it back."

Chris chewed on his burger relentlessly, forgetting all his manners as he shoved another mouthful past his lips and followed it with a fistful of home fries. He didn't respond, but smiled at the waitress as well as she came by with another plate of fries to replace the ones he had almost finished.

Xander reached over and grabbed a few of the salty strips of potato. Chris glared at him from over the top of his burger like an animal did when you tried to take its food, and it took him a moment to remember what the words 'unlimited fries' fully meant.

"Nice place, huh?" he said, motioning around with the fries before shoving them into his mouth. "Found it a while back when I was visiting with some friends. Best fries I ever had."

Chris nodded, swallowing the mound of ground beef in his mouth and then tearing his eyes away from the burger in his hands for the first time since he'd picked it up. "I thought you said yesterday you spent your last two dollars?"

He smiled. "One thing about money: there's always more if you're willing to look."

"That's what Momma used to say, too."

"Food here's cheap anyway. Cheap and good, can't beat that. Not in this city, anyway." He paused and looked around the room again. Most of the tables were empty. There was an old couple sipping tea at the other side of the restaurant that didn't seem to even notice he existed. He turned back to the boy and examined him thoughtfully for a moment. "I take it you're a local?"

He nodded.

"Nothing wrong with that. It's the city that's crazy, not the people."

He said nothing and looked down at his burger again. He picked it up and took another bite, if a little less enthusiastically.

He took another handful of fries and popped them all into his mouth. "So, I know how I survive in this city... I've got to wonder how someone your age does, though."

Chris did not respond, finally finishing his burger. There was a sloppy puddle of ketchup and mustard on his plate that had fallen from between the patties. He grabbed some fries and started dipping them in it, savouring as much of as he could.

"I mean, I assume you're stealing food. I've got no issue with that. You do what you need do to survive, that's just the way it is. It means you're probably going to deal with one or two assholes like yesterday, but it could be worse. But where do you sleep? Do you go to a shelter or a Y or anything?"

Chris finished off the last of the fries, looking longingly at the plate. Xander raised a hand to the waitress again, then pointed down to the empty plate. She nodded, smiling first this time, which he returned.

"You gotta figure that the police or social services would be all over a kid your age, probably get you in with a family or--"

"We don't like cops," he said finally, his words clipped and matter of fact. "Cops don't like us."

Xander regarded him for a moment, then nodded. "Okay. But like I said, there's other options. There's shelters or Youth Centers."

"They check the shelters."

His eyebrow twitched slightly, his head turning to one

side as his interest perked. "Who checks the shelters?"

Chris looked uncomfortable for a moment, shuffling between the two cushions he straddled. The waitress planted the new plate of fries in front of him, still sizzling and bubbling grease. He took one quickly and popped it in his mouth, apparently unfazed by how hot it was.

Xander sighed, falling back against the booth.

"They came for Momma," he said finally, staring at some random spot on the table. "There was a place we were staying but they said I couldn't stay, they said they'd come looking and I had to go away. So they took me down to one of the centers and it was fine for a while, then the man showed up."

He tried his best to keep his face even until the child was done talking, not wanted to do anything that would make him too uncomfortable to continue. "Was it the man that took your Mom?"

"I think so, but there were more of him. They all looked like the same man, all dressed the same."

Xander nodded.

"He didn't see me, but he asked about me. He said he was my uncle but he's not my uncle. I went to a different centre the next day but he showed up there too. When I went to another one I found this." He reached into his pocket and withdrew a folded up sheet of paper, soggy and faded. Xander knew what it was before opening it but did so anyway. It was a flyer with Chris's picture on it, ripped at the corners from where he'd pulled it down. There was a number below his photo to call if anyone saw him. "So I stopped going to the shelters. No shelters, no cops. Momma always said she didn't like no cops."

"Okay, no cops," Xander agreed, folding the sheet in half and shoving it into his own pocket.

The bell above the door rang and Chris jumped, spinning to see who it was. It was a girl with blonde streaks and a bright purple top stretched wide over voluptuous breasts, smiling wide as she finger-waved to the waitress. Chris sighed, and Xander could almost hear his heartbeat slow back down to a near normal. He looked up at Xander with eyes that were almost ashamed of the fear he'd just felt. But there was spite there as well, not toward him but just in general. For a moment he looked like Klarissa, and by proxy a little like her mother.

Xander smiled, as warmly as he could. "Tell you what, let me take care of this for you."

"No!" he protested, grabbing Xander's wrist. "Can't tell anyone, that's what Momma said. They'll know, they always know."

He nodded. "I know, kid, I know. I dealt with this kind of crap before. There are a bunch of them where I come from, really just a bunch of bullies picking on people smaller and weaker than they are." He leaned in a little toward Chris and whispered, as if sharing some trade secret with the child. "Trick about bullies? Eventually they meet someone bigger and stronger than them."

Chris looked weary, squinting at him suspiciously. "No cops?"

"No cops," Xander smiled, raising his hand as if to swear it.

The boy frowned, almost visibly weighing the offer, then nodded.

Xander smiled, the first real smile he'd given in quite

some time. "Okay. Now first things first, I need to get you home for this."

Chris strattled the metal pole between his legs, holding it with both hands as the train picked up speed pulling away from the station. Xander stood next him, holding onto the bar that ran across the ceiling and examining the ads that were plastered around the small space between it and the windows. Three were for birth control, one was for fast food. Another advertised a hair restoration clinic downtown.

There was a thirty-something man in a grey shirt a few feet away, typing something on his cell phone and smiling infectiously. He had a crew cut and was in shape but didn't look to be military, his jeans hanging off him loosely. There was a spill-proof coffee cup balanced precariously next to him, the string of a teabag hanging out of it. He was sitting next to a brash looking man who was covered in tattoos from shoulder to wrist on each arm, at least thirty different designs on each. He was wearing a wife beater and was sweating profusely, but was caked in body spray to cover it up.

A few feet away from Xander was an elderly woman with a white shawl he guessed she'd knit herself covering her shoulders. Her features were haggard and her thinning hair was forced into small grey curls. Blue eyes threw stern looks in the boy's direction every few moments, but other than that she kept to herself.

Across from them and to the left, an attractive young woman with lightly tanned skin sat near the exit. She was wearing tight black jogging pants with a single pink stripe up either side, as well as a large grey hoodie that seemed to be designed to hide her face and figure. It only partially worked and made for an oddly inviting mix.

On the other side of her was a man with a small goatee wearing a dark grey suit and tie. He was wearing thick glasses and sipping on soup from a cup, some of which kept getting stuck in his mustache. The effect was comical each and every time. There was a paper folded up on the seat next to him with its crossword face up and complete except for one word, with many possibilities for the answer written and scribbled out along the page margins.

There was a young African American man with light blue hair wearing shorts and a tee shirt nearly on the other side of the tram. There was an unlit cigarette dangling from his lips that reminded Xander of how long it had been since he'd had one. It had been so long that he was aware he shouldn't even crave it anymore, but did.

He turned away from the sight and forced a smile, tapping Chris lightly on the head with one knuckle. "It's gonna be okay you know."

The boy smiled weakly, then turned back to the floor.

Xander frowned as the train went around a wide turn, jolting them all to the left. Chris nodded at him and he reached over to the wall, pulling down on the wire once. The train immediately started to break, slowing down little by little until finally coming to a stop. The doors opened with a mournful sigh, a rush of warm evening air pushing its way in and forcing their hair back.

The pair got up and stepped out onto the tram and started walking toward the station. The sun was low in the sky behind it, reflecting off the thick layer of polluted smog that hung in the air and turning the rays a barrage of deep pinks and purples. Several other passengers got off behind them and were now pushing past them, not willing to walk at a child's pace.

Xander looked around and frowned. On the right side of the station was a well developed set of houses. Fences were built high around them but he could see the tops of trees and swing sets, as well as hear the children no older than Chris playing on both. To his left was an area of the city that used to be residential but now was clearly trying to become more of a business district. Buildings that were three and four stories high had brightly coloured and well kept exteriors for the first two floors, but became run down and dingy above them. Most of the upper floors didn't even have siding, and some showed serious signs of fire damage. There were bars, video stores, liquor stores, cigarette stores, an atm vestibule... only one building looked to be a residence; it had a sign out front proclaiming it to be a battered woman's shelter.

"I don't suppose I should guess what side of the tracks you're on," Xander observed as they reached the station and he opened the door for Chris.

He didn't respond, and perhaps didn't quite understand the observation.

They walked up the stairs two by two, avoiding the bustle of commuters crammed onto the escalators. They got to the top and turned left, heading over the walkway and stairwell toward the line of businesses.

Chris stopped on the side of the road, turned around, and glared back up at the stairwell.

"It's okay," Xander chuckled, tapping him on the shoulder blade. "There's nobody here but us ducks."

"What?"

"Nothing. Stupid thing my Dad used to say."

He nodded, then stepped away from the concrete base of the stairwell and onto the sidewalk. Xander followed a few steps behind, letting the child lead the way.

They walked down a street running perpendicular to the tracks and followed it down two streets that were more of the same, older homes transformed into businesses. There were one or two that hadn't been converted into anything yet, three that had been demolished into vacant lots or parking lots for the adjacent business, and one that seemed to have been remodeled into an actual home that was well kept, at least by the standards of the others. They turned down one of the streets and walked past a hair salon and a horrid looking bowling alley before coming to a stop at a rundown used auto parts dealer that was currently closed and looked as though that was its typical state of existence.

"You live in an auto parts outlet?" Xander wondered aloud as he stared at the building, one eyebrow raised quizzically.

Chris gave him a *what are you retarded?* look that only children could wear appropriately, then walked around to the alley along the side. There were three dumpsters lined up, each one with a different businesses name scrawled onto it in yellow shoe polish. There was a large puddle in the centre of the alley with a rat next to it, lapping cautiously at the water with both eyes trained on the two intruders. When Chris got close enough it ran for a small hole in the wall and disappeared.

The boy scaled one of the garbage bins and stood on top, teetering onto his toes and just barely grabbing the last rung of the ladder that came down from the second floor's fire escape.

Xander smiled, nodding respectfully at the child before following.

They scaled the rusted stairs and ladders until they came to a window on the fourth (and top) floor. He grabbed it by its ledge and started to pull, old paint digging in under his nails as his face turned red from effort. Xander motioned for him to stop, then slid the window open easily.

"I loosened it," Chris said, ducking his head under the pane and climbing in.

"I opened it," Xander shrugged, following him.

The room was old and covered in charred marks and mold. There was graffiti over almost every spare surface, with vibrant and violent and sexual images in each. They came into what had once been a kitchen. The aqua blue tiled floor was faded and buckled in three square patches against the wall where a fridge, stove and deep freeze had clearly been at one point. What remained of shelves and a sink were there as well, the latter covered with splotches of rot and had been used to dispose of more than one used condom.

The room opened up into a living room of sorts. There was a large trash bin in the centre of it that was almost overflowing with charred strips of newsprint and cardboard. A mirror hung not far from it, strangely out of place and the only actual piece of furniture he'd seen yet.

Along the left wall of the living room / kitchen were three doors. The one in the middle hung open to reveal a filthy, yet apparently serviceable, bathroom. Each of the others had clearly been bedrooms when the home had seen better days. Judging by the size of the building from outside compared to the amount of space left unused, it appeared as though they were both quite large.

"Not bad." Xander smiled, nodding respectfully.

"I sleep in the one on the left." Chris said, motioning toward it and confirming Xander's assumptions about the rooms. "Sometimes an old guy comes in and sleeps in the one on the right, but I haven't seen him lately and he doesn't bother anyone."

He nodded again, craning his head to look back the way they'd come and take in the entire apartment. "Better than some of the shelters."

"There's no hot water or power. It gets pretty cold, the warmest room's the bathroom. I stay there sometimes in the tub."

Xander peeked in, and sure enough there was a ratty old sleeping bag scrunched up in the tub. He turned back to Chris, who was shifting uncomfortably from foot to foot, trying not to make eye contact with him. There was a moment of uncomfortable silence before Xander spoke. "You gonna be okay here on your own?"

Chris rolled his eyes, then turned back into the kitchen and opened one of the cupboards to reveal and saggy old bad of Cheesies. He unrolled it, grabbed a handful and then carefully rolled it back up, making sure there was no air inside before tucking it back into its space.

"Alright," Xander huffed, heading back toward the

window. "I should be back in a few hours and we'll have this whole thing taken care of. Then we're gonna talk about what you should do next."

Again Chris did not respond, now ignoring Xander completely as he had been before their meal.

Xander frowned, ducking under the window and heading back down the fire escape.

It took less than five minutes to get back to the station. He brushed past a police officer and three women in business casual clothes talking about TPS reports and made a bee line directly for a row of phone booths on the upper right deck. He stepped into the closest one and snatched up the receiver. He brought it to his ear and heard nothing, then picked up the chord and realized that it was attached to nothing. Cursing, he slammed it back against the receiver and moved on to the next booth, this time rewarded by a crackling low tone.

Smiling brazenly to himself, he reached into his pocket and withdrew the withered and creased sheet of paper he'd put there hours ago. He unfolded it hastily and then turned it right side up, the grainy photo of Chris staring him right in the face. His hand was just touching the first digit in the number when the phone began to blare that he'd taken too long. Sighing, he hung up the receiver, let it rest there for a moment or two, then picked it back up and dialed.

A curt male voice answered half way through the second ring, high pitched and yet somehow gravelly at the same time. "Winston."

"Yes, hello," Xander smiled, leaning against the solid brick interior of the station. He'd learned long ago that you can hear a smile. It changes the tone and connotation of your voice dramatically and can't be faked any other way. "My name is Mike Harris, I'm calling about a flyer I found at the Y"?"

There was an audible shuffle as the phone switched ears, as well as the mumbled drone of voices too far away to hear over the cheap receiver. When the voice returned it was still gravelly but much more pleasant, although it sounded manufactured and fake. The man wasn't smiling, and you could tell. "Is it about Chris? Did you find him?"

"Yes, yes. He's been staying with me for several days now at my loft. I couldn't believe it when I found that flyer. My son told me he was one of his friends whose parents were out of town."

"Kids," chuckled the voice on the other end of the line. Again, it was fake. "Well, this is just wonderful. We'll be so happy to have him back."

"Where can I meet you?" Xander asked, digging into his pocket and retrieving a pen and brought it to his open palm.

"You know Mulholland Drive?"

It took Xander a second to process where in the city that was. "That's a bit out of my way. Anything closer to West End?"

"Do you know the strip mall just off Olvera?"

"I do. I do know that."

"Excellent. How soon can you be there?"

There was another pause as he calculated the distance

in his head. "Hour and a half. Maybe less."

"I'll leave now. And thank you again, sir. Thank you so much."

"My pleasure, sir. See you soon." He hung up the receiver and the smile immediately fell from his face, replaced by stone carved determination. He turned away from the phone booth and started down the stairs toward the trains, pushing past a large man in a Hawaiian shirt as he went.

Darkness had finally found its way to the streets by the time he went outside. He took a deep breath through his nose and filled his lungs with the cool air. It was never that cool here, not by his standards, but it was just chilled enough after the sun went down that he could take it in and allow himself a brief moment.

The train pulled up beside him, kicking up dust and debris and swirling it around as the wheels squealed to a halt. The doors opened with a angry hiss and he stepped into the mouth of the beast.

The parking lot was deserted.

There was something about an empty parking lot that he'd always found slightly disconcerting. It wasn't the pavement or the lights in and of itself, but simply the act of seeing something in a way he wasn't used to seeing it. It made him uncomfortable and fidgety, and he wished he'd spared the fries and bought another pack of Pal Mals.

The perfectly straight white lines that checkered the pavement created the illusion of depth as they got further and further away from him, making it look as though it was slowly descending into nothing. It gave him an odd sense of vertigo, and he was suddenly very aware of how little he'd had to eat of late.

Cars passed by on the street adjacent to him, their headlights all that was visible to him as the high beams swept across his face. He was waiting almost ten minutes before one pulled in, slowing to a crawl as it went over a speed bump and then swerved in a large arch to get to him, rather than pulling right up. There was a brief, horrible moment when he thought the vehicle might just slam right into him; but it came to a stop five feet away. The high beams shut off and he could see both men in the front. The driver was about Xander's height with a broad, muscular bust. His head was shaved clean and he had a neatly groomed handlebar mustache and thick sunglasses that would have looked at home in and eighties music video. The other was slightly taller and was balding well enough all on his own. There was a layer of stubble on his chubby cheeks that looked less than a day old. Both men wore pressed, clean business suits that made them blend in with the darkness of the car beyond them. They looked at Xander for a moment; then said something to each other, nodded, and got out of the car in unison.

The driver took a quick look around, then cocked his head at Xander. "The kids not here."

"No, he's not," he agreed, smiling.

He looked to the other man briefly, then back at Xander. "You wanna tell me exactly what's going on here?"

Xander stared at him for a moment, a wry smile growing over his lips, then turned to the other. "I'm gonna go out on a limb here and assume that neither of you is the man in charge, and that's okay."

"Don't know what you're talking about."

"Right, whatever. Either of you ever hear of a Black Womb?"

The driver looked from Xander to his partner, and then back again.

"Didn't think so. Just go back to your boss and tell him to cut the kid loose. The trouble he can cause you is nothing compared to what'll rain down on you if you keep this up. You got all that?"

Again the men exchanged glances, the balding one snickering a little to himself and looking at his shoes, unable to make eye contact with Xander.

Xander's brow crunched together, his eyes flickering from one man to the other looking for some sort of answer to the question on his mind, finding none. "Okay, what's so funny?"

"Nothing," the driver said, laughing a little now himself. It wasn't the fake sort of laugh he'd heard over the phone either, it was genuine. "It's nothing, really. You just look so goddamn funny, standing there and telling us how it's gonna be."

"Excuse me?"

"Oh, it's not what you're saying or anything... it's just been so long since anyone's tried something like this is all." He smiled, taking off his sunglasses and rubbing the bridge of his nose.

He looked from one thug to the other again, trying to figure out the attitude he was getting. "I take it you're not going to be listening then?"

"Son, have you ever heard of Stephen Fields?"

"Never."

"I thought not. Let me give you some advice, man to

man: you don't wanna get involved in this. In any way, shape or form. To quote the song, it's like tugging on Superman's cape. It's just not a good plan."

"So, I take it we're not going to be leaving the kid alone?"

Once again the men exchanged glances. The driver shrugged.

Xander sighed dramatically, then let his smile broaden. "Mazel Tov."

He pulled a white handkerchief out of the driver's breast pocket and wiped the blood off of his knuckles. The scrapes and displaced flesh there had already healed themselves, the damaged flesh still pink and rosy.

He picked up the gun that lay a few feet to his left and examined it for a moment before releasing the clip into his palm and thumbing the remaining five bullets out onto the pavement one after another with a series of metallic chimes. One rolled along the grooves and contusions in the pavement until it connected to the driver's head, immediately becoming coated in the redness all around it.

"You ever hear of a Black Womb?" Xander asked again, squatting down to get close to the thug. The other had lost consciousness within seconds of the altercation, and he honestly couldn't recall hitting him that hard at the moment.

He spit up another mouthful of pink tinged saliva, rolling onto his side so that it would fall onto the pavement. He coughed twice, a sickly sound usually reserved for palliative care patients. His throat was filled with fluid that seemed to get worse and worse no matter how often he spat or swallowed.

"That's okay, you don't have to answer." He smirked and folded up the handkerchief, then placed it back in the man's pocket. "I think we've reached a point where the both of us can sit down like men and figure out a way that you and your boss can leave, the kid, alone."

The man coughed once more, then laughed, showing off his teeth and gums, both stained with blood.

The smile left Xander's face and was replaced for the first time by something resembling concern as he raised one eyebrow and watched the man struggle to breathe through his laughter, his chest convulsing freely.

"I can definitely say," he laughed, spewing more blood and bile with every syllable. "That we aren't going to be bothering that kid ever again."

Xander looked at him for a moment, giggling and laughing like some sick clown; the blood on his lips a poor substitute for makeup. His head lolled downward a little, passing by the bobbing adams apple and red stained collar to the rest of him. The suit was expensive, no less than three thousand dollars. It had been tailored to form fit, the fabric falling tight over his form without restraining his movement even now, sprawled out on the whitewash grid of the parking lot. The tie was silk and looked new, the clip on it solid platinum with a diamond button in the center. Slowly, his eyes cast to the balding unconscious man a few feet away. The suit was equally expensive and almost identical, with the exception of a golden tie clip lacking in a diamond. He didn't think it was any indication of rank, but more to do with each individual taste. Not the type of suit you'd see on a this sort of man. Slowly in the back of his mind, he felt recognition spark.

Near the other side of the train was a bald man wearing a tight, form fitting suit and reading a newspaper. He sifted through the pages aimlessly, grumbling incoherently as he did. He was wearing large black sunglasses that hadn't been in style since long before Chris was born, and they reflected the sunlight right at him so that it seemed to be coming from both sides of the tram.

Near him was a tall man with broad shoulders. He wore a suit that was tailored to fit him perfectly. His nails were manicured, and his every hair was in place.

While it never occurred to him to question the presence of two well suited men in this city, he cursed himself for not questioning their presence on a public train. It shouldn't have mattered that he wasn't used to this city: there aren't many men who could afford a four figure suit that would ride public transit. Running into two in the same number of days was a statistical no no.

When he turned his head back toward the driver he was filled with hate, blood rushing to his cheeks and making them hot and uncomfortable. He grabbed him by the collar and pulled him up until they were nose to nose, drawing back his free fist menacingly. His nose shot out each breath like discharge from a steam engine as the man looked at him through half swollen eyes, still smirking. He tried a few times to think of something to say; some threat or retort to end the interaction on his note.

He found none, finally lashing the heel of his hand forward into that man's nose, knocking him unconscious.

"Son of a bitch," he said simply, then turned toward the car and started it. He peeled out of the parking lot as fast as he dared.

As soon as he opened the window he knew.

His nails had dug into the aging wood and chipped white paint of the frame and pulled up, bathing his midsection in a humid breeze from inside. It wafted up into his nose and filled him with the sickly sweet metallic scent he'd smelled all too often and he was sure, so much as he was his own name.

He dropped to his knees on the rusted metal grate of the fire escape and cursed, letting out a long sigh of defeat. He felt tears come but did not shed them, continuing to look down through the lattice below him onto the street for well over five minutes.

He could see people moving around on the street out of his peripheral vision and hated them at once, curling his lip and clutching the metal rail so tight that it sliced at the webbed flesh between his digits. He forced himself to his feet in one swift jaunt, straightening his legs almost painfully fast. Something inside him hadn't wanted to move from that spot ever again and he felt he had to do it all at once, like ripping off a band-aid.

He placed his palms firmly on the underside of the window again, pausing briefly before pulling it the rest of the way up. It rose steadily and with ease, barely making a sound as it found its way to the top and locked into place. Taking one last, deep breath of clean air, he stepped inside.

The smell was exponentially worse inside and seemed to shoot into him and then seep out of his every pore, like garlic. The room itself was not that different from the way he'd left it, the open area that had once been a kitchen still in the neatly placed shambles it had been earlier. The dirt on the floor might have been a little more displaced, he wasn't sure. He hadn't felt the need to pay that much attention the first time he'd been there, but now it seemed of the utmost importance.

As normal as this room seemed, he knew what lay beyond it. Pressing forward, forcing his feet to move as if to punish himself, he stepped around the corner into the other room.

The wall slowly revealed more and more of the empty floor that lay beyond it, and for a moment he dared to think that for once he was wrong. Then the plush forest green of the sleeping bag came into view, more and more visible with every step he took until it was revealed in its entirety.

The zipper was facing him and had been pulled tight all the way around, the draw strings at the top pulled taught. It was unnatural to see it that way, as tightly wrapped as a sausage in such a way that the person sleeping inside could never have done. Even without lifting or touching it, there was a weight to the bag that only happened when there was a person inside. The lans and grooves of the fabric took a certain form when conforming to the shape of the human body, its folds falling over the joints delicately and completely.

The lower inch of the bag had been turned a slightly darker green than the rest all the way around, like it had absorbed copious amounts of liquid. He had a sudden flashback to his father scolding him as a very young child for wetting his own sleeping bag while on a family vacation, and it had looked remarkably like this one did now. He pushed that thought out of his mind as he squat down next to it.

He moved his eyes over it from top to bottom and then back again, his face never once changing expression or poise. He regarded it on the same level with which it regarded him, that sort of moment making everything alive and existential. He briefly wondered at what point a person became an object, and vice versa. If it ceased to be a person simply by definition, or if it was still imbued with life despite its current state.

He reached out, neither quickly nor slowly, and released the clasp keeping the draw string tight. It loosened immediately as he worked it down the line until it reached the end. The top of the bag opened slightly, becoming a small round mouth with all the fabric folding toward it in strained, pulled lines. The smell it let out was toxic, the worst level of that same decomposition he'd gotten the second he opened the window. He did not respond to it, merely moved his fingers from the clasp and onto the zipper.

He brought the metal tab all the way around its track slowly and carefully, getting nipped in the fabric only once on its trek around to the other side. The smell did not get worse as more and more of it opened, having reached the peak of its pungency, he hoped. His hand falling back to his side, he regarded the bag again. It was still in roughly the same shape it had been when he first found it, the changes he'd made changing the thing itself only slightly.

For the first time since entering the home, his expression changed. He closed his eyes and took a deep breath, then opened them again and bit his lower lip slightly.

He reached out and took the bag gently by the top corner, pulling it aside slowly until it was as open as the nature of it allowed it to be. He did not wince or close his eyes or look away. He made no gesture or remark, nor did he even gasp or feel his heart skip. He'd known what he would find from the second he'd peeled out of the parking lot.

Chris's body lay awkwardly on the plastic lined interior of the sleeping bag. From the neck down he looked eerily normal, and at first glance a casual observer may not have noticed that his arms and legs were in a position that wasn't quite normal, twisted and contorted into ways that weren't quite right. That his chest didn't move or twitch the way it would have if his lungs were being filled with air or if his heart had been beating. That his skin had turned the pale peach white color that happened when your blood stopped moving in your veins and started settling inside you.

His head was covered in a light grey plastic bag. It conformed to his features almost perfectly, but removed the details that made the face human. The freckles were gone, as well as the scars and folds of his skin. What was there was a perfect impression of his open lips and teeth, the bag pulled into his mouth as proof of his last breath. His pupils were visible through the thin plastic, tilted up slightly and wide with horror and pain.

Xander let out a long sigh from both nostrils, reached

out and took the boy in his arms, then stood.

Two weeks later.

"It's fifty bucks."

"Fifty?" Dennis scoffed, looking down at the bag that rested comfortably in the palm of his hand. He let out a reluctant sigh and ran his fingers over the faded grey baseball cap atop his head. "It was half that last time."

"Well that's cause this shit is twice as good." Trevor smiled, showing off a mouth of questionable looking teeth. He turned away from his customer for a moment as a couple passed them, taking a quick look around. They stood under the arch of a classic theatre that was between showings at the moment, the streets reasonably empty. At the very least, they were empty of anyone who would think to care about what he was doing. The air was hot and humid despite the time of night, making even his tee shirt cling desperately to the skin of his chest. There was an atm vestibule across the street where a man was taking out money and would throw wry glances in his direction every few minutes, and did so again now. Trevor cocked his head at him, sneering, and the man turned away quickly.

Dennis looked down at the tiny package in his head. It looked light, but at the moment he felt its weight that went beyond physical presence. Something inside him twisted and then released, screaming out like hunger but much more powerful. He felt a pressure in the center of his chest that felt like his entire body was trying to pull itself in to that point, a tightness he'd felt too many times before but always surprised him.

"You all right, man? I ain't got all day."

"Just feelin' the cross, man."

Trevor raised an eyebrow at him. "Sound like you're high enough already."

"No," Dennis laughed, taking the bag in his other hand and sliding it into his jacket pocket. "Something my Mom used to go on with. Said when you get that weight on your chest you were feeling what Jesus did on the cross."

"Hn," he hummed, holding out his hand for payment. "Sounds like your Mom was a few pineapples short, bro."

Dennis curled his lip slightly but said nothing, reaching into his back pocket and pulling out his wallet. He licked his fingers once, then started thumbing through the bills. "Forty five good?"

Trevor rolled his eyes, then snatched the cash out of his hands.

Dennis looked around once, then nodded and held up his hand. Trevor took it and they shook briefly, then he turned and started toward the parking lot of the theatre. Trevor watched him go, shoving his hands and the money down into the pockets of his hoodie. When his customer was gone from sight he turned back to the theatre and stepped inside, feeling the wonderful flow of the air conditioning almost immediately.

The third tier theatre tried admirably to be impressive but fell just shy. The walls were a pale yellow that had been spot painted with slightly different shades in places where teens had taken off the paint, leaving them looking oddly patchwork depending on the angle you stood at.

The main area between the entrance and the concession stand was largely vacant. There had been carpet there at one point, but had been removed after multiple repairs became difficult to keep up with. It was now just concrete, which retained its dusty look no matter now many times it was swept. The frames for movie posters on the walls were empty for the most part, and the only thing decorating the room were felt ropes that stretched between pylons, forming an unnecessarily long maze to get to the concessions.

There were words painted on the wall behind the lanky cashier that read Thank You for Your Patronage.

The man behind the counter looked at Trevor wearily, then went back to work and tried his best to ignore him.

Not far from the stand, three young girls stood in a small huddle talking. One of them turned toward him for a moment, looked him up and down, then turned back to her clique. A few feet to their left was a short man with scruffy cheeks and hair that looked damp even though it wasn't wet out. The man was staring at him, fiddling with his upper lip all the while and peeling away dead skin as he watched.

Trevor shifted from one foot to the other, then looked away. He stared at a random spot on the wall, counted to thirty, then turned back. The man was still there, and he was still staring. "Something I can do for you, Narco?"

The man smiled, but barely moved otherwise. "Actually, yes."

Xander slammed Trevor against the tile wall of the

bathroom stall, his skull making a loud wet snap as it connected. "Paw!" he yelped, pain shooting through his skull as his entire world turned lopsided. He had less than a second to recover from the shock before his forehead connected with the jagged edge of the porcelain sink, spurting red onto the white.

He coughed twice, then turned back to Xander from his place on all fours. His lip curled in disgust and his eyes were filled with fire.

Xander stared down at him with dead eyes that barely registered where he was or what he was doing. He didn't appear to even be looking at Trevor, but rather at some random crack on the floor. His pupils were huge, so much so that Trevor couldn't see the iris' at all.

"You tripping out, man?" he asked, trying to keep his voice even. His hands shook as he reached into his pocket, withdrawing another baggie almost identical to the one he'd given Dennis. "I got your fix, man. On the house. All I got, all on the house, man."

Xander squat down, coming in close to the man. He still didn't really look at him, his eyes now focussed on the bag of cocaine he held in his hand. "Looking for somebody, hoping you can help me out."

"Sure man, sure," he stammered. "Whatever you want. Who you looking for? Jessica for some E?"

"Never met him before," Xander continued, almost ignoring that Trevor had spoke. "But he's big news, at least he thinks he is. Got some thugs, had a friend of mine killed. Don't know his name, but I need to know where I can find him."

Trevor furrowed his brow, his voice changing from

fearful and shocked to angry and annoyed. "Man, I sell crappy ass coke. You honestly think I know anyone that far up the chain, you're crazy."

The side of Trevor's face hit the wall again just to the right of the sink's pipes. One of his teeth came out and clacked along the floor, leaving tiny flecks of his blood dotted along its path.

"Fuck!" he screamed, cradling his jaw in his palm as it seeped blood and saliva. "You fuck! Fuck you, you fuck!"

"Be quiet," Xander snapped, meeting his eye for the first time. Trevor stopped yelling almost immediately, his pain forgotten for the moment. "I know you don't know who I'm looking for. You probably don't even know who your own goddamn father is. All I want to know from you is... who are you afraid of?"

Trevor stopped, raising an eyebrow at him. "What? What do you mean?"

Xander brought his hand upside his head again, this time swatting him away from the wall and toward the centre of the bathroom. "Who are you afraid of? Who, more than anyone else, would you avoid at all costs? That's all I want to know."

Trevor took several deep breaths, trying hard to get a lungful of oxygen but continuously coming up with more blood. He did this for several moments, his forehead resting on his forearm as he stared down at the floor. He sniffed back the mucus that was coming out of both nostrils in buckets and turned toward Xander. "There's a guy called King, hangs out around O'Learys a lot. Reggie King. Motherfucker fucked up my brother once, real bad."

"Thank you," Xander replied politely, then rose to his feet.

"I wouldn't go after him, though. Is just asking for trouble."

Xander paused at the door and looked back at Trevor, then left without a word.

It was a large restaurant, taking up the entire third story of the Malworlo Market on the way to centre city.

All the walls were plate glass that looked out onto the streets around and were miraculously clear of droppings and litter all the way around. Inside, small round tables were tightly packed together across marina coloured floors, creating winding rows between isles for servers to bring food to and from. The air was thick with the smell of fryer grease, so much that it seemed to stick to the walls and skin of all those present. All the tables were full and there was a pitcher of beer at almost every one. There were no drinks other than beer on the menu, except water, which had the same hue as the beer.

Xander sat at a table alone with a full beer and a plate of fries in front of him. The beer was untouched and had gone flat, but the majority of the fries were gone. There was a magazine laid haphazardly on the chair next to him which he'd long since stopped pretending to read and was instead scanning the crowd that surrounded him. Even though it would have appeared to anyone that his eyes were scanning the crowd for someone he recognized, he was actually paying very little attention to anything he was seeing. He was listening.

"I don't know, but I can certainly find that out for   "

"What is this, avocado? I'm not sure I like avocado."

"called from his phone to say that he was out of   "

"This guy, here, is, the guy. He's the guy."

"Do you think we're goin   "

"Never had anything like this type of beer."

"Feeling like a pizza. Anyone else feel like pizza? I feel like pizza."

"Let me get the tab this time, Reg. You get it every   "

"Long as there's no anchovies."

"I think this is avocado."

He got up, turning one hundred and eighty degrees from the direction he'd been sitting. There was a long row of tables between him and the doors, and he walked between them effortlessly without even paying attention to what he was doing, winding between patrons. He brought up his arm suddenly as he passed by a table near the centre of the room, catching a tanned man in the temple and sending him into his plate of Alfredo. Still moving, he grabbed the chair the man was sitting on and spun himself on it, knocking the woman sitting next to him off her chair and taking her place.

The man bellowed as he rose his head, pasta hanging from the ends of his pencil thin mustache, before Xander pushed him right back into the bowl by the scruff of his neck.

"Reggie King," he spat, holding the man down as he thrashed. "Tell me who you fear."

Xander kicked the girl in the ribs. She barely moved,

her weight keeping her planted to the ground that she was hugging for dear life now. She let out a long, wet cough as the pavement she was staring at became blurred and cloudy.

"I'm not going to ask again," he snarled as he reached down, lightly, blood dribbling from the tips of his fingers.

She looked up just as he picked up a large chunk of glass from the burst streetlight overhead.

⋏⋏

He held the man by his ankles off the roof, his tie fluttering defiantly as cars drove this way and that below. A pen fell from his breast pocket and seemed to hang suspended in mid air for a moment before plummeting downward and disappearing into a tiny speck.

He screamed.

⋏⋏

Xander stepped into a large, open area in the middle of the subbasement, his eyes straining against the low light to see everything around him.

There were crates stacked almost to the ceiling on either side, some of them new and some so old that the wood seemed to be sagging and bending under the stress of their contents. Pipes and cables ran adjacent to him overhead, so many that they obscured most of his view of the stucco ceiling.

There were fluorescent lights stuck vertically where the wall met the ceiling every few metres on the right hand side, and each of them let out a soft energy-efficient glow that did not stretch very far past its point of origin. However, each one was working and neither so much as flickered.

The hallway itself was long and narrow and seemed to be curved slightly, always keeping the area about ten feet ahead of him blind. It was an illusion created by the crates he was sure, but it was enough to make every step careful and tedious.

A metal catwalk ran along the upper left side of the room, its doorways opening into the main basement few and far between. It was held by an elaborate system of suspension cables but did not sway or move at all.

The floor was clean and well dusted, without even a trace of litter or rodent feces anywhere. The entire room was a study of contradictions, with some things looking old and unused while others looked new and well travelled.

"Just wants it to seem unused," he mumbled to himself, glaring at the line of crates. "Doesn't want people to think they come down here as often as they do."

"Not that anyone ever asks," came a voice from above.

Xander's turned on his heels, fists out and at the ready as he glared up at the catwalk.

The man that stood there made no attempt to hide himself. He stood close to the rail with one leg bent and relaxed, wearing a blue pinstripe suit that fit him perfectly. The black vest underneath it was unbuttoned and hung open, along with the top button of his eggshell shirt. A red tie was slung around his neck. His face was hard set and square, his cheekbones clearly visible with only the slightest hint of chub on them, and the rest of him appeared to be in equally healthy shape for a man that must have been at least forty five. He was eating a tunafish sandwich that was almost down to the crust, knawing on it as he stared down at the man in his basement.

Xander loosened, adjusting his posture from the oddly hunched over position he'd turned around in to a straighter one. "Stephen Fields?"

He smiled, his shoulders moving a little as though he'd chuckled. "Are you going to ask me what I'm afraid of?"

"Nope," he responded. "Asked a lot of people that these last few weeks. Further and further I go up the line, you know what more and more people say?"

The man did not respond, but finished his sandwich.

Xander poked his finger toward him. "Stephen Fields. You."

"And you figure that makes me the guy you want to talk to?"

"Couldn't care less what you have to say, in all honesty -- don't really care what you're afraid of -- just so long as you know, before we're done, it's going to be me."

The man did laugh this time, a full body laugh that shook his entire blocky form and made him lean forward onto the rail. He laughed like someone who heard a good joke that really needed one, the sound slowly fading out until it was gone.

Xander watched him, moving from foot to foot uncomfortably as the man steadied himself again.

"Sorry," he said, holding up a hand as he regained his composure. "It's been a long time since I've heard something like that, especially from someone your age. It's not funny... just caught me off guard, is all."

"Uh huh," he said, curling his upper lip. "You ever hear of a Black Womb?"

Fields raised an eyebrow.

"Didn't think so. Just wanted to let you know what it was you were dealing with when you did that to Chris."

"Who?"

"Chris... Chris. The child you killed."

Fields frowned, his brow wrinkling down to meet his nose. "Kid, you may have to narrow it down a little more than that."

Xander opened his mouth to respond when something hard slammed into the back of his head with enough force to lift him off his feet. He registered that the sound it made against the base of his skull made him think it was metal before his forehead slammed through the wooden face of one of the crates. Splinters scraped his scalp as well as the sacks inside the crate, spilling white powder out onto the floor and over him. Some of it mingled with the cut on his head and he felt instantly numb, the womb organ screaming out in a way it never had before.

"Fuck..." he coughed, pressing both palms against either side of the hole he'd made to prop himself up. Someone kicked him in the ass and he jolted forward again, then another blow to the back to the knee made him crumble to the concrete floor. He tried to turn around but only managed to look over his shoulder before that same metal thing connected with his jaw and sent him backward onto the floor.

For a long moment all he could see was white. His left hand kept jolting back and forth between his side and his face without him telling it to as different sections of his brain fired random, useless impulses to other sections for no reason. When his vision returned he saw three men standing above him, each looking down and smirking. Only one caught his eye, a largish man with a handlebar mustache carrying an aluminum bat in his hands. He raised it again then brought it down hard. It seemed to disappear just before it made contact, sinking into the blind spot between his eyes. His whole body jolted from the impact, then again as a similar blow connected to his ribs.

Black blood spurted up from his mouth and splattered against the floor next to him, spiderwebbing out in a thousand directions and ruining the otherwise pristine floor. He coughed three times until his throat was clear again, then rolled over onto his side and leaned on his arm.

The blows continued but he didn't feel them, the Womb trying to kick in time and again but just sputtering like a car that wouldn't start. He could feel his blood pressure rise higher and higher as the blood in his veins shared its space with the black ooze that came from deep in his right side. Knew that there were blood vessels in his eyes that were bursting that had nothing to do with the onslaught he was taking. He was moments away from the transformation, despite his efforts to hold it back.

There were footsteps approaching, first on the metal mesh stairwell and then on the concrete floor. His eyes were swelling shut in great mounds of purple flesh, but he managed to open them enough to see Fields standing over him, his hands thrust into his pockets.

"I'm going to go out on a limb here and assume you're

new in town," he said, motioning for his men to back off a pace.

Xander opened his mouth to speak, but instead spewed another dash of blood out onto his own cheeks.

"I thought as much." He nodded, as if he'd understood what Xander was trying to say. "That being said, let me tell you the way things work here. I mean, things work the same way everywhere... but they especially work this way here."

Xander tried to get up, immediately falling back to the floor. His head hit off the concrete and created a shockwave he felt move through his whole brain.

"Most of it you seem to already get. You get fear, you see what it can do. What it can accomplish, how to use it... but you can't do it right. People like you never could, never can. Because you keep trying to be the good guy. Keep trying to run off playing hero. Keeps you from really, really using that fear the way you should."

Xander coughed, fighting to maintain eye contact with him.

"This whole 'hero' thing... it's just not a smart game to play, kid. There're too many people in this world that need help, and too few idiots willing to take this kind of beating to do it. And there's more than enough people willing to be on the swinging side of that bat," he said, pointing one of his stubby fingers beyond Xander, to where the mustached man still held the metal bat. "Hell, there's too many people in this city alone that need help for one person to do anything about. Anything."

Fields stood back up and let out a deep sigh. "It's just not a smart game to play." He motioned to the three men that waited under the light. "Give him a few more memories, then send him out the way he came in. Call him an ambulance if he looks like he needs it."

The mustache man nodded, then took a step forward and raised his bat again, bringing it down in the centre of Xander's chest. Blood shot from his mouth a good eight feet, touching the back of Fields' shoes as he started his way back up the stairs.

Jasper King sat behind the wheel of his Buick Lesabre and looked out at the Mexican Deli he was parked in front of. There were three men inside, each wearing wife beaters. Their flesh was the pale brown of faded timber.

He smiled at one of them and the man smiled back. He got out of his car and slammed the door hard -- you had to slam the door hard on the Lesabre, or else it'd just open again of its own will. Not that there was anything in the car worth stealing.

He took two steps around the car and then felt the smooth pavement under his cheek. He didn't feel the impact against his temple that put him there, at least not at first. When he saw the blood he did.

There were footsteps, fast, receding into the distance.

The trees went by on either side like an emerald blur, melding into the apex of her peripheral vision.

Carol David been running for almost three miles and the weights strapped to her wrists and ankles were starting to chafe, but she was nowhere near ready to stop.

The trail she was on continued for another four miles before emptying out at the Blue Totem café and she was determined to get there. Not just get there, but get there running. Not just get there running, but get there running like the wind.

Her brunette hair bobbed from shoulder to shoulder with every footfall, held clumped together in a ponytail by sweat and her elastic.

Her breath could be heard long before she could be seen.

She paused.

There were sounds in the underbrush around her. She eyed them wearily for a long moment, sweat dotting her acne-inspired brow in random, sporadic bursts.

The brush was quiet and made not a movement. The stillness was too still, as though the leaves themselves were waiting on baited breath to see what would happen.

A few blocks away, a mugger clubbed a young girl over the head, smiling as he rolled up his sleeves, revealing a tattoo on his right arm. "...come 'ere, sweet thing..."

"... no.... please, stop."

"... please... just stop."

"...stop..."

"...please..."

Thirty-seven people heard the screams.

Nobody did anything.

Xander winced as he opened his eyes, the current

coming up from street level making them sting painfully. He still wasn't able to open them fully, the lids a swollen and misshapen variety of colours.

The lights below him danced about as he brought one foot up to rest on the ledge of the roof, then leaned forward on it and let out a long sigh. Cars travelled past and people walked, each looking behind them for whoever might be behind them. Billboards flashed and changed as people bought and stole, created and destroyed, killed and fucked.

He let out a long sigh. "This might well be suicidal," he said to himself, picturing that smug man in the pinstripe suit. "But this is exactly the game I want to be playing."

AFTERWORD

There are a few things here that bear addressing.

The first and least important is that I have, of course, taken liberties with the geography of America. Though I tried to add details where applicable to bring about flavors and tones when I felt they were needed, the story comes first. In this case, I thought of the setting as being "on the road" rather than as each individual setting, and the stories reflect that, I feel.

Some of the locations are legitimate, while others are fabricated. I feel there is enough acceptable precedent for this in my previous work that this should come to a shock to no one.

To put this collection in context: just after the first story, *Remembering*, was written I founded Engen Books and started about the process of preparing my first book for publication. This would have been in April or May 2007. This makes this book unique, as it is the last one that I was able to write with the illusion that nobody would read it but me. This was the last book where any draft was just for me. From this point on you are in mind during every part of the process, dear reader, and I must say that the work is the better for it.

The idea of writing a book of short stories in which every story was a different stop along the road of a long journey is one that I came upon very early in planning the long tale of Xander Drew. It is something I was always strangely enamored with, and in my mind seemed like a cool idea. A fun idea, and chance to really have a blast. It likely owes a debt of gratitude to a television program called *The Littlest Hobo*, which was basically the same premise, but with a friendly crime-solving dog as the main character. It was a strange and comforting part of my childhood.

This book is dedicated to Ellen Curtis, my partner in all things. I met her during the writing of this book, I believe just before the last story got started. Everything that comes after that is owed in no small amount to her support and opinion. Thank you, Ellen.

Some notes on this collection.

This collection of short stories bridges two book series together: the Black Womb series, which finished in April 2013, and the Xander Drew series, which begins in October 2014. It was always planned on happening, and not one word was changed to help in function in its role bridging the two. We made the choice to break up Xander's story into several connected book series' rather than on long book series, and the shift in tone between this book and the next seemed like an appropriate place to do that.

This book, like *Roulette* and *Chains* before it, started as two separate books. The short story *Reprise* was originally very different and was to be its own, separate novel.

Rather than be mostly told from the first person as it is now, it was to start as a straight Black Womb book, with the twist of Xander's departure at the end to represent a cliffhanger ending to shock readers with the sudden change in direction. This book of short stories was to be released over the same weekend, with *Reprise* being sold at a discounted rate to make up for its nature as a "red herring" novel. It was also not originally titled *Reprise*, is was titled *Pain*.

A few things contributed to the change to its current state. The first was that I hated it in its original version. I labored with it and hated every moment of it (though I am pleasantly pleased with it in its current state). The first person to read it, Ellen, felt the same way and for the same reasons. The choice was made fairly quickly to merge the two books into one.

Even then the plan was still for *Reprise* to be placed first in the collection and set up longtime readers with the expectation that while this was a short story collection, the status quo of Xander Drew was still much the same. When we announced that *Chains* would be the last Black Womb book and that this book would bridge into a new series, that became a moot point. People would be expecting the continuity change, it would surprise no one. As such the choice was made to place it out of order in the collection, meaning that for the first few stories we realize that there has been a change, but aren't quite sure what that change is, assuming you read them in order. This seemed best.

For the record, the rest of the stories take place in order of occurrence. The misplacement of *Reprise* does not indicate that the rest are shuffled like cards in a deck. This does make it unique in being the only story to feature Xander Drew to be technically published out of order, so to speak, as telling all the stories "in order" was a part of the original mission statement of Black Womb. I suppose it only fits that this book acts as an epilogue to that series then, if it finally breaks that rule.

As mentioned, this collection was in the creative process when the first Black Womb novel was published. As such it is mentioned in the author's bio of that novel, though under the title *Road to Damnation*. The title was changed very late in the plans for publication to *The Long Road*, partly because the original title never sat well. Similarly, the reference to the title in *Enemy Within* went under the same change. I have since learned not to bother trying to hype the current book I'm writing in the author bio I'm penning, it just isn't a good idea. For those of you wondering when *Road to Damnation* was going to be published, you're holding it. You can calm down now.

I am quite pleased with all of the stories in this collection, each for different reasons. Rather than being straight tales, the thematic choice was made early on was that in addition to telling different stories about Xander, each would also showcase a different aspect of his character. *Remembering* focuses on Xander's romantic nature, *Short Story* on his enhanced senses, etc. If there is one weak link in this it is, in my opinion, *Mikhail*. *Mikhail* is meant to reflect and pay homage to the more action-oriented and comic-book inspired aspects of the character. There has always been action in stories featuring Xander Drew, but in this one (being all action) it falls a tad flat, as we don't have time to get invested in the situation from which the action has arisen. I considered cutting it, but not accepting that part of the series would be equally wrong, and I know there are some out there that will enjoy it. At least, I hope so. So it remains. As for the character of Mikhail, he will be seen again, though likely not in the pages of a novel starring Xander Drew. The Engen Universe is a big place, after all. His actions are a part of a larger narrative, though taken out of context here they may be exceptionally difficult to understand. Such is life.

Interlude features the character of Blackheart once again, who has appeared twice before in stories starring Xander Drew: once as one of the primary antagonists in *Roulette*, and again in a cameo appearance in *Ignorance is Bliss*. Since these stories were written Blackheart has become one of the main characters of the *Infinity* series at the request of my co-author Ellen Curtis. Her interpretation of the character is so revolutionary that we actually have edited the "creator" credits on the character to reflect Ellen's contributions, much in the way Frank Miller is credited with the creation of the modern interpretation of Daredevil. Though being published later, this short story was written before *Infinity* and this interpretation of the character (though it does not interfere with it).

When *Interlude* was written in was intended to be placed in the Engen timeline exactly where it occurs, while Xander is on the road, between *Short Story* and *The Enemy Within*. But because it does not feature Xander or any of his supporting cast its placement can be fluid. Depending on how the next few Infinity novels come out, it may be shifted a little earlier or a little later in the Engen timeline, mostly at the discretion of Miss Curtis.

The Enemy Within was difficult to write, I hope I did so effectively. I enjoy it, as a story, greatly.

I will not comment on *The Game*, except to say that if the collection as a whole acts as an epilog to the Black Womb series, this story is unique among them as it acts instead as prolog to the Xander Drew series. Vague? Perhaps. But we'll soon see what I'm talking about.

On the subject of my next novel, *Cinders*, there's not a lot I wish to say, dear reader. It is complete, so there is much I could say, but I don't want to spoil anything.

I will say that it is a crime drama, and one that was written fairly quickly, around the same time that I co-authored *Infinity* with Ellen Curtis. And that it starts the new series off right, in a way that should make both fans of the Black Womb series and newcomers to our dear friend Xander very happy. I know it has made me so.

And so, dear reader, we have once again reached our end. I sincerely hope that you have enjoyed these stories and are hungry for more, for there are more coming. As always, it has been a pleasure.

Matthew LeDrew
April 2nd, 2014.
St. John's, Newfoundland.

ENGEN TIMELINE

With over twenty novels spread over three different series by many different authors, the Engen Universe of titles is growing every day and into genres we couldn't have imagined! From the original ten book *Black Womb* thriller series, its crime novel sequel series *Xander Drew*, our flagship adventure title *Infinity*, or single-novels like *Jacobi Street* or *light dark*, there's something in the Engen Universe for everyone with more books by more authors on the way soon!

...But how do the events relate to one another, chronologically? While some astute readers have guessed at the potential timeline (some accurately, some not), we're going to finally set the question of the Engen Timeline to rest.

Turn the page for an up-to-date guide of the ever-widening world of Engen, featuring the works of Ellen Curtis, Andrea Hackett, Ali House, Sarah Thompson, Jay Paulin, and Matthew LeDrew!

In the 10 Years Prior Black September

"Reptilia" by Matthew LeDrew
published in *light | dark*.
Danger descends on a small secluded town in the form of a deadly virus with fantastic and terrible side-effects. Can a small group of doctors escape alive?

Compendium by Ellen Curtis
Three short stories forming the basis for the Engen Universe's ties to suspense, genetic engeneering, and the supernatural. Features the stories "The Tourniquet Revival," "Falling into Fire" and "At Midnight, the Dawn."

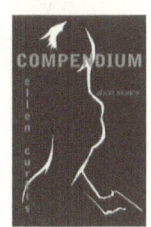

"The Theogony" by Matthew LeDrew
published in *light | dark*.
A tale of young Theo Flaherty of the *Infinity* series and his time admitted against his will to the Black Springs hospital, where he learns to paint, and seeks out his father.

Black September

"Revving Engen" by Matthew LeDrew
published in *light | dark*.
A direct lead-in to both *Infinity* and *Black Womb*, Tasha travels to Coral Beach, Maine on a hot tip about a recently discovered young man with incredible abilities.

Infinity by Ellen Curtis & Matthew LeDrew
Faced with a destiny he's uncertain of, the enigmatic Victor must bring together four unique people with very special abilities... or face the tasks ahead alone. Guaranteed to excite!

Black Womb by Matthew LeDrew
Fifteen years ago, something happened in Coral Beach, Maine that resulted in the present death of a seventeen-year-old boy. Now four high-school students must try to solve the mystery… before the killer picks them off.

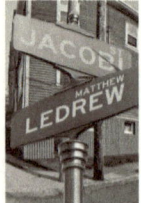

Jacobi Street by Matthew LeDrew
When a mysterious painting shows up at an art gallery he works at, Bob must work with Eddie and Sloan to track down its sinister origins and convince the people living on Jacobi Street of them, before its too late!

Transformations in Pain by Matthew LeDrew
When two girls are assaulted and one is hospitalized, the residents of Coral Beach must put their shared tragedies behind them and stop the man responsible, as well as unlock the secrets behind the true nature of the Womb…

Year One: October

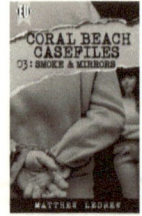

Smoke and Mirrors by Matthew LeDrew
The approaching trial of Genblade brings closure to the people of Coral Beach, until people start showing up dead in the same manner they did when he was at large.

"Scarlett" by Andrea Hackett
published in *light | dark*.
Introducing Scarlett, the slightly damaged hunter on a mission to save others from the monsters from her past.

"The Inevitable" by Ali House
published in *The Lightbulb Forest*
A young woman must contend with the emergence of a frightening new power alongside the emotional high of a first date.

The Tourniquet Reprisal by Curtis & LeDrew
A man lives in Atlanta, Georgia that people don't talk about, but everyone knows he's there. He arrived a year ago and turned a gaggle of uneducated youth into something new, something to fear.

Roulette by Matthew LeDrew
As the teen suicide rate in Coral Beach starts to climb astronomically fast, Xander travels to Los Angeles to fight his most terrifying adversary yet… and learns that the only thing worse than looking for release… is finding it.

Year One: November

Exodus of Angels by Curtis & LeDrew
Victor's enigmatic past is illuminated when Jaycee accompanies him to visit a new friend in the paliative care ward of the Black Springs hospital, where Theo also happens to be searching for a cure for Leigh.

Ghosts of the Past by Matthew LeDrew
Coral Beach faces its most awesome threat when one of Engen's past mistakes is unleashed upon the unsuspecting populous. Friends and enemies unite to fight a common enemy… but will even that be enough?

Touch Your Nose by Matthew LeDrew
Simon Monk must infiltrate the San Fransico branch of Shane Industries, a massive company with deep ties to the Engen Universe. Where do his true loyalties lie? And can he get out without causing harm?

Ignorance is Bliss by Matthew LeDrew
After being set through the ringer one too many times, Xander decides that his life with Julie needs a little more attention… which is bad news because a new villain has come to town with his sights set on Adam Genblade.

"Gristle While You Work" by Jay Paulin published in *light|dark*.
A short story centering around the rise of a new, and possibly cannibalistic, serial killer in the Engen Universe.

Becoming by Matthew LeDrew
For months Xander Drew has been doing his level best to keep the streets of Coral Beach clean, which means it's time for the forces of darkness to strike back… all at once.

Inner Child by Matthew LeDrew
Julie is hospitalized with life-threatening wounds to both body and soul. But the real threat comes from the hospital walls themselves, as a demonic presence makes itself known to Xander and his friends.

End of Year One

Gang War by Matthew LeDrew
The Tees, a homicidal gang of evil men, has finally been taken down by Xander Drew. But his victory is short lived, as retired Tees are mysteriously killed. With a town of suspects, anyone can be the culprit… including one of their own.

Chains by Matthew LeDrew
Sociopath Derek Smith has been freed from prison and is praying on the weak; and none are weaker than August Styles: a pregnant girl with Down Syndrome who has run away from home.

"Omega" by Ellen Curtis
published in *light | dark*.
A sinister division of Engen begins a series of experiments on pregnant women in a fashion eerily similar to those that created the original Black Womb project.

The Long Road by Matthew LeDrew
Xander meets the American people — and realizes that the world is harsh and wicked, but can also be soft and gentle, even loving. Xander Drew comes of age on the road, and sets his new direction.

Year Two

Cinders by Matthew LeDrew
Detective Horton enters a violent and dangerous world he didn't know existed beneath the veneer of order and structure that he has based his entire deductive method around.

Sinister Intent by Matthew LeDrew
One of the killers Detective Horton could not catch has resurfaced: a serial killer who flaunts his sinister intent in front of the Los Angeles Police Department, making it so that no one is safe.

Faith by Matthew LeDrew
Xander's mysterious and troublesome past returns to haunt him on the streets of Los Angeles; a place where even more people can get caught in the crossfire of the games of death and deceit that makes up his life.

Flickers in the Night by Matthew LeDrew
Lisa Rowdan is hunted by her haunting -- and powerful -- ex-boyfriend Ryan through a lonely city street. Can she escape him?
One of over twenty great sprine-tingling short stories!

Family Values by Matthew LeDrew
Xander and his new friends Crowley, Lisa, and Tim investigate a series of kidnappings and murders that stretch back decades, all of which have the same similar twist: victims being found after years of being missing.

The Future

"Remers" by Sarah Thompson
published in *light | dark*.
In the not-too-distant future of the Engen Universe, young athletes are the targets of a scouting program to create the next stage of super soldier with cybernetic enhancements.

ABOUT THE AUTHOR

Matthew LeDrew holds an Honours Degree in English from the Memorial University of Newfoundland with a minor in Anthropology, and studied Journalism at College of the North Atlantic in Stephenville, Newfoundland. He was honoured to be a jury member of the 2018 NLBA awards.

He has written twenty novels for Engen Books: the ten book *Coral Beach Casefiles* series, *The Long Road, Cinders, Sinister Intent, Faith, Family Values, Jacobi Street, Touch Your Nose, Infinity, The Tourniquet Reprisal,* and *Exodus of Angels* the latter three of which with co-author Ellen Curtis.

He lives in St. Johns, Newfoundland.